The Men

THE MEN

Anthony Masters

Constable · London

First published in Great Britain 1997 by Constable & Company Ltd
3 The Lanchesters, 162 Fulham Palace Road, London W6 9ER
Copyright © 1997 by Anthony Masters
The right of Anthony Masters to be
identified as the author of this work has been asserted
by him in accordance with the Copyright, Designs and
Patents Act 1988
ISBN 0 09 477140 5
Set in Linotron Palatino 10pt by SetSystems Ltd, Saffron Walden
Printed and bound in Great Britain by MPG Books Ltd, Bodmin, Cornwall

A CIP catalogue record for this book
is available from the British Library

With much love and thanks to Julia, friend and researcher

Prologue

4 July 1951

Spirals of dust flew from the baked ground as Lucy pushed her shopping trolley up the Cut and past Conifers.

The crackling sound had seemed part of the noisy wheels of the trolley as they rattled along the stones on the path. She knew one of the wheels was rasping and had asked Tim to do something about it. Of course he hadn't. Crackling? Rasping? Surely there was a difference. Then she saw the smoke.

Abandoning the trolley and clutching only her purse, Lucy Groves ran to the gap in the hedge that Peter had recently filled with wire. But it had been pushed aside and the smoke was drifting across the Cut, making her choke. Ducking down underneath the privet, she stumbled through, trying to see what was ablaze. Then Lucy saw the flames, heard the crackling increase in ferocity and caught sight of Sally running down the lawn still in her dressing gown.

A period of withdrawal? One of Sally's depressions? But now she was bounding along and they both arrived at the potting shed at the same time.

'It's those horrible boys,' Sally shouted. 'I saw them in the Cut from the window, but I had no idea they'd come in here. Look what they've done!'

The smoke was blowing the other way now in the breeze, and as glass shattered Lucy caught a glimpse of upturned paint tins twisting in the heat and what appeared to be some kind of scrawl on the wall.

'I should get the fire brigade,' shouted Lucy. 'Those flames might catch the trees.'

An hour later, with hoses snaking up the Cut, the brigade had doused the flames and the shed was a mound of damp blackened ashes. But the trees had been saved.

'Pure vandalism.' Sally was outraged. 'Those awful boys.'

'There was something scrawled in paint on the wall. I think it said WILL TELL.'

Sally's lips worked for a moment and her skin was grey under the summer tan. 'Of course. That's him.'

'That's who?' Lucy was bewildered.

'William Tell. The boy I saved from those bullies. A scrawny child. They were laying into him on the green. I told them to leave him alone and so did the local Bobby.'

'How did you know him?' Why *should* she know him, wondered Lucy.

'Will's from Hersham. He sometimes gives Baverstock a hand.'

'What a strange name. Is he really called William Tell?'

'I hadn't thought of that.' She half-laughed and then looked alarmed. 'Here comes a police constable.' Sally zipped her dressing gown up to her throat. 'Those louts might have burnt the shed to pay me out for rescuing the little lad – and wrote his name up.'

Lucy was puzzled. Then she said, 'You'd better tell the policeman then. Tell him about William Tell.'

They looked at each other and burst into nervous laughter.

Adrian was determined he'd have her.

Sweating, trembling with excitement, he strode ahead, leading Molly up the steep rise to the wooded hill, the July sun shining limply through rolling dark clouds. Please God, don't let the rain start.

Glancing back, Adrian could see Molly was gazing up at the sky apprehensively, and at any moment he knew she would demand to go back. Somehow he had to persuade her to leave the path and head for the bushes. She might not give it to him even then, but it was worth a try. Bugger the weather. When they got off the bus the sky had been a promising blue.

'Adrian!' Molly called with her usual authority.

He plunged on, the path between the beech trees narrowing, the foliage comfortingly thicker. Glancing back he saw she was still following, although rather more reluctantly. Should he stop and grab her now, start snogging and inch her knickers down? What about her clothes getting in a mess? Would she complain, or could he work her up enough to forget about them? He had never tried it like this before and the intensity of his anticipation was almost unbearable.

'Adrian!' Her voice was curt.

'Yes?' He swung round to look hungrily at her heavy body and large breasts, just contained by the red blouse. She was wearing nylons. Well, they'd have to come off too. She'd never do it in those. She was too particular. Was there a chance? Could he afford to be a little more optimistic? 'What's up?' he asked, grinning at his unintentional play on words, trying to wipe the randy smile off his face.

'It's going to rain.'

Very much the weather-wise prophet, Adrian squinted knowledgeably at the sky. 'I reckon it'll hold off for a while longer.'

'What makes you say that?'

'Let's get off the path,' he said, too casually. 'Do a bit of exploring.' Adrian felt so self-conscious that he was sure she would laugh at him. But Molly was still gazing up at the sky doubtfully.

'Wasn't that a drop of rain?' She made it sound like Armageddon.

'No!' He grabbed her. Might as well be the wild beast right away, he thought. If he didn't act now, his chance would be gone and his massive erection would have to be dealt with less pleasurably.

'I told you. I'm not doing nothing in the wet.' Her lips were pursed and Adrian felt such desire he could hardly control himself.

The smell of fern and bracken and last year's leaves increased his excitement still further and he began to run, pulling her with him.

'Come on!'

'Where're we going?'

'Somewhere quiet.'

'It's going to rain!'

But she didn't struggle and Adrian knew that his luck might hold after all.

They were waist high in bracken on a ridge just below the hill when another smell assaulted his nostrils, a smell that wasn't in the least erotic.

He choked, the noxious aroma in his throat, and Molly dragged him to a halt. They were just below an old oak tree, dead, lightning blasted, its roots exposed.

'What the hell is it?' she whispered.

'Dead animal,' he suggested. 'Let's go the other way.'

'Oh Christ!'

'What is it?'

Adrian saw the thing at last. What he had taken for part of the root system of the blasted oak was a pale limb.

'It's a deer,' he said in a vain attempt at reassurance.

'No.' Molly was insistent, and letting go of his hand began to walk purposefully through the bracken. He hurried to join her.

The young man lay on his back, naked, one leg nestling in the roots of the tree, the other twisted grotesquely and brokenly beneath him. He had red hair which was cropped short and his cheeks were freckled. Ants had taken residence in the gash in his throat and a couple of bluebottles crawled lazily from the dried blood.

Adrian tried to pull Molly away, but she was resistant, fixated.

Then, mercifully, the drizzle began and she remembered that she hadn't wanted to get wet. It was some time before Molly really understood and began to scream.

1

Lucy Groves was making sandwiches in the pavilion as the mellow sun swamped the cricket pitch in glowing tea-time light. She was acutely conscious of the strong scent of sandwich spread mingling with the dank smell of well-trodden grass. God, how she hated this ritual. Lucy gazed up bitterly at the stained wooden wall opposite her, with its rows of framed West End First Eleven photographs, some yellowing, the backgrounds as bland as the cricketers' smiles.

In front of Lucy was a trestle table bearing an all too slowly increasing mound of sandwiches and a pile of equally slowly reducing fillings. They included the wholesalers' jar of sandwich spread thoughtfully donated by the Chief Constable's brother who was 'in grocery', the ham given by Glen Mackintosh, a local farmer, the hard lump of cheddar the Ladies' Catering Committee had proudly provided, the sausage meat that Lady Grayson had manufactured in her own kitchen and the tomatoes from the vicar's greenhouse. Not bad with rationing being such a bugbear. But the troops had rallied round for the sacred cause of leather on willow.

If only Tim wasn't a cricketer. How good it would be to potter in the garden or run down to Ferring instead. She could have walked along the cold south coast beach, watching the sea lick at the pebbles instead of the teams munching their sandwiches, homaging the game, their flat jokes as sharp as the lingering taste of sandwich spread in her mouth.

Lucy knew she should never have started eating while filling, but purloining scraps of the valedictory feast was compensatory, despite the fact that the ham was leathery and even Lady Grayson's sausage meat thin and tasteless.

Tim's illness was, as usual, central to Lucy's thinking. Was she romancing what he had once been, colouring his memory purple? Had he really been planning to travel in austere and contemplative places and to take her with him? Or had she

11

created some absurd fantasy? What he *had* been was so far from what Tim was now that Lucy couldn't possibly connect the two.

As she automatically trimmed the edges of yet another sandwich, Lucy remembered their first expedition, walking desert and ocean-side trails through the barren interior of Baya California after Tim's graduation in the summer of '36. She had photographed him under an enormous flowering cactus, in his shorts and khaki shirt, so full of life and so different from other men in his restlessness, his need for change. They had planned to travel the world. No, Lucy told herself firmly, I never made Tim up. He was there. Once.

'He's a free spirit,' his mother, Susan Groves, had told her. 'He's not going to settle. Tim's a doer.'

Now he was more like a changeling. The little people had stolen the old Tim and put someone else in his place.

After the war was over, the shadow Tim had worked for her cousin's estate agency. Soon there was an additional tragedy; Lucy had been told she was barren.

The word gave her a vision of bare fields under a winter's leaden sky. A single crow picked at the arid loam.

A fearless flying ant, having hovered for some time on the edge of her bowl, suddenly fell into the powdered egg mayonnaise. With considerable pleasure, Lucy briskly added the insect to the mixture.

She glanced up at a burst of muted clapping, observing through the open door Tim slowly walking back from the pitch in the hazy sunshine, his white-clad figure shimmering as if in a desert mirage. The desert? Little chance of that now. All she was likely to see for a good long time were the mock Tudor gables of Esher High Street and all she was likely to hear was the chirpy buzz of chatter in Caves Café. Unless she intervened.

As Tim came nearer to the pavilion he seemed more emaciated than ever, his features gaunt and craggy, his wrists and forearms under his rolled-up sleeves painfully thin.

'Tim's been run out.' May Latimer arrived, plain, staunch and stoic. She always managed to oppress Lucy with her total lack of imagination. Not for May the call of the leopard, virgin sand on a Mexican beach, the pleasure of uncertainty. She often felt more like a gaoler than a friend, a continual reminder not to ask for too much, accept the status quo and, above all, put down roots that would be relentlessly encased in concrete.

'Who by?' asked Lucy, boredom making her voice dull.

'Gerry Warburton.'

'What a fool that man is.'

May smiled tolerantly. She had long since given Lucy the label 'rogue', an arrangement by which they managed not to quarrel.

May was married to Martin Latimer who, along with Peter Davis, had shared Tim's wartime escape. Lucy had tried to like them at first, making them welcome for Tim's sake, but she had soon almost convinced herself that Martin and Peter had deliberately moved to Esher after the war to watch over him, rather than to cement a friendship from which their wives would always be excluded. Now, five years later, she sensed they were still watching.

The Men, Lucy thought bitterly, bastions of a masculine world that had become a fortress. Tim's guardians, his trustees.

At other times, Lucy was sure she was exaggerating the situation, creating a fantasy based on her own antipathy. She had to accept that the three men were simply bonded together by their experiences. But unlike Tim, Martin and Peter were unscathed, and for her they had come to epitomise the Surrey suburbs and their relentless conformity. Both had found their officer status useful in peacetime employment. Peter had joined the Prudential Assurance in Holborn, Martin the Midland Bank, professions to which they would depart on the 7.43 each morning, bowler-hatted, pinstriped, swinging their umbrellas, leaving Tim behind in his baggy tweeds, jobbing clerk to Lucy's cousin in Lyle and Watson. She was sure Bruce had employed him out of charity, regarding him as yet another war casualty likely to make a 'slow recovery' with his 'bad nerves'.

'Lot of flies in here,' commented May as she advanced on the trestle table, ready to resume her duties as fellow sandwich-maker.

'It's like a charnel house with Lady G.'s sausage meat.'

'Talking of charnel houses,' May commented in the strained *risqué* voice she sometimes assumed when she wanted to gossip, 'did you hear about the murder?'

'Murder?' Lucy imagined May was joking. 'Someone done in the Chief Constable?'

Guy Bretherton, Chief Constable of Surrey, was one of West End's finest bats.

'Actually, his wife told me.' May blushed. 'A young couple found a corpse at the Clump.'

'A corpse at the Clump?' Lucy stared at her, unable to take in what she was saying. The phrase seemed to have a rhythm of its own, almost like the beginning of a popular song.

May gazed down at the egg mayonnaise as if seeking a solution.

'Has anyone identified – '

'It was the Davises' gardener.' May's voice shook. Murder was impossible in Esher's leafy tranquillity.

'Good God!' Lucy found it hard to believe such an event could really have occurred. It seemed to belong to the special territory created by *The News of the World*. 'The gardener they've just taken on?'

'He came from over Hersham way,' said May, as if that explained everything and then added casually, 'Someone cut his throat.'

'On the Clump?' Lucy's unease was now directed at the location rather than the act. She often tramped alone over the hill with its ancient oaks and dense undergrowth. 'Do the police know who did it?' she asked woodenly.

'I've no idea.' May was a teacher at Beacon House, the local prep school, and strongly believed in keeping anything out of the ordinary well under control. A corpse on the Clump definitely came into this category. Yet, despite all May's reserve, Lucy had once sought her advice, largely out of desperation and loneliness. It had been a mistake.

She and May had been strolling the banks of the River Mole and had sat on the trunk of a fallen silver birch, gazing down into the lazy, muddy water. Suddenly, surprisingly, Lucy had found herself telling May about Tim.

'If only he'd talk to me.'

'Martin won't discuss the war either, and I know Sally says the same about Peter.' May had spoken brusquely, as if the subject was improper. The conflict was in the past and should be kept there. War was the men's business. It had been started and finished by them. Their women had no part in its aftermath.

Lucy had wondered if May secretly despised Tim for not keeping a stiff upper lip, for dwelling on the morbid that must be swept aside. The men were back in Esher now. Outside life lay safely in the City of London rather than the battlefields of Normandy.

'Sometimes I think I should go back to France with Tim, walk where they walked.' In fact, Lucy had only just had the notion and had never envisaged such a course of action before. The unlikely idea, she remembered, had considerably surprised her. May's response had not been encouraging.

'I don't think that would be a good idea,' she had said firmly, as if to some idiotic request by a wilful child. May's thumping good common sense had seemed as thick as the grey loam that lay heavily in the fields around them. Barren.

'This murder,' Lucy said abruptly, realizing she was holding the jar of spread aloft, as if she was about to make a sacrifice to the gods. 'What on earth did the Davises say?'

'I don't know. Of course, the young man had only been with them a month. They don't have much luck, do they? First that nasty piece of vandalism. Now their gardener.'

So he could easily be disposed of, thought Lucy. Forgotten because he hadn't fully penetrated Esher's chintz and damask surface. Forgotten because he came from Hersham. The gardener's funeral oration would be made over the coffee cups at Caves Café and then he would not be mentioned again. The vandalism and the burning of the shed were different, more outrageous in their full frontal attack on the middle classes by the Hersham mafia.

'Does he have a name?'

'Baverstock.'

'Was he married?'

'He was only seventeen.' May's lips were set as if she wanted to bring the subject to a close rather than continue to explore it. Her morality had beaten her curiosity. As always. 'Anyway. We must get on. They'll be off the pitch soon, hungry for their teas.' She made it sound as if she and Lucy were about to be besieged by a ravening horde, rather than twenty-two men and an umpire who would have preferred beer to the thinly-spread sandwiches and brackish urn tea.

May and Martin were childless too, although May wasn't barren. Martin had wanted to 'wait a bit' and not have babies until there was 'a bit more cash around'. Always accepting, May didn't seem to mind.

Lucy knew that she and Tim might wait for ever. Five years of tests and specialists had lowered Lucy's morale, made her feel inadequate, but she was also increasingly aware that she was already nursing her own frightened child. What kind of father would Tim have made? Even if fatherhood had been possible. She had not confided in either May or Sally because she didn't want their pity or comfort – bustling in May's case, thrusting in Sally's. Only Tim knew and he had never referred to the 'matter' since Lucy had told him. Nor had he reacted to her talk of adoption. It was as if she had mentioned the war.

'Did you hear?' Sally stepped over the threshold, as elegant as ever in her white blouse and tailored slacks. 'Did you hear about our gardener? The murder's going to be on the radio tonight.' Her voice held a mixture of excitement and shock. 'We're having a real week of it, aren't we? What with the fire – and now this!'

'May's just told me,' said Lucy flatly.

Predictably, Sally pushed her long blonde hair out of her eyes and gave the plucky little smile that Lucy found so irritating. It was a slight consolation to know that her artificial 'grit' profoundly irritated May too. With her fresh good looks, her undoubted abilities at tennis and golf, her much displayed competence as a housewife, Sally appeared on the surface to be invulnerable.

She had sex-appeal, bore a slight resemblance to Diana Dors but didn't display her style. She did have the breasts, although Lucy suspected Sally also wore a brassiere upholstered with foam rubber to enhance them. She pushed her appearance to the limits, but she also often withdrew from life, taking to her bed for long periods with blinding migraines. During these absences her young daughter Alice had to be one hundred per cent in the care of the nanny instead of the normal ninety per cent. Sometimes Lucy imagined that because Sally lived at such an intense level of perfection, she *had* to lie low and regenerate new and glossy skin as well as a sheen of revitalized enthusiasm, not to mention the breasts.

Lucy was still slightly puzzled by the shed burning episode.

Sally had never had a social conscience before. So why should she berate bullies on Esher green? Lucy, however, supposed there was a first time for everything – even Sally's crusade. Then there was the matter of the boy's name. William Tell. She saw an apple on a child's head sliced by an arrow. The child looked foxy. But he would, wouldn't he? He came from Hersham.

Sally walked across to the bowl of watercress. Lucy wondered if she was going to soil her hands for once, and help fill a sandwich, but she simply looked at the stuff in some distaste and said, 'Baverstock worked for the Dowsetts and the Rentons, too. He'd only been with us a month. Isn't it awful?' She lowered her voice, the doll-like features perplexed. 'He did a wonderful job on the dahlias *and* he promised to get rid of all that ground elder. He was even going to build us a new potting shed.'

Clearly his violent death was an inconvenience, thought Lucy. He could at least have got the essential jobs done before allowing his throat to be cut.

Conifers, the Davises' Victorian dwelling with its extensive grounds, was just opposite Lucy's own more modest red-brick home in Shrub Lane. She had liked Gables when she and Tim had bought the house just before the war, but now it felt dull and suburban, dwarfed by Conifers, whose windows seemed to stare watchfully into their own. Martin and May Latimer's house, Old Linden, in the same thirties style, was only two doors down.

'I just wondered if Baverstock was one of those types,' said May awkwardly, concentrating on furiously carving ham. 'Do you know what I mean?'

Lucy felt a rush of flurried embarrassment. There then followed a stunned silence. Sally made a quick stab at changing the subject for they all knew what May was talking about. Something that was utterly taboo.

'The police have done nothing about that fire. Not a dicky bird.'

'Really?' asked Lucy, a slight blush on her cheeks.

The term 'homosexual' was hardly ever used, certainly not in the cricket pavilion. But of course May worked in a prep school. She would know. She would be able to speak about the problem, clinically and with thumping common sense.

'I saw him from the Cut,' continued May, ignoring the attempts at evasion. 'He was with someone. A man.' May paused, embarrassing herself now. She often 'spoke out', but this was clearly too much and Lucy wondered whether she was beating a retreat.

The Cut, the path between the border fence of Conifers and a stream that ran down the length of Shrub Lane, was partly masked by foliage. May and Lucy, taking the path up to the High Street, often listened to the smack of tennis balls as Sally played with her friends on the court to the right of the house. Neither May nor Lucy could play, despite Sally's persistent offers to teach them. Nor did they want to. She could be determinedly patronizing and, besides, in tennis clothes her breasts were a threat. May's were matronly. Lucy's were modest.

Then May doggedly enlarged on what she had seen, as if she wished she hadn't begun and wanted to get it over with as quickly as possible. After all, homosexuality was a criminal offence, punishable by law, and criminal offences didn't happen that much in Esher. Unless you counted arson and murder. 'I was walking up to the High Street and Baverstock was on your land with this chap,' she said in her 'I've got a duty to tell you' voice. 'Of course, it was only the most fleeting glimpse.'

Sally brushed the hair out of her eyes again. How many times a day does she actually do that, wondered Lucy. Why doesn't she get a hairdresser to alter her style? Or does she *need* the gesture?

'The man disappeared into the woods. He moved fast but I couldn't tell whether they'd seen me or not.'

'Did you speak to Baverstock?' asked Sally, looking away, forcing herself to ask.

'No.' May paused. 'I just went on up to the shops.'

'Why do you think this was – *that* kind of business?' demanded Lucy, hardly able to bring out the unfamiliar. phrase, the blush creeping down her neck.

'I thought when I first saw them – ' May paused – 'that they were in each other's arms.'

In anyone else, Lucy would have suspected gossipy melodrama. But May wasn't like that. She was too full of practical morality and was only remarking on this apparent deviance because she thought it might have a connection. All too obviously she was 'trying it out' on Sally but was, at the same time, awkward, as if she was really 'talking dirty'.

'They sprang apart?' Lucy asked, realizing that she was using

18

the vocabulary of the books in the romantic section of Boots library. Denise Robins, or even Ruby M. Ayres. She glanced at Sally but she refused to catch her eye.

'I almost told Maggie Bretherton, but in the end I didn't,' continued May. 'I mean – I don't want to start anything. I'd really like your advice.'

'You should tell the police what you saw,' said Lucy immediately.

'Yes.' Sally was nodding encouragement. 'There might be a perfectly acceptable explanation. You might have made a mistake. But you've got to tell them.'

May nodded, frowning, clearly unsure, embarrassed again.

The sandwiches were finished with minimal and preoccupied help from Sally and determined effort from May. Her Ladies Committee duties over, Lucy walked out into the hard sunlight, squinting at the white figures on the smooth turf, glancing down at her watch and hoping it would soon be time to draw stumps.

'Hallo, old thing,' said Tim, turning round awkwardly in the deckchair that he had placed at some distance from the small bunch of spectators.

'You're being antisocial,' said Lucy, her love for him hurting inside. She had always been determined not to be protective, not to treat Tim like an invalid, to dignify what he had suffered. Yet she continually found herself fussing, watching, hoping for the first signs of recovery that never came. In fact, she knew he was getting worse.

Despite the hot summer, Tim looked ashen out here in the sharp light, the lines on his face hard and dry. His fair hair was so bleached by the sun that it had a curious flat, limp quality and shed dandruff over his blazer collar.

'Fraid I was run out.'

'Bad luck.' She noticed he had that familiar distracted air and was tapping a finger on the frame of the deckchair, as if he was waiting for something to happen, someone to arrive.

'Did you hear about young Baverstock?' Tim asked her, his voice taut.

'It's awful,' Lucy replied as expressionlessly as possible.

But he seemed over-excited, wanting to communicate. 'To think it could happen here. Esher of all places. Peter's very shocked. Baverstock was a good worker. Came from Hersham. What with that fire and those ghastly boys, the Davises aren't having a good week. I gather the vandals came from Hersham too.' Like May, he spoke as if they had all come from some far-flung country. Hersham contained a large council estate near the reservoir, and allotments and light industry from which Esher determinedly held itself aloof. 'Bit much,' Tim added, gazing down the field. 'Well played,' he called, as one of the batsmen hit a six.

'It's almost time for tea,' said Lucy. 'Not made you feel bad, has it?'

'The cricket?'

'The murder.'

'Well. It's not pleasant. I don't know what's happening to this country. Was it worth fighting a war for?' Tim was giving off a familiar rank body odour. She wondered yet again what caused it for he bathed regularly.

Lucy felt a wave of self-pity. She had married a man who had led her into the light. Now she was trying to cope with an invalid in a deckchair, with scrawny arms and hair like fur, who would be thirty-one next month. It was as if a confidence trick had been played on her.

'Ever felt like moving house?' she asked, taking a risk and trying to jerk him out of his inertia. Lucy immediately felt shocked. She was usually so careful. But her father had died a few weeks ago, leaving her even more rudderless than before. While he had been alive she had just been able to cope with Tim's withdrawal; now she felt completely isolated, with no one in her life to rely on.

Her father had lain in the last bed by the door of the ward (he had claimed they always put no-hopers there so they could be wheeled out quickly when death was pronounced). He had said to Lucy, 'Try and get Tim on his feet again. Why not move? You'll have my money.'

Now, for the first time, she was trying it on.

'Move?' Tim sat bolt upright, his veined right hand gripping the side of the chair.

'Go down to Devon.' Lucy felt a guilty rush of adrenalin.

Tim gave an angry bark of laughter. 'My dear girl – ' The phrase hung limply on the summer scented air. 'What on earth would we live on?'

'I'll have Dad's money and you could get another job with an estate agent. You're experienced now.'

'I'm just on the bottom rung of the ladder,' he replied with gloomy relish. 'Haven't earned any kudos yet.'

'It was only an idea.' Her voice was neutral.

Tim reached out to take her hand. His grip was damp and Lucy felt a wave of self-loathing. What the hell was the matter with her? Why was she so insensitive? Why couldn't she accept mental illness on the same level as a physical injury?

'Toby's serving up some terrific googlies.' He spoke as if he was still at prep school, trying to impress a prefect or even a teacher. *Was* the real Tim in there somewhere? In this bony bundle of subterfuge?

Doctor Wayland had recently told her that Tim was hanging on to normality like a dangling man whose fingers were slowly slipping off a ledge. Yet, once again, Lucy recklessly dived into the attack, almost angry now, determined that he should tune into her feelings for once.

'Have you thought any more about the adoption?' The words were out in a rush and her trepidation rose. It was like being on a kamikaze bombing mission. How had she slipped into this foolhardy course? Lucy felt slightly dizzy and wondered if she was coming down with something.

'Sorry?'

She could see that he had heard, had probably been waiting for her to say this for months and had set up his own rehearsed programme of prevarication.

'This is hardly the time or the place – '

'It's important to me.' She spoke awkwardly. 'To us. You know how – '

'It's a big issue,' he broke in. 'A very big issue. Bad form to bring it up here. What with the murder.' Tim made it sound as if Lucy had dropped her knickers in church.

Her eyes filled with tears.

'Grand game,' Tim muttered as the umpire at last pulled stumps.

Peter and Martin strolled off the pitch together, heading towards them, faces tanned, jerseys over their shoulders, casually self-satisfied.

Tim didn't rise from his deckchair and the two men

approached him as if visiting a patient in a hospital bed, cautiously, with a little embarrassment and far too much bonhomie.

Captain Peter Davis, who had been Tim's senior officer, was the shorter of the two, stocky with a mass of dark curly hair and an assertive manner that showed in his stride. He had a generous moustache, short but bushy, and Lucy noticed as she always did the black hairs sprouting from the open neck of his cricket shirt. She often wondered if he was too much of an animal in bed and that was another reason why Sally closed down so frequently. Peter Davis's soft, gentle voice, however, belied his looks.

Second Lieutenant Martin Latimer, who had been his second in command, was tall, amiable, lean and fit, and much less assertive than Peter. The dark blue eyes in his clean-shaven oval face were benign. He also had an authority to him, a casual efficiency and sporting prowess that had won him the captaincy of the cricket team. Of the two, Martin was the one she related to more easily, although he could be just as oppressive as Peter in his apparent watchfulness. Sometimes Lucy tried really hard to dismiss the men's oppressiveness as overblown imagination, but when she was with them, her suspicions immediately resurfaced. Lucy had conveniently stereotyped the men as marauders. Tim's jailors. She thought of them with a capital M. The Men were the Enemy.

'What-ho!' said Tim. They loomed over him with an almost parental air, grinning affectionately, their shadows cutting him off from the sun.

It was a strange sensation that Lucy didn't like. She always felt uncomfortable when the three of them were together, as if she was an intruder.

'Bad luck about the run-out. Gerry should have known better,' observed Peter.

'One of those things,' muttered Tim. He was trying unsuccessfully to get out of the deckchair and Martin had to give him a hand – or a 'paw' as Tim might easily have said, Lucy thought with a surge of irritation.

'Bit stiff, old boy?'

Now he was on his feet, Tim was giving a rueful grin.

'How about a run one of these evenings?' said Martin, yawning slightly.

'Great idea.'

'Put some muscle on those pins of yours.'

The pavilion was crowded with white-flannelled cricketers and their ladies in summer prints, consuming Lucy's sandwiches with boarding school appetites. There was a slightly institutionalized conviviality; hoots of laughter, raucous banter rose and fell as wasps buzzed the trestle table. The atmosphere was rapidly heating up until both teams and their supporters were running with perspiration.

The war burnt us all out, thought Lucy, and we're only just starting to recover. Pale creatures, battered and torn, like flowers rising out of frost, desperate for a hazy glimpse of the sun. We've endured so much, muddled on for too long. Now all we can do is to pretend to be what we used to be until we begin to thrive again. But Tim hadn't surfaced. France was dragging him back. Only his veined hand had a grip.

Gradually the news of the young gardener's murder began to circulate and voices were lowered conspiratorially, with an undercurrent of excitement.

Lisa Warburton, however, had either not heard of the incident or had chosen to dismiss it as too sordid for discussion. She was a large florid woman with a booming sense of fun, who had gallantly struggled through the war until her man had returned intact and had slipped back into her vice-like grip. Now her mind had raced on to other, more positive issues.

Lisa was talking vivaciously to Lucy, who was only half listening, her mind on the unreasonable demands she had made on Tim. The timing couldn't have been worse. Why hadn't she been more in control? She usually was.

'Gerry and I had quite a fling at the festival on the South Bank,' droned Lisa. 'You and Tim really should get up there. I know he's been off colour but it would take him out of himself to see the Skylon and the Emett railway's a real hoot. And do you know – despite the rain – we danced under the floodlights – even though Gerry was wearing a trilby and we both had mackintoshes. We must have looked a sight but then so did everyone else.' Lisa paused. 'But the best thing about the festival is the people. They're so full of fun. They haven't had a foreign holiday in years or seen café tables with umbrellas or even any fresh paint.' She paused again, this time rather breathlessly, even warily. 'After all, Tim fought for what we've got, didn't he? Like all the men did. The Festival gave us new heart. At least it promised some kind of future. I'm going to redecorate the house. I want that bright, clean "Festival" style.'

We're all still stuck with mock Tudor, thought Lucy. You won't make Esher change that easily. She could imagine Lisa's plans. 'Contemporary' wallpaper with jazzy patterns, the fire-place wall being made to 'stand out' with an even more vibrant wallpaper. Then there was the carpet. She would probably choose 'Skaters Trails', the latest best-seller, an equally jazzy pattern of thin curved lines on a background of grey or burnt red. Very modern. Very bold.

Lucy and Tim hadn't been to the South Bank yet. He kept putting the outing off. Besides, she didn't really want to go. She didn't want to be modern and she couldn't imagine Tim dancing in the rain. In fact, she couldn't imagine Tim dancing at all.

Lisa lowered her voice conspiratorially. 'Is your husband any better?'

'We're going back to the specialist.' This was Lucy's most recent standard reply. It was suitably vague and shut most of them up. Except Lisa.

'I know how worried Peter and Martin are about him. They went through so much together. But they didn't catch bad nerves, did they?' She made it sound as if Tim had had a particularly long run of chicken pox.

After the match, most of the home team, with their wives or girlfriends, attended Evensong in the tiny church by the green. It was the cricketers' tradition, Tim had once explained to Lucy who was not a believer. 'Bad form not to show.' Before the war, cricket or no cricket, Tim would not have attended either. 'Lot of tommy-rot,' she heard him say, as if from the depths of half-forgotten history.

Peter and Sally Davis, Tim and Lucy Groves, Martin and May Latimer sat in the front pew, the men still in their grubby whites, the women in their creased prints, except Sally of course who had found time to drive home and change her immaculate slacks for a smart skirt.

Peter Davis led the singing with his fine tenor, as Mrs Cronin, head down and lips pursed, played a liberal scattering of bum notes on the organ. Her inadequacies, however, didn't put Peter off his stride.

> For thee, O dear, dear country,
> Mine eyes their vigils keep;
> For very love, beholding
> Thy happy name, they weep.

Tim's lips moved but no sound came out, and Lucy's contralto was muted. Sally and May contributed thin sopranos and Martin's bass was largely inaudible. The rest of the congregation boomed lustily, still grateful for the end of the war, realizing that as the Defenders of the Right it was fitting that they should pay homage to their Maker, at least for a while.

Gazing round the small church, Lucy's sense of isolation increased. I'm hemmed in, she thought, crushed by complacency and sterling common sense. Esher had been fought for. Esher had been won. Now the Festival of Britain was still celebrating victory, flags and bunting were out over every shop and many householders had run up the Union Jack. There was more jingoism now than on VE Day.

Lucy tried to imagine Esher in Nazi hands, but the idea was impossible, unthinkable; all she could produce were unlikely images of Oberleutnants strutting through Woolworth's, or taking the salute outside the electricity showroom, or checking the 4th Esher Scout Group for signs of circumcision. Perhaps that's why we won the war, she thought. We couldn't even *imagine* an Occupation.

> The mention of thy glory,
> Is unction to the breast,
> And medicine in sickness,
> And love and life and rest.

Love and life and rest? Where was Lucy going to get that? Only somewhere far from Shrub Lane, away from the men. They were a cabal. Even now, she realized, Martin and Peter were standing on either side of them, like guardians. Like conquering heroes.

Of course it would be a story to tell their grandchildren if they ever had any. Cut off after Dunkirk on the Havre peninsula, the three men, instead of remaining behind with the wounded to surrender to the Germans, had started walking through Occupied France. Having failed to find a boat at Honfleur, they tramped from house to house, barn to barn, relying on the good will of local people, sometimes staying for a few days, or even just one broken night. Typical of the English, none of the trio had much grasp of the French language. Yet, by sheer tenacity they had muddled through. Except something had happened out there to destroy Tim and no one had told her what it was. Not even Tim.

> With jasper glow thy bulwarks,
> Thy streets with emeralds blaze;
> The sardius and the topaz
> Unite in thee their rays.

Lucy had a degree in French and spoke the language fluently. That's why she admired Tim's escape so much. It must have been a terrifying ordeal, stuck in a country with none of its language.

Nevertheless, Tim and Martin and Peter had walked and eventually cycled through Vichy France to Franco's Spain, where they had managed to board a cargo ship bound for London. It had been an amazing feat and, for a while, all three men were fêted in the press. There had been talk of a book, but it had come to nothing. Nor had any military decorations been conferred on them, which Lucy found distinctly odd. But the oddness had been swallowed up by Tim's breakdown.

When the men had arrived back in England in 1942, after a reconciliation with their wives and a suitable rest, Peter and Martin had rejoined their regiment and were based in Bournemouth in various administrative capacities. Tim, however, went from one shell-shock clinic to another. They seemed to make him worse.

Lucy regularly visited him in army requisitioned country houses with still smooth lawns and fountains. Tables with umbrellas were grouped under spreading chestnut trees and men in wheelchairs and dressing gowns closed drugged minds against brightly discreet relatives. Tim was usually the only man who was ambulant. He slept a lot, often through Lucy's visits,

26

and she was forcibly reminded of the dormouse at the Mad Hatter's tea party.

Having endured him being posted missing for close on three months, having almost given Tim up for dead, Lucy found him 'missing' again. There had only been traces of the man she had known so intimately, had loved so deeply. The rest of him was no more than a hollow shell, as if someone had scraped the real Tim out.

The clinics and their psychiatrists had been able to do little for him, and gradually the tag 'shell shock' became blanket coverage for everything and anything that was the matter with him. Meanwhile, Tim was refusing to attend the clinics any longer.

Recently, Vera Lynn's voice had beat hollowly in Lucy's ears, dozens of times a day.

> We'll meet again, don't know where, don't know when,
> But I know we'll meet again some sunny day.
> Keep smiling through, just like you always do,
> Till the blue skies drive the dark clouds far away.

Would she ever meet the old Tim again, or had the war taken him away for ever?

When he was discharged from the last clinic, spat out like a gnawed bone, Tim had moped around the house. He was barely capable of taking a decision about paying a bill, posting a letter, turning on the wireless, taking her out in the Riley, even cleaning his teeth. He would look at his toothbrush for a long, long time. Then he would put it away.

Tim sat and worried, getting his concerns out of all possible proportion. Did his demob suit fit? Were they eating too much? Paying exorbitant amounts for food? Had the drains been inspected recently? Was the bathroom damp? Could he smell gas? Was the milkman overcharging? Should they stop the newspaper delivery? Should he sell some shares? He was also obsessed with the post, always tense before its arrival, inevitably going out to meet the postman halfway up the garden path, taking the letters and using the same phrase every day, recited for some obscure reason in a mock Welsh accent. 'Thank you, Postie.' The daily repetition got Lucy down. She reckoned it got the postman down too.

When Lucy had got Tim the job at her cousin's estate agency

27

he was immediately over-anxious. Was he too slow? Did they think him careless? He was sure he had bad breath. People were shrinking away from him. Had he been rude? Too familiar? Were his clothes wrong? What about his shoes?

Of course, Tim, like Peter and Martin, would never talk about the war and what had actually happened to them. He had always claimed he couldn't say any more for 'security' reasons. But of one thing Lucy was sure: something had happened, something so momentous that it had broken him. The doctor had tried to arrange for more psychiatric help, but Tim had refused. 'No more trick cyclists,' he pronounced. 'I'm feeling better every day.'

In fact, he was getting worse, and whatever had happened in France held him in a vice.

Although May was sympathetic in her plodding way, Lucy had never wanted to confide in her again. Sally chose to ignore the problem and Martin rarely mentioned Tim's 'condition'. He and Peter just watched over him. Carefully.

Lucy remembered the one occasion when Peter had talked to her, just after he and Sally had moved in. Tim had been mowing the lawn when he had knocked at the front door and she had warily invited him in, inhibited by his assertiveness.

'Don't disturb Tim for the moment,' he had said as she ushered him into the lounge. 'I just wanted a word.'

In the intervening year before they moved into Shrub Lane, the Davises had rented a flat in Teddington and the Latimers had lived with Martin's parents in Cobham. It's as if the Men had both been waiting in the wings, waiting for their opportunity. It had been unfortunate, Lucy thought, that so many houses in Shrub Lane had been up for sale at the end of the war. The enemy had easily been able to take up positions.

Yet surely the three men were just friends, bound together by their survival. Lucy had tried to rationalise the problem time and again. It was natural they wanted to be together after all they had suffered, although some might have thought they would have preferred to be apart, to start afresh.

Peter had settled in the big armchair with his back to the window and Tim, intent on his mowing, still hadn't seen him.

Or if he had, thought Lucy, he wasn't letting on. She enjoyed his occasional evasions, which seemed to have all the artfulness of a naughty schoolboy. Evasion was healthy – in the circumstances.

Peter had gazed at Lucy, his dark eyes holding hers, level, honest, pulling no punches. The kind of chap she should trust. But she didn't. 'Tim's rough, isn't he?'

'His nerves,' Lucy had replied. 'They don't get any better. In fact I think he's worse than ever.'

'He had a terrible ordeal.' Peter's voice had been steady, blunt, condescendingly attempting to share.

'I appreciate how awful it must have been.' Lucy had been determined to try and make the most of his visit. 'But I've never known what really happened.'

Peter had shaken his curly head brusquely. 'He was a fine soldier. But wasn't he – always the nervous type?'

Lucy had been immediately indignant. Peter had not only ignored her question but had also been quietly patronizing.

She had first met Tim on a trip she and her father had taken to Austria. He had been climbing with a friend while they had been hiking. Towards the end of the holiday, they all spent a day together, striding up a valley on to a path that wound its way to the top of a mountain. She could still recall the startling radiancy of Tim's youth that had bathed her in a new vitality. She had never been confident, always thought things out too carefully for comfort. Tim made her realize that, as he often said then, 'Life is for living'. Now he was merely passing the time.

The climb had made Lucy hot and thirsty and rather light-headed, but the sense of elation she had experienced on reaching the summit had always remained with her. 'Going the extra mile.' The cliché hovered on her lips as she gazed back at Peter's stolid features. That's what Tim had shown her.

'He was only the nervous type *after* the war,' she had retorted.

Peter had nodded acquiescently, as if humouring her. 'Obviously I'm very concerned about Tim, but the trick cyclists didn't do him much good. You're supplying more than adequate support. The cricket helps, of course. Tim loves his cricket.' Peter had leant forward, candid now with his confidences. 'If I can do anything, you'll give me a shout, won't you?'

Lucy had nodded acquiescence, knowing she was under orders.

Then Peter had risen to tap on the glass of the French windows.

29

His broad, sports-jacketed back had cut off her view of Tim, but she imagined him turning from the noisy mower and saluting.

With a leaden feeling, Lucy returned to the pious dirge.

> Upon the Rock of Ages
> They raise thy holy tower;
> Thine is the victor's laurel,
> And thine the golden dower.

Lucy's thoughts turned to her father, who had been her own rock of ages. A furniture maker, he had had a small workshop in the nearby village of Claygate where he had lovingly crafted the regular commissions that had come to him from all over the country. Gerald Newton had been an artist in wood, a lifetime conscientious objector, and a Fabian. Lucy knew how deeply he had valued her, his only child, and she had always confided in him. She had loved him to distraction, dreaded any illness, couldn't bear to imagine life without him.

Lucy's mother had died a few days after she had been born and she and her father had become so close that they knew each other's every thought without causing irritation. Now he was dead and she was alone. More than that, she had lost part of herself.

'Tim should see another specialist,' her father had told her. 'He's not going to get better on his own.'

'Do you think they were captured in France? Or tortured?' she had asked her father for the millionth time.

Gerald had shrugged. 'I don't know, and Peter and Martin aren't going to tell you either,' he had replied as he always did. 'They come from the stiff upper lip brigade and believe in putting the war behind them, not blubbing to the ladies.'

'Can't *you* ask Tim what happened?' she had pleaded. 'He might talk to another man.'

'Me? A Conchie?' He had laughed. 'I'm no better than a communist to them.'

'They respect your views,' she had begun.

'They're polite. Discreet. You're Tim's wife. They won't want to rock the boat. But they won't tell me anything. Why – I don't even play cricket! I'm a pariah.'

Now he was a pariah no longer. Just in a coffin under a mound of raw earth in the parish graveyard. She had yet to commission a headstone and was still toying with ideas for the inscription.

If only we could move, thought Lucy. If only I could adopt a baby. If only I could heal Tim.

She took his hand as the hymn continued and found that it was no longer moist but dry and strong. Tim smelt of crushed grass; the inexplicable rank smell had gone.

As the pious chorus died untidily away, the vicar slowly mounted the pulpit. There was coughing and an air of curiosity. Would he mention what everyone had been talking about? From the rigid set of his pink-and-white old-man's face and from his downcast, distrusting eyes, Lucy knew the Reverend Watson-Byte would do just that.

He had been rector for many years, since well before the war, and was responsible for the parish church just off the High Street as well as this tiny place of worship by the cricket field which served the small West End community, largely comprising a market garden and its tied cottages. Italian prisoners had worked the land during the war and some had married local girls and stayed. Because the Catholic church was some miles away, the families were sitting at the back, at a respectful distance from the indigenous population.

The rector was a theologian, an academic who had always seemed surprised and rather daunted to find himself in charge of a parish, despite his many years of incumbency. Lucy had liked him ever since she had met him at a cocktail party and found him watching the more up-market inhabitants of Esher as if they were specimens of an alien society that he didn't want to relate to.

He was married to a thin, angular woman named Teresa who ran the Guides with grating enthusiasm and whose only other interest was archaeology. She left the parish for months at a time for foreign digs and was the subject of much disapproval from the Parochial Church Council, whose female members tried, unsuccessfully, to fuss round the rector. But he was determined to live off sardines and soup rather than the little messes his devoted parishioners brought him, retreating to his study to write a treatise on Norman ecclesiastical architecture. His sermons were normally theological, so much so that they induced a torpor in his flock which often turned to a deep sleep. Lucy sometimes wondered if this was his way of exacting revenge. In his quiet way, the Reverend Watson-Byte was a rebel and Lucy respected his tactics.

'My dear friends.' The rector gazed at the congregation quizzically, unused to so much attention, his voice so soft that they had to strain to hear him. 'I was going to speak about the Sermon on the Mount, but I've now decided to mention one of our Lord's commandments. Thou shalt not kill.' He paused, waiting for the buzz of interest to die down. Lucy glanced round at the back pew and saw the Italians whispering. She suddenly realized they might come under suspicion. 'Eyeties', in Esher's opinion, 'needed watching.' Especially ex-prisoners of war.

'Many of you will have heard of the tragic death of a young man at our beauty spot, the Clump, yesterday. It is normally not my place or function to impart such grim news from the pulpit but, as some of you may be aware, this was not an ordinary death. Someone had taken the life of Graham Baverstock who was a local gardener.'

There was a ripple of shock from the few who had not as yet heard the news and a child began to cry at the back of the church.

'I realize how upsetting this will be to you all, but I felt it my duty to warn you that the police have informed me that, so far, no one has been apprehended for this dreadful act. Therefore I must ask you to be vigilant and to lock your doors tonight. I have no doubt in my mind that the young man's assailant was a marauding stranger who came from outside Esher, perhaps even from outside Surrey. But we must take precautions. I've spoken to the Chief Constable, and he assures me that the police are doing their utmost and he is confident that an arrest will be made soon.' The rector's voice took on a more comforting, less jarring note. 'Extra officers are being drafted into the area and the Chief Constable joins me in requesting you to take every precaution. And now, let us consider our Lord's commandment – '

The congregation settled back in their pews to consider – or even to relish – the situation. The war had come and gone, and peacetime had been uneventful. Too uneventful.

Lucy gazed around the congregation to see if she could spot the Chief Constable. Maggie Bretherton was in her usual place, but her husband was nowhere to be seen. She realized that the local population would no doubt have greater faith if he was seen to be 'on the job'.

2

Lucy was in shallow sleep when Tim woke screaming. Immediately, she could detect the rank smell again.

They had recently chosen to sleep in separate beds, but at least they were in the same room. She dragged herself up and took Tim's hot, sweaty hand.

'The angels are dying,' he muttered.

Lucy shivered apprehensively in the cold room. He hadn't mentioned angels before. His bad dreams had always ended with incoherent shouting.

Tim sat up, his pyjamas soaked, the perspiration standing out on his forehead, his hair matted and damp. His lips were working but no sound was coming out.

Suddenly Lucy felt deeply afraid. Was his breakdown reaching a new peak? Would he need to be hospitalized?

'Don't make me,' Tim said abruptly. He was staring ahead at the chintz curtains, as if he was watching something crawling on them.

She tried to keep calm herself. 'No one's going to make you do anything you don't want to.' But Lucy knew she sounded like some unctuous nurse. Her fear surged.

He was coming to now, blinking his eyes, gazing at her in bewilderment. Shaking his head Tim pulled his hand away. 'I'm not fit to be his father,' he said muzzily, but he was watching her, as if waiting for some kind of reaction that she wasn't giving. 'That's why I won't adopt,' he added, licking his lips, saliva caked into the corners of his mouth.

'Tell me what you were dreaming.' It was a fatal question and Lucy cursed herself for she could see the shutters coming down in his eyes.

'Don't worry, old girl.' His jaunty tone was forced as he continued to watch her closely.

'Don't you remember?' Lucy didn't want to repeat what he had said, but now she had gone this far, she realized that she might as well keep going. The damage had been done.

'Damn dreams.' Tim smiled ruefully. 'Can't seem to get rid of them. Any chance of a cup of cocoa? That'll send me back to sleep so the bedbugs don't bite.'

Lucy was still not prepared to give up. 'What do you see?'

He laughed impatiently. 'Running on the spot, pursued by demons, that kind of thing.'

'French demons?'

He said nothing, but looked as if he was trying to remember. 'That poor lad,' he commented slowly. 'The gardener I mean.'

Lucy realized he was using guile, trying to change the subject. To ease the tension, she decided to go along with him.

'It was horrible. Were you dreaming about him?'

'Of course not.'

'Don't make me,' she heard the sleep-slurred voice again. Lucy turned Tim's words over in her mind, increasingly afraid. 'Do you reckon someone round here did it?'

He started and then shrugged. 'What nonsense.'

'Apparently May saw the gardener with a stranger.'

'Where?' His voice was querulous.

That'll teach him to get off the subject, thought Lucy, and then realized how petty-minded she was becoming. Let me in, she pleaded with Tim in her mind. You've *got* to let me in.

'On the Davises' land. She was walking up the Cut to the High Street. She saw them in the woods.'

'Couple of unsavoury customers.' He spoke slowly, as if trying to establish something. Tim cleared his throat. 'How about that cocoa?'

'I'll get it.' Lucy got up reluctantly and went to the door, aware that she hadn't finished, couldn't finish. She knew she had to confront him, shock Tim into some kind of submission. 'These dreams can't go on,' she said, deciding to risk everything, turning back to face him.

'I'm fine,' he asserted. 'Nothing wrong with my cricket, is there? Nothing wrong with my work?'

'Of course not.' She knew Tim was on the defensive now. He had that familiar questioning, agitated, obsessive look, as if he thought she had information that she had not revealed to him, rather than the other way round.

'Are you sure?'

'Yes.'

'No one been saying anything?'

'Of course not.'

'Saying things about me?' He was determined to worry away at the problem, dropping his defences at the same time.

'I'd have told you if they had. There's nothing wrong with your work.' She knew the reason for this particular concern. Her cousin gave Tim only the lightest possible tasks. A little filing, checking a few details here and there, taking minor or weekend clients round.

'He's a sick man,' Bruce had told her. 'Over-conscientious in the office, and that's an understatement. He's driving the staff crazy with his neuroses. I respect what he did in the war and what happened to him. But some of the younger girls – '

'And there's nothing wrong with your cricket either.' That was certainly true for Tim remained a very competent sportsman. Presumably it was automatic, a habit, an inheritance that couldn't be tampered with.

'What did I say in that darn dream?' he asked suddenly, gazing at Lucy intently, almost threateningly.

'Something about angels dying. And then you said, "Don't make me."' Lucy paused, shocked by the look of betrayal in his eyes. 'You also said you weren't fit to be a father, but I think you were awake then,' she added awkwardly.

'Anything else?'

'No.'

'You sure?'

'Quite sure.'

'It's all nonsense, of course – ' His voice tailed off ineffectively.

Lucy said nothing, hoping she had unsettled him enough.

'Had a grenade chucked at me. Thing is I got blasted. Do you see?'

She was thrown by this unexpected confidence. Could they be getting somewhere at last? Sometimes she imagined the old Tim beckoning to her from a doorway halfway up a street in France – and then slamming it in her face. She saw the evasion back in his eyes. He was trying to outwit her.

'Fortunately I was at the tail end of the blast. Got bumped and bruised of course. It was the worst incident we had. No wonder I keep dreaming about it.'

Tim's voice was stilted and he stared at her glassily. He's trying to convince me, Lucy thought as he paused for breath. He's made it all up.

'This debriefing's for you only, old thing. I don't want you to go and burden the other chaps. We all had a bad time and I know it's got to me, even if it *was* years ago. So it's for your ears only. Eh?' Tim was speaking fast now, his words falling over each other.

'Of course I'll keep it to myself,' said Lucy with assumed gentleness. 'But Tim, you've *got* to get help.' Now she was all sweet reason. She would defeat these lies, this veneer. Tim was in there but she had to outmanoeuvre his determined façade, his instinct to destroy himself still further.

He gave her a little-boy-lost cheeky grin. 'What shall I do then?'

Lucy could feel the contest between them sharpening. Was the old Tim nearer the surface, fighting to break out?

'See the doctor.'

'You mean the shrink. Well, I won't do that again, old girl. We've been through this before.'

'You won't be hypnotized.' She tried to make a joke of it.

'What do you mean?'

'You'll be in control,' she promised, but was immediately aware that Tim was mentally scanning ahead.

'Do I *need* to be in control?'

'Can't you talk to *me* about it?' she countered.

'I'm afraid I'm bound by the Official Secrets Act. Isn't that enough for you?'

He look so smug that Lucy could have hit him. 'And the aftermath?'

'I can deal with that.'

'You're not at the moment. You've got to get help from someone, so if it's not the shrink then it'll have to be me.'

'*Have* to be? Are you giving me orders?' Tim tried to smile, but she could sense that he knew he was losing.

'Yes, I am. For your sake.'

'And if I don't obey?' He gazed at her calculatingly. 'What will you do?'

Lucy's mind went blank. Tim had suddenly cornered her. 'I need you to get better,' she said haltingly.

'You're not answering my question.'

Without thinking any further she blurted out the half-formed notion, just as she had done that afternoon when she had shattered the sanctity of the cricket. 'Will you come to France with me? Take the car and retrace the route. Talk to me about what happened.' Her words were running away with her.

'That's absurd.' He was impatient now, before ducking down in the face of her unexpected fire.

But Lucy was already running across no-man's-land, heading towards him, blazing unwelcome ideas. 'You have to face up to – whatever happened.'

He's so afraid, she thought. Lucy wondered why. Could it be that he had detected an ultimatum. Then she realized what it must be.

'And if I don't obey?' he repeated, trying to mask his fear with sarcasm.

'Why can't you just agree to go to a psychiatrist? Give it another try.' For a moment she put off the next part of the bout.

'Because it didn't work for me. However many more times do I have to tell you?' He was sulky now, petulant, aware that she might have other weapons.

Lucy could see that he was adamant, that for some reason he now feared the psychiatrists. So could the return to France be an easier option? She knew that this was her moment and that if she dithered she might never regain it. The risk had to be taken.

'If you don't come to France with me, Tim, I'll leave you.'

'You'll leave me?' He sounded absolutely incredulous, but she could see in his face the slow realization that she meant what she was saying. You've got to get Tim on his feet, her father had said. Was *this* a way of doing it?

'Yes.' There, she had done it. Lucy was appalled, but she knew there was no other way. Why hadn't she realized that before? She could have saved so much time. A sense of uneasy power filled her. Why had she been so flabby for so long? Why hadn't she made up her mind?

'I can't believe this.'

'I should start trying.' Lucy deliberately made her voice cold, although she could hardly bear to see his distress.

'For God's sake – ' He was floundering now.

'I mean it, Tim. We can't go on like this. You're like a shadow on a wall. I need you to be real again. I love you.'

'And what do you think jaunting back to France will do?'

'I want to hear about what you went through, share it. We

always shared before. Now there's months of your life that I know nothing about. Can't you see?' she shouted, wanting to shatter the aridity. 'Don't you *want* to see?'

'All right.' His shoulders sagged.

'You mean you'll come?' Lucy was amazed that he had given in so quickly. Had he wanted this all the time? Had *she* been afraid to suggest it?

Tim nodded, but there was no hint of relief, only more anxiety. He lay back on the pillow, exhausted, his eyes on the ceiling.

Was he just agreeing to pacify her? Evade everything between them all over again?

'I never imagined you would threaten me like this,' Tim complained. His voice wobbled.

'You know I can speak the lingo,' she said brightly, trying to lighten the atmosphere and failing. 'That's more than you and your lot could. So you won't have to do a thing but sit back and talk.'

Tim said nothing.

'I'll go and get the cocoa.'

Lucy walked self-consciously to the door. Before opening it she turned round again, wanting to catch him out, but Tim was simply staring at her blankly. She hurried down the stairs, dazed at her success but worrying about what she was going to do next.

Next morning, after Tim had left for the estate agents, Lucy set off up the Cut between Conifers and the stream without thinking.

Breakfast had been largely silent, and throughout the wearisome repast Lucy now realized she had given herself the role of blackmailer, with Tim as victim. 'I'll book the dates for France,' she had told him and he had nodded acquiescently. 'It'll do us both good to have a break. We can cross Newhaven to Dieppe and then we won't have so far to drive.'

Lucy realized she was gabbling, and after Tim had given yet another barely discernible nod, the silence returned, a barrier between them but at least a release from her chatter.

She had been so preoccupied with her daunting plan that she had completely forgotten to turn on the radio at breakfast or even remember what the vicar had said. Now, halfway along the dank little path that led uphill through thick foliage, Lucy remembered the murder at the Clump and what May had seen when she last used the Cut.

Lucy glanced back to the road and wondered whether or not she should retrace her steps. Traffic crawled past reassuringly. After all, how long was the Cut? Two or three hundred yards at most. Pulling herself together, Lucy hurried on.

The ground was covered with last year's leaf mulch and she could smell its dampness, sharpened by dog excreta despite the official notice down by the road that read in stencilled ferocity DO NOT ALLOW YOUR DOG TO FOUL THIS FOOTWAY. STRICT PENALTIES.

Lucy suddenly realized how sharp her sense of smell had become and she laughed aloud, the sound breaking the silence, almost making her jump. Maybe it was she who should go to the trick cyclist. 'I keep smelling foul smells,' she would tell him, and he would reply, 'Mrs Groves, the world, your father, your husband, are rotting about you. You can detect the decay.'

Lucy hurried on, refusing to look back. Like her father, she had always been an independent spirit. I'm not tramping all the way back to the road. I'm not being frightened off. But she also knew she was being stupid.

The fetid smell of the mulch and the swollen rain clouds above her made the Cut deeply claustrophobic, and Lucy increased her speed, dragging her trolley, the uneasiness building up inside her. She fancied she could also smell burnt wood and she saw that Peter had plugged the hole in the hedge again, this time with barbed wire. William Tell. The wretched boy's name kept coming into her mind with a banal regularity. Hersham or not, it was an odd name. She saw the apple on his head again, split by the arrow.

Lucy turned the corner with relief. Now all she had to do was to reach Clive Road, flanked by large imitation Tudor mansions, all of which would contain house-proud wives cleaning their house-proud homes while the radio played *Music While You Work*. Nothing untoward could happen in Clive Road. All should be Electrolux energy. Hoover happy.

Then she saw the man in the hat and raincoat. He was striding down the passage towards her, a fixed smile on his face.

*

Lucy stopped walking, gazing back at him, knowing she should turn and run, but finding herself unable to move. He came on relentlessly, polished shoes glinting in the gathering gloom, the smile rigid, arms swinging, hat pulled slightly forward over his forehead. Lucy looked to right and left, knowing there was no means of escape, realizing the hedgerows were far too thick and wiry for her to penetrate.

Penetrate? Would he rape her first? Throttle her or cut her throat? Lucy ran over the options, screaming inside, knowing she was a fool to stay where she was, hardly conscious of the first few droplets of cold rain. Slowly a pain spread in her stomach and her throat was so dry that it felt as if it was caked with soot.

Instead of clouding her senses, terror gave Lucy an unexpected mental clarity. The Cut stood out in sharp black-and-white relief, rather like a negative. She could smell woodsmoke and hear the slapping of the man's polished shoes on the wet leaves. If only she could force herself to turn away from him, but any movement appeared to be out of the question. Her heartbeat became as loud as the sound of the slapping shoes.

The man was almost on her now and Lucy could see he was older than she had thought, clean-shaven, with lines round his mouth and under his eyes, his face long, his brow wrinkled, one of his eyes puffy, reddened with a sty.

Lucy tried to run back down the Cut, ludicrously banged into her shopping trolley, gave a little whimper and thrust it away.

'Wait!'

She gave a rasping cry, almost fell, and then turned to face him.

'Police.' He had pulled out some kind of identification and Lucy froze.

'Didn't you hear me call?'

She shook her head numbly.

'I'm sorry to have frightened you.' His voice was soft, slightly nasal. 'Really sorry. I'm Inspector Frasier.' He was very close now, still holding out the card. Suddenly Lucy realized he must be authentic. 'I've just been checking on the regular users of this path.' He cleared his throat. 'Are you a regular user, madam?'

Lucy nodded, the blessed calm spreading, indicating her

shopping trolley. 'It's a short cut.' She paused, and then added, 'To the shops.'

'Do you live down there? In Shrub Lane?'

'I'm Lucy Groves,' she said. 'I'm married to – '

'Timothy Groves? Who works at the estate agents in the High Street?'

'How do you know?' She felt foolish, as if she ought to have understood the police investigation was so far advanced, ought to have realized how comforting that might be.

'We've already had a chat with him at the office. You know about the murder?'

'Of course.'

'We're just eliminating as many people from our inquiries as we can. I gather you're friends of Peter and Sally Davis at Conifers down there.'

'Yes.'

'And the victim, Graham Baverstock, was their gardener.'

Lucy nodded.

'Did you – had you ever met the young man?'

'No.'

'Or seen him?'

'I suppose I must have seen him in the garden. But I can't remember when. I just took him for granted. He was their gardener.' Lucy wondered if she sounded insufferably snobbish, but Frasier's expression, now one of official interest, didn't change.

'Did you ever see Baverstock with another man?'

'No.' Lucy realized that May had rightly reported what she had seen. She didn't feel so embarrassed this time. Frasier was like a doctor. These things could be made clinical.

He paused. 'If you don't mind me saying so, Mrs Groves, I think it's a little foolish to come up here on your own – even if this is a short cut to the High Street.'

'With this man about?'

The policeman said nothing, making her feel stupid.

'Do you think he's hiding somewhere?' Now she sounded too gossipy. Lucy just couldn't get the tone of the conversation right. Maybe it was the shock.

'We've searched the vicinity and found no trace of anyone so far. But you can't be too careful.'

41

'Of course not.'

'I'll let you get on, Mrs Groves.'

'Were you trying to see Mrs Davis?' she asked him. 'Because that's where I'm going now.' She gave a strained half-laugh. 'I mean, I'm going to meet her for coffee. At Caves Café in the High Street.'

'No. I don't need to see her again at the moment. I'm just taking a stroll. Having a think.'

Lucy paused. 'Oh, by the way – did you ever get anywhere about the shed fire on Mr Davis's property?'

'We're looking into it, madam.'

'I'll be getting on then.'

Frasier raised his hat to her and passed on, his shoes shuffling the leaves, his back comfortingly matter-of-fact.

Lucy walked on for a few yards and then turned round to see how far he had got. She saw Frasier was watching her, a benign presence, raising a hand in reassuring farewell.

As Lucy trudged up Clive Road, she felt exhausted. The broken night with Tim, the decision she had forced on him, the game they were playing, the discomforting walk and the meeting with Frasier had taxed her almost beyond endurance. All she wanted to do was to go home to bed. Having locked the doors first, of course.

Tim would protect her when he got home. Despite all his troubles, Lucy had no doubt about that. That's what she had once thought men were for. Her father had always protected her. Then she and Tim had bought Gables and she swapped one protector for another.

Suppose the men had not returned from the war? How would she have coped on her own? But Lucy already knew the answer. She would have gone on living with her father. Another thought surfaced, this time more deeply buried. Living with her father had been such a certain experience. When Tim had come home as an artful shadow, life had become so dreadfully *un*certain.

Protection. The image of last Guy Fawkes night returned. The men outside, gumbooted and overcoated. Setting up the display. Locked into their own pomposity. The women inside, chattering over sherry, their conversation eventually cut short by a muttered command. Then, with Alice Davis as the statutory child, the firework display was begun by the three men, the women herded into an enclosure between the wall and the flower-beds. The little ladies had been made safe.

Why couldn't she and May and Sally have lit the fireworks? Why couldn't the men have watched? Why couldn't the men have been 'made safe'?

Later they had all repaired to the chintzy lounge in Conifers to watch the 'goggle box'. The Davises had been the first to have a television and the thing stood in their lounge behind a pair of double doors veneered in walnut, looking like a rather ugly cocktail cabinet. The little screen inside was only about ten inches across, but Lucy and Tim had often been invited to watch a variety of bland transmissions which had forcibly reminded her of an evening class. Gardening hints from Fred Streeter, cookery lessons from Philip Harben, even Eric Robinson's *Music For You* had a light, ephemeral flavour to it. Lucy had also suffered extreme boredom at the hands of clog dancers, cabaret artistes and Czech jugglers. Only *What's My Line* with Lady Barnet, Lady Boyle, Barbara Kelly and in particular the irascible Gilbert Harding cheered her. She had liked his acerbic pronouncements. May had not. Sally had been flustered. The Men had roared hearty, masculine appreciation. Tim had slept.

Caves Café buzzed with home county accents, and the closely packed tables were crammed with women sipping the weak coffee and munching a dry biscuit or a plain piece of Madeira cake.

Rain had set in outside, lashing the High Street; the interior fug had steamed the windows and there was an underlying smell of wet mackintosh. Lucy felt a twinge of irony. Smells again. She was developing a complex.

May, Sally and Lucy sat at a table in the corner of the café. They met here once a week, confirming their friendship with news of what had happened to them since they had last met – usually only a few hours ago.

Lucy found the company and the café oppressive, particularly of late, and she had made several excuses to stay at home, excuses that had been greeted with some disquiet, as if she had temporarily resigned the membership of a compulsory club.

Now she was back, explaining what had happened with the

policeman in the Cut whilst her mind was dominated by Tim and what she had forced him to agree to.

When Lucy had finished, Sally began to protest. 'I'm sure they haven't thoroughly searched the neighbourhood. There were a few officers in the garden yesterday, until they wandered off somewhere else. Of course that man Frasier was with us both for a very long time. He seemed surprised we knew so little about poor Baverstock. But why should we know the personal history of a gardener from Hersham? And they've got nowhere over the fire.'

William Tell, split apple and all, ran across Lucy's mental horizon. Was the wretched Hersham brat becoming an obsession like the smells?

'I've told Nancy Dexter to keep Alice away from the Cut,' continued Sally firmly.

May was more conciliatory. 'I've seen a lot of police on the common. I'm sure they're being thorough.'

She relies on authority, thought Lucy, but then why shouldn't she? She's married to Martin.

Sally continued to talk about the incompetence of the police and how much Lucy had been at risk for some time, until May looked impatient. Abruptly Lucy changed the subject.

'There's something else,' she said anxiously, needing their approbation but knowing instinctively that she wasn't going to get it. 'Tim and I are going to France.'

The statement was followed by a long, startled pause, during which Lucy noticed May and Sally giving each other a brief covert glance. Are they the enemy within, she wondered. The men's lackeys? Co-conspirators?

'When?' asked Sally abruptly.

'I'm not sure. Soon. Tim's owed some holiday,' she replied limply. 'And I've got the language.'

'Where are you going?' May was brightly curious.

'To the Havre peninsula.' Lucy suddenly felt like giggling, watching the astonished expressions spread across their faces.

'There?' Sally's jaw was set. 'Why there?'

She glanced across at May, but she was looking down at her plate, at the biscuit crumbs on the table, anywhere but at Lucy. 'Tim was ill again last night. He's adamant he won't accept any more psychiatric help.' She paused. 'He seems to think he might give something away.'

44

'What on earth makes him think that?' demanded Sally. 'I mean – what *could* he give away?' The reasonableness in her voice sounded ludicrously phoney.

'It's just a feeling I've got. I could be wrong,' Lucy added, wondering if she was now seeing deception everywhere. 'Perhaps it's just his bad nerves.'

'You – you're traipsing off?' demanded May.

'I don't know about traipsing. We're going to take a couple of weeks touring in the car. I'm hoping we can talk.'

Sally lit a cigarette with savage concentration, looking absurd in her sudden pent-up fury. 'Do you think that's wise?'

'Yes,' said Lucy calmly. 'I do.'

May looked up from her plate. 'Isn't the idea a little dangerous?'

'Do you know what they went through?' asked Lucy quietly. 'I mean – *really* went through? Because I don't. I mean – do Peter and Martin talk about it to either of you?'

'We've had this conversation before,' said May. 'You know they don't.'

'I wish they would,' volunteered Sally unexpectedly. 'But Peter told me they weren't allowed to discuss what happened.' She paused and then rushed on quickly. 'As you know, the army have offered more psychiatric help, but if Tim won't take it they can't force it on him. To go back might make him much worse. I wouldn't go if I were you. I have to say I think May's right.'

'So what else do you suggest?' asked Lucy flatly, angrily. Sally seemed to pronounce the word 'psychiatric' with considerable, almost distasteful, awkwardness.

'There *is* another alternative,' said May, with her usual thumping good common sense. 'And I'm sure it lies with his specialist.'

'You mean pills? He won't take those either.'

'He doesn't exactly help himself, does he?' Immediately penitent, Sally hurriedly took Lucy's wrist in a firm, cool, cologne-scented hand. 'I'm sorry. This awful murder's made me so anxious and what with Alice and Nancy – '

'Of course it has.' Lucy was anxious to appease, to avoid any more confrontation. 'It was the wrong time to bring all this up.'

'No, it's not,' said May, pouring more coffee into Lucy's cup in a brisk motherly way. 'I *know* Tim's in a bad state but I'm not sure France is the answer. I mean – have a holiday. I think that's a very good idea.'

'But not, perhaps, in the Havre peninsula.' Sally smiled with sweet admonishment.

Lucy was seething with anger, but none of them had ever quarrelled and it seemed a particularly bad time to start now.

'I wonder what would have happened if the men hadn't come back?' she asked spontaneously and immediately wished she hadn't.

May, however, surprised them all, perhaps even herself. 'They didn't come back in the old way. They've all changed.' She paused, stirring at the grouts of her coffee. 'But that's what happens, isn't it?' She hesitated again and then continued rather lamely. 'I expect we've changed too.'

Lucy fumbled in her bag to find change for her share of the bill.

'There's a minuscule currant in this piece of cake,' said Sally, holding it up for inspection. 'I call that a good omen.'

Lucy walked back down the hill that eventually led to Hersham, still shocked by how near she had come to an argument with May and Sally. Even now they must be finishing their shopping, talking about her reprovingly, bonded by their mutual antipathy to what she had proposed. *Was* she about to embark on a journey that she might regret, that could irreparably harm Tim in some way? But how? Surely the damage had already been done? Surely she couldn't make matters worse? Of course she could, Lucy told herself. She might make them much worse.

As she unlocked the front door, however, the anger returned and swept away her indecision. They were all so negative. No one had offered a solution. She was alone.

'The balloon's gone up,' said Tim, hurrying into the kitchen that evening. He was the naughty schoolboy again, on the one hand a bit of a dare-devil, on the other looking shaken. The effect was unsettling, disturbing. How far had she pushed him, Lucy wondered. Too far?

Then she saw them walking purposefully up the path. She automatically half-waved at Peter and Martin but they didn't appear to see her.

'Where are you going?' Lucy demanded as Tim hurried out of the back door into the night.

'The lawn mower seized up on me yesterday. Better take a look.' He disappeared with near farcical speed.

The knocker pounded with a familiar jaunty tattoo, and when she opened the door they were both standing on the steps. They would have been shoulder to shoulder if Martin hadn't been taller. Tweedledum and Tweedledee, Lucy thought venomously, trying to imagine them as ridiculous but only managing to make them more menacing.

'Sorry, old girl,' said Peter. 'Wanted a word.' She could see the nicotine stains on his moustache. Peter and Martin smoked Craven A voraciously whilst Tim now abstained. 'Given up the weed,' he had told Lucy, 'or the weed's given up on me. Can't get any pleasure from it any more. Don't know why.'

'Come in,' Lucy said brightly. 'Tim's out in the potting shed.'

'Leave him there.' Martin's tone was brusque. Was she under orders again?

They sat heavily, legs crossed, and Lucy stared at them, noticing that they had both changed from their city suits into sports jackets and flannels. Neither of them spoke, but Peter hauled up his navy-blue socks while Martin cleared his throat.

'Do smoke,' Lucy said, pushing the ashtray across the coffee table. 'Can I get you something?'

'No thanks.' Martin seemed to be the spokesman. 'I'll come straight to the point. The girls have told us about this French stunt.'

'Stunt?' Lucy had a sudden vision of Tim and herself walking a tightrope across the English Channel. Then she realized the image was not entirely inaccurate.

'Trip.' Peter replaced the word. 'Look here, you *know* things happened out there that we can't discuss.'

'We both think you're making a terrible mistake going back,' added Martin gently.

'Why?'

Peter sighed as if he knew she was going to be difficult. 'It'll just make him worse.' His voice was as gentle as ever but he didn't fool her. Not one bit. They were both out to stop her. Well, she *wouldn't* be stopped.

47

'How do you know?' Lucy's voice was querulous now and the men averted their eyes, hoping she wasn't going to make a scene.

'I've been in touch with a couple of other chaps with chewed-up nerves. One of them took a trip back to a battleground and he landed up in an asylum.'

There was a long, melodramatic pause.

'Who were the dying angels?' Lucy asked quietly.

'Dying angels?' Peter repeated incredulously. They both gazed blankly back at her, as if she, too, was a case of 'chewed-up nerves'.

'Tim was talking in his sleep. He said the angels were dying and then he added, "Don't make me."'

The blank looks deepened. In God's name why couldn't they come clean and share what they knew about Tim and try to help her? Or was the Official Secrets Act really such a barrier? What secret could they share? For a moment she tried to be reasonable, to see it from their point of view, but objectivity was quickly replaced by pent-up anger.

'I'm sorry,' said Martin. 'I haven't the faintest idea what he was talking about.'

'Nor me,' added Peter sympathetically. 'But surely this is further evidence – if we needed it – of Tim's illness.' He grinned ruefully, every inch the embarrassed man of action, the clumsy, sporting male who saw mental breakdown as something that wasn't quite playing the great game of life.

'The Official Secrets Act?' Lucy sneered.

'You've got to see sense, old girl,' said Peter jovially. 'Why not take him down to Cornwall? It would be lovely at this time of – '

'We're going to France,' she insisted. 'Tim's agreed. He *wants* to go.'

'That's not the point.' Martin's patience had so much conde-scension built into it that Lucy snapped at last, getting to her feet, smoothing down her skirt, talking as softly as Peter but with such venom that both men were taken aback.

'You're not his keepers. What the hell do you think you're doing? Telling us how to run our lives?'

'Look here,' began Peter, and she could see he was already dismissing her as a hysterical little woman. Perhaps she was,

Lucy thought, and for a moment her resolution wavered, but she knew she had to fight them.

'Get out,' she shouted, not caring whether Tim heard or not.

To her surprise the men rose abruptly to their feet and did exactly as they were told, walking slowly into the hall, shrugging away the public embarrassment that, in their view, could only be caused by a woman.

Peter opened the front door and Martin followed him as they strode awkwardly down the path. It was hard to tell what they felt because she didn't know them. Who are they, she wondered, under all that bluster.

Suddenly, Lucy's victory seemed hollow and she felt a wave of hopelessness creep over her.

She found Tim in the potting shed, staring blankly at the wall.

'They've gone?' he asked and gave her a grin which cheered her. 'They don't want us to go to France?'

'And how!'

Tim laughed with just a trace of his old self. 'They mean well,' he said quietly.

'They're not used to mutiny.' Lucy smiled awkwardly. 'Do you still want to make the trip?'

'If you do.' His old indecisiveness had swiftly returned.

She knew, however, that she had given him no choice.

'I thought you were repairing the lawn mower,' she said, looking at the empty workbench.

'It went out of my head.'

'What *have* you been doing?' Lucy demanded but she spoke gently.

'Having a think.'

'What about?' Her voice was sharper now.

Tim shook his head impatiently. 'Let's go back inside,' he said. 'It's getting chilly.'

3

Soft summer rain fell on to the deck of the ferry bound for Dieppe, and Tim, wrapped in blankets, sat in a chair at the stern, watching the wake and the following gulls. The sky was grey and overcast. He had been largely silent ever since Lucy had driven the Riley down to Newhaven and she could sense an increasing anxiety that he was trying to conceal. Yet he had seemed to sleep deeply the previous night.

Lucy felt both triumphant and guilty. She was not used to taking the initiative and could hardly believe that she had actually got this extraordinary journey under way. Yet here they were, making their 'jaunt', soon to reach France and her quest to 'put Tim right again'. The phrase rang in her ears, alternately trite and optimistic.

But the tentacles on the English side of the Channel had been slow to release them, for last night May had phoned, undermining Lucy's already tenuous confidence still further.

'I just wanted a word,' she had said tentatively and had then breezily attacked her with no holds barred. 'I know how worried you've been about Tim, but I *do* think you should cancel this trip. Martin and I have been talking it over. He's concerned that going back could trigger a complete breakdown.'

'Why?' Lucy had demanded, trying to think of convincing counter-arguments and finding that her mind had gone horribly blank.

'Of course Martin couldn't *divulge* anything. As you know, they all had to sign – '

'The Official Secrets Act,' Lucy had finished for her. 'Frankly, I think that's a load of shit.' She deliberately used the word, knowing how much May would hate it, pleased that she had been able to hit back so quickly, if childishly.

'My dear Lucy. You're courting disaster.'

'I'm taking a chance, probably the only chance I'll get. Tim never came home to me. Do you realize that? The real Tim's still somewhere in France.' Tired and feeling guilty at his tactical withdrawal to an early bed, leaving her to pack and to organize, Lucy had let herself go, with an uneasy rising excitement. Her new role of rebel was going to be hard to carry through, but at least May would no longer see her as a charming 'rogue'.

'I *do* understand how awful it's been for you. It's a long, slow mend, I'm afraid.' May had tried to be ameliorating.

'I *can't* wait.' Lucy had been driven to new heights of fury as the deadening complacency in May's voice had enveloped her. She was surprised at herself for being so openly hostile. But she had held back for a very long time.

'You're doing him harm. We *all* think so. We're very concerned – '

'Please mind your own business. And that applies to *all* of you. Tim and I have made up our minds.'

'No,' May had replied sharply, 'you've made up his mind *for* him.'

She had put the phone down abruptly, taking Lucy by surprise for she had been hoping to put the phone down on May.

'Tim?'

As she gazed down at his pallid, indoor face and closed eyes, Lucy's hard-won but paper-thin courage really began to founder. What was she doing going to France with this worn-out wreck of a man? Could May infuriatingly be right after all? For the first time, Lucy lost control and panicked. They had to go home. She had to take the decision now. What was she doing, exchanging chin-up Esher for post-war France? They might as well be setting out for Kathmandu.

'Tim?'

He opened his eyes and grinned weakly. Lucy was bizarrely reminded of Sally's plucky smile.

'Yes, old girl? Sorry. Was I being bad company? Just getting a bit of shut-eye, that's all.'

'I've been a fool. You're not up to this. We're both ill-prepared. We're going to stay on the ferry and go home again.'

Tim gave her a puzzled look. 'Wait a minute.' He said nothing for a while and then muttered, 'Rotten weather.' She gazed at him blankly and he added, quite firmly, 'But of course we're not going back.'

51

'What?' she demanded unbelievingly. She hadn't heard such authority in him for years, not since the beginning of the war.

'Of course we're not going back,' he repeated testily. 'In for a penny, in for a pound, I say. Unless you want to, of course.'

Lucy shook her head. 'Everyone thinks I'm being irresponsible.' What Tim had said had been like a golden streak of pre-Raphaelite sunshine in the dull grey of the Channel sky.

'We're on our way. Don't let's back out now.' Tim huddled back into the blankets. 'I thought we'd go to a village I know called Navise. Base ourselves there for a few days and then amble.' Once again, Lucy was shaken by the decisive note in his voice. 'I'll have to map-read carefully.' Tim closed his eyes again against the unfamiliar burst of energy and she felt a transient joy. Despite all her fear and self-recrimination, at least the patient seemed to be partially responding to treatment.

Lucy thought of May and her accusations. Yah, boo, sucks, she said to herself in childish delight, mentally thumbing her nose and watching her stout opponent scamper for cover. Then she condemned herself for being so cravenly childish. A few seconds later, however, she was enjoying seeing May run again.

'I'll drive,' Tim volunteered as they clambered down the companionway to the car deck.

There were not many passengers disembarking and the absence of the ship's thrumming engines made Lucy oppressed by the lack of noise, the lack of purpose. There had been a certain rhythm to the voyage. Now Tim was insisting on driving, something he hadn't done in years. She would be completely irresponsible if she allowed him his way and they would sure as eggs end up in a ditch and then what would May say? What would the whole bloody bunch of them say? She saw Peter pulling up his socks and frowning, Martin giving a tight smile, Sally rolling her Diana Dors eyes. Even so, Lucy didn't want to sap Tim's confidence.

She watched him reach the car deck, unsure, trudging, but with an invalid's precision. One hand shook slightly. Was she witnessing a new sense of purpose, or was it just febrile enthusiasm? Either way, Lucy knew she had to take a decision.

'I'll drive and you navigate,' she said crisply.

Tim nodded slowly, as if he had already thought the matter over and decided she was right.

Dieppe was dismal. A crane loomed with a skeletal arm, stranded amongst the fishing boats, and the trawlers were moving on a tide that sent water slapping against the rusting bulwarks of the dock.

War damage proliferated. A warehouse still hung at a rakish angle, half collapsed, a huge crater full of water adjoined the ship's berth and a wharf had been cut into two separate sections. The air of desolation was heightened by the gulls that mewed and wheeled, searching for scraps.

Tim was silent as Lucy slowly drove through the Customs clearance, hunched in his seat, a little old man again. Yet she still marvelled at the tiny chinks of light she had witnessed on the ferry. Were they good omens like the currant in Sally's cake? Was the old Tim going to re-emerge, even in the most fractured form?

The overcast sky grew swollen again and more rain fell, the steady hum of the wipers comforting. When Lucy glanced at Tim he was gazing down at the road map, totally absorbed, frowning, his lips slightly parted. It's all right, old thing, she thought. We'll muddle through.

'We didn't book anywhere in Navise,' Lucy reminded him after they had driven for some while in silence. 'Is there a decent hotel?'

He nodded vaguely, still gazing down at the map, a shaky finger following the route.

Yesterday, Tim would have been driven to panic over such uncertainty. Now Lucy had the strange feeling that the real Tim had never left France, only casting his shadow across the Channel. The idea made her at first gloriously elated and then slightly apprehensive. Why Navise?

Lucy's spirits rose again as she drove over the flat landscape. Even the grey, monotonous sand dunes and the renewed rain didn't spoil her optimism.

'You're quiet,' she said recklessly.

'I'm working something out,' he replied abruptly, and Lucy knew she shouldn't have spoken. She realized how careful she would have to be. It was as if she had just met Tim again after a long time apart and had forgotten how to talk to him.

He took the map from the side pocket, studied it for a while and then began to give her directions. Lucy followed his route without question, taking the minor roads he suggested, pretending a confidence that she didn't have.

Tim had the map on his knees, meticulously checking and re-checking, while the rain lessened and streaks of watery blue appeared in the sky.

There wasn't much traffic. It was a Friday afternoon but only the odd lumbering tractor or battered, high-sided truck held them up. Gradually the wet tarmac began to steam as the sun came out and the dark clouds drifted away.

Why hadn't she suggested this trip earlier, Lucy thought, trying to stop herself from becoming over-confident. She really should have done so, just for the hell of it, just to spite them all. Had it been the feeling of taboo that surrounded the past that no one could talk about, least of all its victim? Or had she known instinctively that Tim had to bottom out and get as low as he could, rather like an alcoholic? Either way she still felt they were both, for once, in the ascendant.

Slowly, the nature of the countryside was changing and small fields began to emerge, with windbreaks made of beech trees. The earth looked lush and there were steaming manure heaps and patch-eyed cows.

In the still misty heat, Lucy's triumph waned and she felt a sense of entrapment. The landscape seemed ancient, alien, rooted in its own past, hugging secrets.

Apart from a burnt-out house and a bomb crater in the middle of a village square, there was now little evidence of war damage. Dozens of conflicts could have raged here, Lucy thought rather wildly, now masked by the lush foliage. In her mind's eye she could visualize hundreds of corpses under the soil, mouldering, unidentified. Then she was conscious of the violence of her mood swings. She had to calm down, not expect so much, not expect anything at all.

*

54

Lucy saw half-timbered manor houses emerge from the trees, barns criss-crossed with dark oak beams, their lathe and plaster walls lime washed.

'Does it look different now?' she asked quietly, wanting to break Tim's reverie, anxious to make contact but trying to do it casually, as if it was the most normal thing in the world for them to be driving back to his route march.

'I thought we'd never get out, that we'd always go round in circles. The roads double back on each other.'

'Were you in Navise long?' she asked hesitantly, acutely aware that she was leading him on.

'A few days.' But there was a finality in his voice now, as if he had already said too much. 'There's a small hotel. I can't remember the name, but Navise is right off the beaten track. They shouldn't have too much trouble putting us up.' He closed his eyes against another excess of words. 'I say, old thing. Do you think all this was wise?' he asked suddenly.

Lucy's hopes plummeted and she knew that whatever she said now would be crucial. It was the first time he had expressed doubt and in a few clumsy words she could wreck everything she had gained -- that they had both gained.

'Yes,' she said baldly. 'It had to happen. You were going down.'

He gave an odd chuckle. 'Is this up?'

'It is if we're together.' Lucy spoke briskly.

Tim suddenly stroked her shoulder and she felt tears in her eyes. He had hardly shown her any affection recently, unless she counted his wary dependence, his need for her to reassure him on so many dozens of depressingly trivial details.

'Is it strange coming back?'

'It's unnerving. Do you mind stopping for a moment? I'm feeling a bit queasy.'

Lucy drove on to a rutted layby and bumped to a halt, switching off the engine.

She turned to Tim and saw that he was shaking, crouched down in his seat, the sweat pouring off him. 'Do you want to get out?'

'No. I'm just wondering if – '

'What?' She knew she had interposed too quickly.

'Nothing.'

Once again a feeling of awesome responsibility overtook her. He should never have come off the medication. Suppose he had to be taken into hospital here? In this remote countryside. Lucy had a fleeting image of a tall building amongst fir trees, the echoing slam of its front door and Tim, separated from her, escorted down endless corridors to some desolate cell. Probably padded. She tried to pull herself together, attempting self-ridicule. She was merely being dramatic, Lucy told herself. But then so was her situation.

His shaking continued and Lucy impulsively put her arms around Tim, hugging him tight, but his body was rigid and she quickly let him go, realizing her mistake, making the excuse of opening the sun roof of the Riley. The scent of honeysuckle filled the stuffy interior.

'I couldn't reach you in England. I *want* to help.'

There was an uneasy silence. Then Tim spoke unwillingly.

'I wouldn't have agreed to come here if I hadn't felt I had a sense of purpose.' The admission made Lucy turn to face him, but he wouldn't meet her eyes and was staring ahead into the damp, grey landscape.

'Purpose?' She tried to probe gently.

'I have to come to terms with some things that happened.' His voice was trembling now and he kept clearing his throat. 'I can't do that in England. I keep – I've been turning it all over in my head for too long. Naturally I haven't been able to confide in you.'

'The Official Secrets Act?'

They grinned at each other and there was a renewed hint of conspiracy. Hope swept her again.

'Bollocks to that,' he replied, leaning back in his seat and closing his eyes, the smile still on his lips. Sunlight bathed his pale skin, showing a line of blackheads around his nose. Tim tapped the steering wheel with mock joviality. 'Drive on, Macduff.'

Lucy switched on the ignition and pulled back on to the road. She felt some progress was being made, however small.

Navise was small and disappointing. A shanty-like garage dominated the outskirts with a yard full of wrecked German tanks

56

and armoured cars, the scrap value of which had clearly not yet been realized.

Beyond the battered petrol pumps and sun-baked forecourt was a patch of waste ground on which crouched half a dozen mangy-looking cats, nonchalantly gazing at the dusty road.

As Lucy drove the Riley down the long approach with its attendant plane trees, more nondescript buildings appeared and she glanced at her watch. It was just after 4 p.m. A man was slowly unlocking the door of a boulangerie with scarred paint and partly boarded-up glass. Leaning against the chipped wood he yawned and stretched, watching them pass with little interest. The cats had offered a better welcoming committee, Lucy thought.

As the Riley turned the corner and they drove into the afternoon shadows of a medieval square she was pleasantly surprised. The place was equally shabby but quiet and dusty and somehow timeless, its very drabness appealing. The slightest lick of paint would have broken the spell.

'It never was a pretty place,' said Tim. 'But it's even more neglected now.' He paused and said, 'Not exactly Esher High Street, is it?'

Lucy was just about to ask him if he had stayed here during the war but stopped herself just in time. Instinctively she realized the cross-examination she so yearned to undertake would be premature.

She gazed round the dull little square, taking in the battered tourist sign which read CHATEAU PAVILLY.

'We stayed there,' Tim said absently. He wasn't sweating any more but he was still agitated.

'Do you *want* to stop?' she asked him. 'We could move on to Honfleur.'

But he wasn't listening. 'We had a night in the cellars of the hotel over there and then we moved into the château for a couple of days. Martin had a dicky foot and we had to rest up.'

Lucy felt almost in shock as she brought the Riley to a halt in a spare parking space by a dry fountain that had once gushed water from the mouth of a battered stone shepherd boy. Was Tim going to blurt out the whole story?

'Who owned the château?' she asked when he didn't say anything more.

'The Goutins. They're merchant bankers in Paris but they

57

never appeared.' He paused. 'They had employed a caretaker.' Tim paused again and Lucy could smell the rank odour she had noticed so many times in England. She had never decided what it was. His lips worked, but no sound came out.

The sight of his distress made Lucy look closely at her surroundings. She knew she had to give him space and time. A couple of cars were parked beside the Riley in front of the hotel on the north side of the square. There was a signpost indicating Honfleur in one direction and Robic in the other. Opposite was a small Norman church with a half-open wooden door, surrounded by a graveyard. Next door was a three-storeyed eighteenth-century building which looked as if it had once been some kind of agricultural co-operative. On the ground floor was a tightly shuttered shop without a sign.

The other two sides of the square consisted of a crumbling medieval house which had been partially boarded up, and a flat-fronted monstrosity which now sold tractors.

The hotel was long and low with dirty white walls and shutters that had once been blue and were now peeling, the paint hanging in shards. Clematis grew up to the first-floor windows and there were a few tables and chairs scattered about on the pavement outside with Martini-sloganed umbrellas and Ricard ashtrays. Flowers in tubs brightened the area around the door. A sign read HÔTEL DES ARBRES, BAR AND RESTAURANT.

In the middle of the square, around the fountain, were half a dozen bay trees in a straggling semicircle. They looked under-nourished. So did the dogs that lay in their shelter. One of them had a cut paw that was encrusted with dried blood.

Yet despite the slightly squalid nature of the square Lucy felt more buoyant and hopeful than she had ever done over the last few years of gathering misery and apprehension. In contrast, she recalled the discreet 11 o'clock murmur of the coffee drinkers in Caves Café.

'Nothing much has changed,' said Tim softly, almost as if he was talking to himself. 'The tractor showroom's new.' He paused and Lucy wondered if she should speak or just wait and let him run on again.

'How long had you been walking?' she asked, too casually.

'Two or three weeks,' he answered, and Lucy felt as if she was hacking away at the ice on the edge of a frozen lake. She didn't want to get out of the car for fear of changing his mood.

'We'd managed to get hold of some casual clothing and I don't mean French smocks.' He laughed at the feeble joke.

Lucy watched a silky grey cat pad across the road and wind itself around the legs of an old man who sat on one of the seats in the centre of the square, head bowed, eyes closed, gripping his stick.

'Some of the locals were helpful, but we still slept much of the time in ditches or in the forests and we were damn cold. The country was pretty low on rations during the Occupation, and several times we had to grub up what we could get from the fields. We even ate raw chestnuts, which were surprisingly tasty! We'd hoped to look like labourers but we were getting so unshaven and filthy that we didn't think we'd pass muster if we were stopped.' Tim laughed. 'Anyway, none of us could scrape up more than a couple of words of the lingo. So we slept by day and walked by night but even that had its risks. There were quite a few German patrols and the local dogs had a habit of barking incessantly once they were disturbed. Then we got help from a farmer who knew we were escaping British soldiers. He told us that the owner of the Hôtel des Arbres would be sympathetic.'

'Why?' asked Lucy quietly, risking an interjection. Could she begin to steer him, she wondered, or was that going to be too ambitious? Too dangerous?

Tim paused, but didn't seem inhibited. 'Philippe Madol had an English wife. Not that she was there – he'd sent her home – but he *was* sympathetic. He hid us in the hotel for a night and then arranged another couple of days at Pavilly. The château hadn't been requisitioned by the Germans and still had the housekeeper in residence.' He hesitated and Lucy risked another question.

'Is Madol still here?'

Tim shook his head. 'Not according to Peter, who tried to phone and thank him in 'forty-six. Madol sold up after the war apparently. I'll always remember him. I don't know who owns the place now.' Tim paused, looking directly at her for the first time. Suddenly it seemed almost unbearably hot in the Riley and Lucy wound down the window as quietly as possible.

'Who did the map-reading?' she asked.

'Peter. He was soon prompting us to move on.'

'From the château?'

He nodded again, impatiently, glancing first at the hotel and then back at her as if he had suddenly realized they had spent an inordinate amount of time sitting in the car.

'What was Martin's role?' Lucy asked quietly, determined to make the most of an opportunity that seemed nothing short of miraculous.

'Supplies officer.' Tim gave a cracked laugh. 'His aim was to keep our bellies full and our spirits up. But he didn't have much luck.' He looked exhausted now. Was she pushing him too far? Or had he simply run out of steam?

'And you?'

'Tail-end Charlie.' He laughed the cracked laugh again and gripped the door handle. 'Shouldn't we be checking in?'

Lucy didn't move, wanting more, and was relieved to see his grip on the handle relax.

'Peter and Martin were the finest pair of chaps I could ever have served with.'

This time, she forced herself not to speak, hoping the flow would continue. But it didn't. Instead the words came haltingly.

'I know you've always found Martin and Peter rather over-protective. I don't mind admitting that I feel much the same. That's why I always head for the shed. But they mean well, you know.'

He paused for such a long time that Lucy almost asked another question. Resolutely she remained silent.

Tim began to fiddle with the ashtray and her already taut nerves screamed. At the same time, she had the strong feeling that he was trying to summon up the strength to tell her something.

'We're here, aren't we?' he said at last. 'Back in France, after all these years.'

Lucy knew the chance had gone and plunged in shakily. 'Was I right to make you come?'

'I didn't want you to leave me,' he said. 'I'm no good on my ownio.' The attempted joke was painful. 'Anyway – ' his grip was back on the door handle – 'let me introduce you to the delights of the Hôtel des Arbres.' The cracked laughter was working overtime now.

The interior of the hotel was very different from the drab exterior. Directly Tim opened the front door Lucy saw a galleried hallway with a wide staircase sweeping up to the first landing. There was the smell of dark, cool, fragrant wood, floor polish, garlic and cloves.

To the right of the staircase was a small reception counter with a bell on its dark surface. Nobody was around, and as they stood there in silence they could hear the melodious ticking of a clock. There was also the angry buzzing of a trapped bee as it nudged a windowpane.

Tim walked slowly across the high-ceilinged foyer, gazing up at the galleried landing with its oak balustrade and ragged stair carpet.

Lucy followed him across tree-patterned tiles, the branches stark and leafless, a winter design that was stained and, in some places, almost completely faded.

Around the walls and up the staircase were woodcuts of more trees, this time in full leaf with Latin inscriptions. A large painting of traditional poplars lining a road was positioned over the reception counter, the narrow strip of tarmac fading into the distance beyond the trees.

A photograph underneath the picture showed a similar poplar-lined road with three familiar figures on bicycles.

Lucy felt dizzy, the shock waves sweeping her, and she clung to the counter for support. Then the dizziness receded, leaving a dry mouth and a pricking at the back of her eyes.

Tim gazed at the photograph for a while without comment, a little smile playing on his lips. 'We're famous, then,' he said at last, and chuckled. 'Bit of a local legend, don't you know. Just you wait till I tell the chaps,' he said with locker-room enthusiasm.

The photograph showed the three men perched on the saddles of heavy-looking bikes. They were dressed in ragged pullovers, shirts and corduroy trousers and each had a bag flung over his shoulder.

'Who took it?'

'The caretaker at the château. She thought she ought to take a snap for posterity.' He was silent for a while, and then added reflectively, 'I've changed somewhat, haven't I?'

Despite the fact that the photo had been taken less than ten years ago, the three men looked quite different, quite French in fact, Lucy thought. They seemed relaxed enough, as if on a cycling holiday.

Peter was shorter and squatter and more vulnerable looking than he was now, while Martin was thin, with stringy brown hair sticking out from under his cap. But Tim was the old Tim. Tall, spare, his head thrown back almost challengingly. Of the three, he was the only one who was smiling. The expressions of the other two were neutral.

'It looks as if the life suited you,' she said without thinking.

He didn't reply.

'Did you know the photograph was here?'

'No one's been back,' Tim reminded her. Then he gazed round him again, humming a little tune, trying to appear calm but looking anxious. 'No sign of anybody. The restaurant's down there, if I remember correctly. Let's do a recce.'

They walked down a narrow corridor into a large, square room with a low ceiling and latticed windows that looked on to a formal garden with roses, heavy double begonias and gravelled paths. Rain still glistened on the shiny dark-green leaves of the begonias and drops were falling from the almond tree. A coil of hose lay near the well-ordered flower beds and there was a trug basket full of cut flowers by the French doors. The garden was walled, with hollyhocks and lupins at the back of the border and clematis entwined with moss roses clambering over the old stone. The British would have let them run wild, Lucy thought, but the French had tamed them with trellis and pole.

She turned away from Tim and pressed her face against the cool glass of the windows, her attention absorbed by the lovingly tended little paradise that was such a marked contrast to the forlorn square outside.

'Monsieur?' Tim sounded unsure.

A large man, tall, bearded and run to fat, had come out of the kitchen in a dirty chef's apron, yawning, with a splashed cup of coffee in his hands. '*Oui?*'

'*Je voudrais une chambre à deux. C'est possible?*'

'Yes,' replied the man in more than adequate English. 'It's possible.' He smiled apologetically, aware that he had made Lucy look foolish. 'In fact you can have any damn room you like.'

4

Tim seemed at a loss. 'I'm sorry. I would have thought in July – '

'Here in Navise? It's not exactly what you would describe as a beauty spot, is it? That's what you say in England, don't you? A beauty spot?'

He was staring straight ahead at Lucy with a questioning look.

'Yes,' she said in English. 'We do say beauty spot. The surrounding countryside is lovely and the square is – is – peaceful. And as for your garden – that's a *real* beauty spot.' She smiled at him, but he nodded disconsolately.

'The restaurant just about pays. We serve good food. But the rooms are a problem to let.'

'The place hasn't changed,' said Tim, and received a curious glance.

'You've been here?'

'Once. In the war.'

'You are familiar.' He took a couple of steps nearer. The man's face was doubtful and then slightly embarrassed, as if he was about to insult them and immediately lose their custom. Then he remembered and his face lit up with surprise and pleasure. 'You are one of the heroic Englishmen in the photograph. Of course, you've – '

'Aged?'

'I was going to say you've lost weight. My name's Louis Dedoir.' He offered Tim a large fleshy hand that seemed to be covered in dried blood. Noticing its condition he wiped it on his apron but didn't offer it again. 'I'm sorry. I have beef on the menu. I was just cutting it up. I'll get my wife to take you up to the most agreeable of the bedrooms. There are several that overlook the garden.'

'It's so lovely,' said Lucy, conscious that Tim had grown tense.

'It's my solace,' said Dedoir. He glanced at Tim again. 'I'm honoured to have you as guests.' He paused slightly. 'The photograph was here when we arrived.'

Tim said nothing and there was a silence which deepened alarmingly. Lucy was over-conscious of the ticking of the foyer clock.

'My husband – prefers not to talk about the war,' she said, startled at the stuffy, schoolmistressy tone to her voice.

'I'm sorry.' Louis Dedoir was immediately penitent. 'I was clumsy. Forgive me.' He was clearly anxious for some kind of forgiving comment, but she decided against giving it to him. Tim wasn't to be bothered. He had to be a total priority.

'I'm glad I haven't changed beyond recognition,' Tim said, making an effort to brush the slight awkwardness aside but only succeeding in increasing the tension. 'But Lucy's right. I don't make a habit of discussing the war.'

'Ah, my wife has arrived. Monique,' Dedoir shouted in relief, 'we have guests. Guests who need a room.'

'*Quel surprise.*' Her voice was dry and measured as she walked down the corridor. 'Has the age of miracles come again?' Monique Dedoir was in her mid-fifties, tall and rather austere with chalk white features and hollow cheeks with broken veins spreading from her nose into the rigid powder of her cheeks. But her eyes held an ironic, intelligent humour.

She shook hands with Tim and Lucy with a firm dry grip, glancing wryly at her husband's filthy apron. 'He looks more like Sweeney Todd than a chef, doesn't he?' Her English was equally good. 'No doubt you will be amongst our last guests. We are putting the hotel up for sale next month.'

'How long have you been here?' asked Lucy with artificial interest.

'Four years and there were two owners before that. We were running a restaurant in America during the war, but we got homesick. Like fools we came here.'

'Did you know the area?' She knew she was brightly, automatically backing her into a corner as if they were at a cocktail party in Esher.

'No,' Monique Dedoir replied. 'It was my fault. I saw some idyllic country village where we could build up a business – and got Navise! Naturally, the hotel came to us at a knock-down price. So we bought it. The village didn't make such a bad impression on us then. Now it's like a vice, slowly tightening.

My husband has got the garden. All I've got is ulcers. Can I show you upstairs?'

The room, like the garden, was an unexpected surprise.

There were dried flowers on an oak chest, a small wooden chair and a marble wash basin rather shakily attached to the wall.

'Dinner is at any time from seven,' said Monique Dedoir. 'Louis is a good chef so you're in for a treat. I'll let you recover from your journey.'

It was five, and suddenly feeling exhausted Lucy lay down, while Tim opened the shutters. The bed was austere but the mattress was not as hard as she had suspected. There were woodcuts of willow trees on the walls which were washed a pale lime green.

Gazing round her, she felt a little more relaxed, and then saw with surprise that amongst the tree prints there was one that reminded her of home. At the back of her father's workshop there was a single, straggling willow that leant over a pond. The willow on the wall overlooked a lake, but there was something about the shape of its slender frame that reminded her of the much loved original. Then she realized that if anything happened to Tim she would be alone. Her only relative was a cousin in Australia that she had never met. As for children – Lucy firmly shut away the negative thoughts.

'Shall we have dinner in the hotel?' she asked Tim abruptly.

'I'm sure the Dedoirs would be upset if we didn't,' he replied with a forced smile. 'Anyway, they speak English which is a help. I hope that hasn't put you out. I know what a crack linguist you are. But at least I'll know what I'm ordering.' He gazed at her almost imploringly, as if he wanted Lucy to bring his nervous torrent of words to a stop.

She tried to help. 'The trouble with the English is they expect foreigners to speak their language. Insist, in fact.'

Tim seemed put out. 'I'm sure you're right,' he said rather frigidly.

'How long?' Lucy asked.

'How long what?' He was impatient.

65

'How long are we going to stay here?'

'A day or so.' Suddenly he seemed to make a decision. 'You don't mind if I go out for a bit?'

'Go out?' Lucy sat up against the headboard. 'Go out where?' She felt a childish pang of desertion. Why was he leaving her alone? She stared at him accusingly, panic welling up.

His face was completely expressionless, but Lucy thought she could detect a hint of resolution in his eyes.

'Just for a stroll.'

'I'll come with you.'

Tim was silent, and she waited for a while. When the silence became unbearable Lucy repeated her offer.

'I'd rather go alone. Just get a breath of air and have a think.'

'Where are you going?' she demanded.

'Nowhere in particular.'

Lucy was sitting on the edge of the bed now, not knowing how to cope with what Tim was doing. But what *was* he doing? Just going out for a stroll. What in God's name was the matter with her? She tried to apply logic and found none.

'I shan't be long.' Tim came over to the bed and sat down, holding her hand. 'I love you,' he said. 'I'll always love you.'

The situation suddenly seemed to have got out of control. What had started out as the greatest risk of her life had taken an unpredictable turn. But surely, that was what risks were about. All he'd done was to suggest a walk. What was wrong with that?

'I shan't be long. An hour. Maybe less. Just to have a think. Why don't you take a rest?'

'You never go out on your own.'

'I haven't had the gumption, old girl. But you've given me some confidence.'

'Have I?'

He bent down and kissed her. 'You bet.'

Strangely enough, Lucy slept, dreaming of the willow tree overhanging the pond at the back of her father's workshop. It was a late summer evening and they were both sitting on a blanket having a picnic that she had prepared. She was about ten, and often 'mothered' her father in this way. On this occasion Lucy had made him tomato sandwiches with plenty of salt, the way he liked them. She had also produced sandwich spread, Battenberg cake and doughnuts, cherry slices, bread and butter and plum jam. They ate silently and companionably, watching the willow leaves rustle in a fleeting breeze.

When she woke Lucy felt the pain of her father's death far more acutely than at any time before.

She glanced at her watch and saw that over an hour had passed, but her grief, long delayed, temporarily overlaid any doubts she had about Tim and she began to cry for her father for the first time since the funeral. The tears came easily, and she was grateful they were flowing at last.

Ten minutes later Lucy got up and walked over to the wash basin where she swilled her face with cold water. She knew the tears were just the start of her grief for the man who had been her rock and comforter, who had loved her unconditionally and who had never faltered in his depth of feeling. What was more poignant, unlike Tim and herself, Lucy and her father had never kept any secrets from each other.

She went to the window that looked out on to the garden and glanced at her watch again. It was a quarter past six. Wasn't it deeply insensitive of Tim to stroll off so casually? Injured innocence, a sense of martyrdom, a feeling of being left out irritated her. Lucy went back and sat on the bed, trying to reach the pain of her father's death again but only feeling an increasing anger against Tim. ·

It wasn't fair.

Lucy gazed at her watch again.

It was six thirty.

Where the bloody hell was he?

The knock was hesitant.

'Tim?' she called expectantly, her anger evaporating in blessed relief, but when the door opened Monique Dedoir stood on the threshold.

'Is your room satisfactory?' she asked tentatively.

'I was just waiting for my husband.' Lucy was immediately defensive, as if she'd been caught doing something she shouldn't. 'The room? I rather like it.'

'It's simple.'

'And welcoming.' It was such a surprise seeing the photograph,' said Lucy artificially, determined not to give herself away. 'I was impressed Monsieur Dedoir could recognize my husband. He's changed a lot. But I gather you find it difficult to let the rooms.' She realized she was running on like Tim had been and she brought the flurry of words to an abrupt halt.

'My sister-in-law's offered us a job running the restaurant in their hotel in Paris.'

'It's lucky your family's in catering.' Lucy smiled.

'Yes.'

Their eyes met and Monique Dedoir shrugged. They both laughed for no apparent reason, but it was more the laughter of embarrassment than anything else.

'Will you be dining with us?'

'We're looking forward to it,' said Lucy, starting to talk in French, determined that despite Tim's lack of punctuality she would practise the language. Gazing down at her watch again, she frowned.

'Are you worried about something?' Monique slipped helpfully into her mother tongue.

'Sorry?'

'Forgive me – I just thought you looked worried.'

'I am rather.' Lucy wanted to confide, to reach out for the woman's sympathy. 'Tim went out over an hour ago. He said he'd be back well before now.' To her annoyance, Lucy found her voice was trembling. 'Typical man! No sense of time!'

'I saw him pass the window. As he set off,' she added quickly.

'You didn't see him again?' Lucy asked foolishly.

'No.'

'What direction was he taking?'

'Pavilly.'

'The château?'

'It's not far.'

'Perhaps he went in,' said Lucy hopefully, 'to have a look. You know – for old times' sake.'

'It's boarded up.'

68

'The château's deserted?'

'It was burnt down just after the war. Most of it, anyway.' Monique Dedoir's face was inscrutable. 'The caretaker lives in the lodge.'

'The Germans?'

'The French.' She gave Lucy an ironic smile. 'It was before we came here.'

'An act of vandalism?'

'I don't think so. There was some trouble.'

'What sort of trouble?'

'Some young Frenchmen were accused of collaborating with the Germans. They were executed by local people.'

'I see.' Lucy was nonplussed. 'That was rather barbaric, wasn't it?'

'So was the Occupation.' Monique sounded slightly impatient. Was she implying that no Englishwoman would be able to understand? Lucy had to admit that she was probably right.

'I'm sorry,' she said. 'You all had a terrible time.' Fatally, Lucy knew she was giving the wrong impression and being patronizing.

Monique shrugged. 'I wouldn't know. We were in Chicago at the time.' She paused. 'I must congratulate you on your French. It's good.'

Lucy hardly heard, glancing down at her watch yet again. 'Could Tim have got lost?'

'He might have done if he decided to come back a different way. Those small roads are confusing – even if he has been here before. There's not a lot of variety in the landscape. That's one of Navise's problems. I expect you've noticed.' Monique Dedoir paused. 'I tell you what – if he's not back in the next ten minutes, my husband will get the car out. I'd do it myself but I don't drive.'

'I can't put you to all that trouble,' Lucy protested.

'It's no trouble. He likes to drive and his assistant chef comes in tonight from Vernise. There's no problem.' Monique opened the door. 'Give it ten minutes.'

The time crawled by, the fear inside her mounting. I should be reasonable. Logical. Practical. Less hysterical, thought Lucy. But I'm away from home for the first time since the war. I'm in a foreign place. And I've lost my father and now my husband. She wanted to cry again but this time like a young child. The sense of sanctuary, of the grey square and the simple room, had been replaced by alienation.

There was another knock on the door, but it was much more purposeful this time.

'Tim?' she cried out.

But when the door opened it was Monique Dedoir again.

'What is it?'

'A call. A telephone call.'

'From Tim?' asked Lucy wildly. Of course he *must* have got lost and was phoning her, feeling a fool.

'I am sorry.'

'Sorry?'

They looked at each other helplessly.

'It is not your husband,' said Monique Dedoir unhappily.

'Who is it then?'

'A Monsieur Latimer.'

Her heart pounding, feeling slightly sick and very bewildered, Lucy followed Monique back to the foyer and the telephone which was on the reception desk.

She picked up the receiver and almost dropped it in her agitation. 'Hello?'

'Lucy?' The voice was jovial and joltingly familiar.

'Is that you, Martin?' She was incredulous.

'Thought I'd give you a buzz.'

'How did you know where to find me?'

'Tim gave me the number.'

'*What?*'

'Before he went off. I say – is everything OK?'

How would Tim have known the number, wondered Lucy in bewilderment. He'd never been back. Why should he have given the number to Martin without telling her?

'Hello?' He was shouting now.

'Yes?'

'Are you sure you're OK?'

'I'm fine. Just waiting for Tim. Where are you?'

'Where else?' he chortled. 'Good old England.'

Safe old England, she thought. 'Your voice sounds awfully near.'

'It's the system. They're getting it better all the time. Except that on my end you sound faint and crackly. Where is the old devil? Chatting up the local crumpet?'

'He thought he'd take a stroll.'

'And why not? You know I don't want to interrupt anything but I've got a confession to make.' Martin was still exasperatingly jovial.

'A confession?'

'We all got a bit heavy handed about this trip, didn't we?'

Lucy tried to sound more confident. 'We're having a wonderful time.' She paused, still wondering why Tim had given Martin the number. 'Have they found the murderer yet?' she asked suddenly, trying to make conversation. Where are you, Tim? Would he come through the door while she was on the phone? Lucy gazed out on to the square but saw only the dog with a cut on its paw rooting in the gutter.

'Who?' Martin was saying.

'The murderer. Baverstock's,' she replied automatically.

'Oh, that sordid business. I'd completely put it out of my mind. He came from Hersham, didn't he? Probably got done in by a chap from one of those council estates. Now I mustn't hold you up any longer. Where are you dining?'

'At the hotel.'

'You mean – '

'Des Arbres.'

'Has he told you we took shelter there?'

'Yes.'

'Even in those days – under those conditions – the grub was good. Have lots of wine and relax. I won't phone again. Wouldn't want to spoil a second honeymoon.' Martin rang off, booming with laughter.

Lucy knew she was still under surveillance.

'Everything all right, madame?' Louis Dedoir asked in French. He was standing in the shadows of the corridor, dressed in a dark suit and a bow tie. Lucy wondered if he served the food in his own restaurant.

71

'An old friend,' she muttered.

'Has your husband returned?' Dedoir asked gently.

'No, monsieur.' She was trying to conceal the fact that she was shaking.

'Let's go and find him,' he said, detecting her anxiety without being intrusive. Suddenly he seemed immensely reassuring. 'Why do you not call me Louis? It would be more comfortable.'

The road was narrow and thickly hedged. Distant hills were on the horizon but Lucy couldn't see fields or even farms. Occasionally a chimney loomed up and once a flinty track to a yard in which chickens scratched in front of a barn. Although she knew how near they were to towns like Honfleur, Lucy felt threatened by this remote and shut-off countryside that seemed so much more claustrophobic than England.

Yet now she was with Louis, some of her panic had dispersed. Obviously Tim had lost his way and must still be on one of these endless roads that seemed to go nowhere.

A flight of birds wheeled up above them and a couple of pheasants emerged from a copse. Louis blasted the horn of his battered Citroën and they scurried towards a dense hedgerow, somehow managing to squeeze through.

Louis sat squarely behind the wheel, his large hands relaxed and protective. He was such a strong bull of a man. He would find Tim for her. Nothing untoward could happen with Louis around, Lucy told herself. He represented order, predictability, the solid march of time. Soon he would be serving Tim and her a delicious dinner in his dark suit, complaining about Navise and its parochiality, the lack of guests and the likely difficulties of selling the hotel. She and Tim would half listen and then go to bed, sleeping heavily after the wine and the rich meal, to wake in each other's arms.

Martin's call, although initially irritating, had been reassuring as well. Fancy him climbing down like that, she thought. A twinge of irritation remained and Lucy wondered yet again why Tim had given him the hotel number without telling her. She would have to challenge him about that. Maybe in their cabalistic way Martin and Peter had forced him to comply. 'Keep in touch, old boy,' she could hear them saying in chorus. 'Give us the hotel number – just in case.' In case of what?

The large black battered Citroën smelt of old leather and Gauloise as it nosed through the silent roads, until the hedges gave way to a stone wall that was half-strangled with ivy.

'The Château Pavilly.' Louis slowed down. He sighed. 'A disaster – a fine building destroyed by idiots.'

The Citroën crawled round to a gap in the wall that had been filled in with galvanized iron sheeting. A little further on there were gates and a small lodge with a vegetable garden.

'The caretaker, Solange Eclave, lives there. The family still pay her to keep an eye on the ruins.' Louis gave an angry shrug. 'The inhabitants of these parts are atavistic. They'd destroy their own if they felt strangers had been near them. They're like dogs, staking out their territory. We made a big mistake buying the hotel. We were both fools.'

'I gather you don't like Navise.' She tried to be arch but he didn't understand.

'It's not Navise. It's the peasants who live here.' Then, realizing he might seem too vehement, Louis resorted to polite conversation. 'There are long-term plans to rebuild Pavilly.' He paused. 'Do you think your husband knew Madame Eclave? She was here during the war. Could he have gone to call on her?'

'Perhaps,' Lucy said hopefully. 'They might have got talking and not noticed the time.'

'It's a possibility. They would have a lot to talk about.' Then he continued hurriedly, as if the comment required an immediate explanation. 'Madame Eclave's husband and two other men were executed by local people during the war. They were said to have collaborated with the Nazis. The Eclaves' farm is abandoned now, and Solange lives in the lodge. I'll go and ask her if she's seen your husband.'

'Shall I come with you?' she asked.

'Please do. I wouldn't worry. There's a perfectly normal explanation for all this. I'm sure of that.'

Lucy nodded, still reassured, gathering confidence all the time.

The gravel on the drive that led up to the gates of the château was overgrown with grass and weeds, but some attempt had been made to keep the path to the lodge clear. The squat one-storey building had small windows and green shutters, and the place had a run-down look to it like the square in Navise. Paint was flaking and the stone walls were stained.

Louis went up to the front door and Lucy followed. He knocked loudly. There was silence and then he knocked again. Still no reply.

'If this is the way your husband came he can't have got far. No doubt, like us, he found Solange was out and has taken the other road back. I'm sure we'll catch up with him.'

'It's very good of you to go to all this trouble,' said Lucy, getting back into the dusty heat of the Citroën.

Louis didn't reply, and as the car moved down the lane she asked curiously, 'What does Solange do exactly – as caretaker to a ruin?'

'The family have employed an archivist to sift through what's left of the Pavilly documents, to try and rebuild the château on paper before plans are drawn up for the restoration. Solange helps in this task. I rather like her but, because of her husband, she's very isolated. In fact she has become – quite ill. It's a tragedy but Monique and I don't know all the details. Navise looks inward. We are still outsiders.' The Citroën turned an almost full circle and then headed down a narrow road. 'Solange comes over to us for an occasional game of cards.' Louis paused and then gripped the wheel harder. 'She stayed on as caretaker on behalf of the family, and the German high command never requisitioned the château. I know she worked hard to put them off. The place is everything to her – or was. Something she aspired to. Anyway, her husband Claude spoilt all that by recruiting some local girls to have – relations with German soldiers. Of course it's difficult to tell what collaboration really is. Is it sitting passively doing nothing while your country is occupied by the enemy? Is it obeying Nazi orders? Working with them as a bureaucrat? But the locals say Claude would do anything for money. He'd have sent his own mother to Dachau for a few francs.' Louis paused again, clearly wondering if he had said too much or appeared too prejudiced.

Lucy, however, had only barely taken in what he had said. Why couldn't he drive faster? Why couldn't they find Tim?

'That's all I really know. Solange never discusses her husband's death or the local animosity.'

'You say she's ill?' asked Lucy.

'Nothing physical. It's all to do with her mind. Something went wrong. But the family doesn't seem to be aware of her problems and believe she's doing an excellent job for them. I'm sure she is.'

'They overlooked her husband's activities then?'

'A good reliable honest caretaker can make anyone overlook anything,' Louis replied. 'They're very hard to find. Of course the irony is the local people burnt the château down because they thought Solange had been up to the same tricks as Claude.' He sighed and began to drive slightly faster. Lucy was relieved, scanning the dense hedgerows for a sighting of Tim. 'Nevertheless, the Goutins still kept her on. They rely on Solange a great deal.'

Louis steered the Citroën down a narrow lane which had become a tunnel of trees. On either side the banks were torn by great sinewy roots. Very little light was able to penetrate, and moss, lichen and sallow toadstools grew amongst the spreading tentacles.

'Is this the only way back?'

'Unless he went across the fields. But there are no footpaths.' Louis was driving slowly again now, gazing around him, as if Tim might be concealed somewhere amongst the roots. A rabbit ran across their path and narrowly avoided being mashed to a pulp under the Citroën's wheels. 'The law of trespass,' said Louis, 'is very important here. Territorial rights are sacred. That's why the Occupation was such a terrible imposition.'

'You're *sure* there's no other way back?' said Lucy, ignoring his digression, her agitation mounting.

'Yes.'

'How far is Navise from here?'

'A mile or so.' He seemed less reassuring now and she had the odd feeling that Louis had shrunk in bulk and was sitting less solidly behind the wheel.

'I expect your husband will have returned by now,' he said with a self-conscious laugh.

'No doubt,' she replied woodenly.

But when they got back, Tim wasn't there. He had now been missing for more than two hours and the Hôtel des Arbres had all the aura of a jail with Lucy a prisoner on parole. Now she was back to face her warders.

Monique Dedoir was in the foyer, exuding a calm common sense which Lucy couldn't share.

'He must be in the vicinity. You have explored all possible routes?' Monique eyed Louis critically, as if she suspected him of not being sufficiently conscientious.

'Unless he went beyond the château,' he began guiltily.

'You didn't check?'

'I'll go back and see.'

'You can't go out *again*,' Lucy protested, but knew she wanted him to. She was still trying to convince herself that there was some simple explanation, but failed completely, renewed panic surging at being back at the shabby hotel without Tim.

Louis Dedoir hurried out of the foyer, back to the Citroën parked in the sun-soaked square outside, no doubt anxious to get away from the accusation of a duty not done.

'I'll go up to my – our – room,' said Lucy. She had the unsettling sensation that this woman knew what she was thinking and was putting her down as a panicky fool.

'I wouldn't,' she replied briskly. 'Come and have an aperitif with me. I'm sure Louis will find your husband and there will be a perfectly ordinary explanation. This is all just a muddle. Please call me Monique.'

What kind of muddle, wondered Lucy as she followed her through a door at the back of the reception desk and into a small, neat office that, like their room, had a view of the garden.

'Please sit down.' She went over to a cabinet and produced a bottle of St Raphaël. 'This is good. You'll join me?'

Lucy nodded, apprehension tightening her stomach.

As Monique poured the aperitif into two glasses, she asked, 'Do you have children, madame?'

'No. We haven't started a family yet.' The words rushed out too defensively.

'Ours are grown up. Henri is a lawyer in Lille and Sylvain is at university in Montpelier, reading architecture. No grand-children. Not yet.' Monique smiled her spare smile. 'Was your husband a well man?' she asked suddenly. 'Or do you consider me interfering?'

Lucy didn't. It would be a relief to talk about Tim.

'He had this breakdown after the war.'

'So did poor Solange. I do understand how difficult it must have been for you.'

'This is the first time we've been away together since – ' In a rush, Lucy began to explain how the three men had travelled from the Havre peninsula to Spain. Then she realized that she must know all about this anyway, or they wouldn't have kept the photograph. Lucy felt increasingly stupid, very much the little lady from insular England. Nevertheless, Monique listened attentively.

'And the others? Was their – their mental stability affected too?'

'No,' said Lucy bleakly.

Monique got up and poured herself another St Raphaël. She turned back guiltily. 'Do you want another drink?'

'I haven't finished this one yet.' She tried not to sound smug. She certainly didn't feel it.

'I drink too much,' confessed Monique. 'I keep trying to cut back, but it doesn't work.' She smiled warily, wanting understanding but finding none.

'*Did* anything happen here that might have affected my husband?' asked Lucy abruptly. The drink was going to her head and she knew she was in danger of giving Tim away.

Monique shook her head. 'Apart from the Occupation, nothing has ever happened in Navise. If something *had*, then I'm sure we would have heard about it.' She paused. 'Of course there was the execution of the collaborators.'

'Your husband told me about the incident.' Lucy took a few more sips of the St Raphaël. She would give anything to be back in Esher buttering bread in the pavilion with Tim in his deckchair outside. At least she would have been able to check on him from time to time. Now he was lost in France. She suddenly gave a half-sob and her hand shook so much that a few drops of the red liquid fell on the threadbare carpet.

Monique Dedoir was on her feet at once, taking Lucy's glass, setting it down on a mat on a paper-strewn bureau. The clock outside in the foyer chimed a quarter past nine.

'I'm sorry – '

'You are upset. Is there any other way I can help you?' Monique's pale, set face seemed far too near her own.

'No.'

'I think Louis has returned.' She hurried out and seemed to be gone for an inordinate length of time during which the sun began to sink into an orange glow of fire, hanging over the secret garden until the dull red ball disappeared below the window frame. Dark shadows crept into the room.

At last Monique returned.

'It's getting dark,' she muttered as she switched on a too-hard light bulb above the bureau.

Why doesn't she have a shade, Lucy wondered, trying not to think about what was going to happen next.

'I'm afraid he hasn't found him.'

'Hasn't – '

'Louis has gone out again.'

'To keep searching?' Was Tim lying injured in some field? Why had she been sitting here drinking?

'He's just rung Monsieur Metand at the Prefecture in Honfleur. He dines here sometimes with his wife and we've got to know him well. He is a detective. He also plays chess with Louis. I'm hoping that you won't mind.'

'Mind what?'

'We've asked him to drop by. More as a friend than a policeman.'

Lucy's gaze swept the mantelpiece, resting on a couple of Dresden shepherdesses, one of which had a broken arm. The limb was placed just behind her crook, covered in little slivers of china.

'Isn't it too early to worry the police?' she asked almost defiantly.

'It's getting dark.'

'This woman Solange. Would Tim be with her?'

'Why should he be?'

'He knew her in the war when she hid him at the château. I told your husband and he very kindly knocked at the door of the lodge but there was no reply. Would she be anywhere else?'

Madame Dedoir shook her head. 'It's the only habitable building on the estate apart from the summerhouse where the archivist has a room.'

'Does Solange have a car?'

'A blue Deux Chevaux. But I haven't seen it in the square all day. Not that she comes to Navise much.' Monique Dedoir paused, looking confused and unhappy, as if she had been about to say something but had thought better of it. Then she gave an uncomfortable little laugh. 'She visits us here occasionally. She isn't particularly well.'

'Louis told me.' Lucy used his name rather self-consciously. 'Does she ever talk about her husband?'

'No.'

'What's her background?' asked Lucy curiously.

'She was originally a farmer's daughter who was ambitious. She loves Pavilly and is still distraught about its destruction, but after all she's only the caretaker. Solange had no education, no chance at all to better herself except to work for the Goutins. The rumours say Claude beat her and I'm sure that's true. He hated his wife rising above him and I believe he did everything he could to pull her down.' Monique paused, slightly flustered, and Lucy knew the drink was making her talk. It's unfair, she thought. I don't want to hear all this.

Monique hurried on, wanting to finish the saga, realizing perhaps she should never have started.

'Claude collaborated in the most stupid manner and Solange would have lost her job if the family hadn't valued her so much. The Goutins believed that she could keep the Germans from requisitioning Pavilly and she succeeded. Ironically, it was the French who burnt it down.'

'Why did they do that?'

'To pay Solange back for getting a job above her station, to make an example of the collaborators. Who knows? They're all peasants.'

'When were the executions?'

'In the late summer of 1940, I think. But no one talks about them now.'

'Tim might have been in the château then,' said Lucy hesitantly. 'Do you know the exact date?'

'No, I'm afraid I don't.'

An uncomfortable silence grew between them, rather as if they had both been indiscreet.

Monique finished her second glass of St Raphaël and got up to pour a third. This time she didn't offer Lucy one.

'Has Solange ever mentioned Tim?'

'Not to my knowledge, madame.'

'Call me Lucy,' she said softly, wanting the comfort of her name. 'So what *does* she talk about?' Too late, she wanted to lead Monique on. But Lucy realized that her questions had become too probing and she had frightened her off.

'Our conversations are rather restricted. Solange only talks of the château in its former days.'

'But not about the Nazis or the collaborators, or Claude?'

'Never.'

'She didn't have any children?'

Monique shook her head.

'How old is she?'

'Mid-thirties.'

'Why did she stay on? You would have thought she would have moved away after what happened,' she said eventually.

'Yes. I suppose so. But she loves her job.'

There was another pause, mercifully shorter this time.

'I'm sure you don't have to worry about Solange,' Monique said quietly. 'She's not a person who could harm anyone. Except herself,' she added as an afterthought.

They sat silently again until Monique rose as if she couldn't bear it any longer and flung open the window. The scent of mimosa drifted into the room. 'It's so hot,' she complained. 'The time we spent in America has made Louis and me restless here. We often think Navise is closing in on us.'

'Will Monsieur Metand come here?' asked Lucy. 'Or is he going to search with your husband? I'm very grateful for all you are doing, but – '

Monique began to apologize, saying she was sorry she hadn't made the situation clear. She sounded slightly slurred. 'He'll be here soon,' she said.

Lucy looked at her watch. It was now quarter to ten.

'Can I get you something to eat?'

'No, thank you.'

'Are you sure? You must be starving.'

Lucy's exhaustion and anxiety were now beginning to tell. 'Please – my husband is missing. I don't know where he is. I *don't* feel hungry.'

The clock in the foyer ticked mercilessly and a white moth

flew into the room from the half open window, fluttering around the light bulb.

'Damn. I shouldn't have opened the window. I'll get it out.'

Monique picked up a feather duster and made ineffective attempts to flick the moth away. In the end, Lucy got up on a chair and began to try and drive the frantic insect towards the window.

Eventually she failed and the moth returned to the light. Lucy watched it in silence and then decided to phone Martin. She suddenly needed to hear a familiar voice and she couldn't care less how overbearing he might be.

'Could I make a phone call?'

'Of course.'

'I'd like to phone England. Speak to an old friend.' Lucy gave her Martin's number, and as Monique went back to reception, Lucy had an alarming thought. Could Tim have left her? Then she dismissed the idea as the wanderings of an exhausted mind. But it didn't quite go away.

Lucy took the receiver with a brisk nod of thanks. Monique returned a little unsteadily to the office and the bottle of St Raphaël.

'Martin?'

'Lucy.' May's voice was incredulous. 'What are you doing on the phone? Is something wrong?'

'I want to speak to Martin. He called an hour or so ago.'

There was a short silence during which Lucy tried to work out what May was thinking. Was she still angry?

'You say he phoned you?' She sounded more perplexed than harbouring any resentment. Besides, thought Lucy, it was she who had put down the phone after their last conversation in England.

'About three hours ago.'

'Not from here he didn't.'

'I don't understand.'

'He's gone on a business trip to Birmingham. It's only for a couple of nights and I don't have the number. I wonder why he called you.'

'He said he thought that he'd made a mistake – that he and Peter had both made a mistake.'

'A mistake?' May made it sound an unheard of event.

'Martin told me that he and Peter thought it *was* a good idea for us to come out here. On reflection.'

'How extraordinary. He never gave me that impression.'

'Is there *any* way I can get hold of him?'

'I told you, I don't have the number.'

'Would Peter know?' Lucy tried to hide her frustration.

'I don't see why he should. Is there something I need to know?'

Suddenly all Lucy's hostility against May was swept away by the need to confide.

'Tim's gone missing,' she said, breaking down, the tears blurring her eyes so that she could hardly see.

'Missing? I don't understand.'

'He went for a walk. Hours ago. He didn't come back!'

'And you say Martin felt that going to France was a good idea! He must have been trying to cheer you up.'

Or check we were actually here more likely, Lucy thought.

'What have you *done*?' May continued.

Rather than getting the unqualified support she needed, Lucy was amazed to find she was being attacked. 'Did you hear what I said?'

'You said Tim's gone missing. He probably couldn't take all those memories. Went wandering off – '

'Shut up!'

'But wasn't that the danger?'

'Shut up!' Lucy screamed and then screamed again without words, letting the sound shrill out as loudly as she could. 'Just shut up!' she finished.

May, recognizing hysteria, tried to be comforting. 'Give me your address and we'll come straight out. I'll phone Peter, get hold of Martin somehow. Now you *must* give me the address.' She was full of direct, compassionate action and it gave Lucy a frisson of delight to slam down the receiver this time. Tit for tat, she thought. And bugger you, May Latimer.

*

Lucy could smell the drink on Monique's breath but she was no longer slurred.

'I lost control.'

'It's not surprising. Who were you talking to?'

'A dutiful wife.'

'And her husband?'

'One of Tim's fellow officers who shared the escape. Who came here.' Lucy paused. 'We all live in the same road.'

'That doesn't sound a good idea,' said Monique with surprising perception.

'They were his guardians,' Lucy explained. 'I don't know why.'

'Will you come back into the office? I'm going to get a brandy for you.'

'Could I have it in the garden? I mean – could we both walk in the garden?'

'If that would help. I expect Louis and Metand will be here soon. Let me get the brandy and then we'll go outside.'

She hurried away. This time Lucy knew she needed the alcohol. As much as she could get.

The air smelt of honeysuckle as they walked around the little garden that Louis had so lovingly created.

A sense of unreality had gripped her and Lucy felt as if she and Monique were floating rather than walking sedately along the meticulously laid gravel paths. She felt completely reliant on her; the large brandy she had quickly drained had just as quickly made her drunk. A bat dived over Lucy's head. She didn't cry out but would have slipped and fallen if Monique had not steadied her.

'You'll be in no state to talk to Metand. Louis will be furious with me. Your husband can't have been spirited away. Maybe he *did* find Solange and started to talk and didn't notice the time.'

Lucy nodded, eager to accept almost any reasonable suggestion.

'Come into the office – no – into our sitting room – and I'll organize some coffee.'

'Won't you have anyone in the restaurant tonight?'

'It's too early in the week. Come on. You've got to sober up.' Monique put a hand on her arm and began to lead her back to the hotel. She seemed to be quite upset. 'It's usually me who is like this.' She laughed and Lucy joined in out of sympathy and confusion.

She collapsed into an armchair and must have slept for a short while. When Lucy woke with a stinging headache she was alone in a large room with a low ceiling that was full of shabby furniture, books and family photographs.

Slowly and painfully the memory of Tim's disappearance filtered back. What could have happened, she wondered over and over again until her head ached even more.

A few minutes later, Monique returned with a plate of cold meats and a basket of bread. She put them down on a table that was piled high with magazines that looked untouched, as if they had never been read.

'Is there any news?'

'Not yet.'

'I'm not hungry,' Lucy muttered.

'You've got to eat.' Monique was gently pressing. 'Louis and Metand have returned. They checked all the roads in the area.'

'They've given up?' Lucy asked belligerently, the cold yearning for Tim working its way up from the pit of her stomach.

'Metand is going to make the search official.'

'Doesn't he want to see me?'

'When you've eaten.'

'Don't you mean sobered up?'

'That was my fault.'

Lucy got up and lurched towards the table, still feeling sick and light-headed, but when she began to peck at the cold meat she found she was ravenously hungry. The meat was succulent and deliciously light and the bread was warm and crisp.

'Can I see him now?' Lucy asked when she had finished.

Monique nodded but didn't move from the hard chair she had sat down on. 'Are you feeling better?'

'Don't you mean, will I start drunkenly abusing your French policeman? The answer is no.'

'I'll go and get him.'

Whilst she was out of the room, Lucy tried to make up her mind about Monique Dedoir. She had been immensely kind but she also detected a deep-seated bitterness. Had the Hôtel des Arbres done this to her? Or was it being land-locked in Navise?

Monique returned with two black coffees on a tray. She was followed by a small, lean man with glasses and a receding hairline. François Metand was somewhere in his mid-forties and had a slightly hesitant, rather donnish air to him.

'Mrs Groves. I'm sorry to hear about this business. I shall do everything to help you.' His English was not as fluent as the Dedoirs'.

'I speak French.' Lucy tried to steady herself.

Metand looked grateful.

They both sat down on the uncomfortable leather chairs at the magazine-strewn table and sipped at their coffee as Monique withdrew.

'What purpose did you and your husband have for visiting Navise, madame?'

Once again she appreciated his directness and decided to edit nothing. 'Tim hid here in the war. He has never discussed what happened.'

'Their presence is well known. They were brave men.'

With the two simple phrases, Lucy felt even more drawn to Metand. She felt she could trust him, that he wouldn't evade the truth. Whatever that was.

'You weren't here then?'

'Like Louis and Monique, I am a comparative newcomer.'

'My husband was not as fortunate as his companions. He suffered a breakdown when he came home and he's not fully recovered. We came here in the hope of laying some ghosts.'

Lucy was aware that Metand had been watching her carefully, but she didn't resent his scrutiny. At the same time she wondered if he thought she was lying. 'Did he want to come?'

'No.'

'What changed his mind?'

'I said I'd leave him unless he did.'

Metand nodded, relaxing the eye contact, looking down at the table.

'He was deteriorating.' Lucy was defensive.

'What convinced you that coming here would be an answer?'

'I didn't think it would be an answer, but I hoped I might reach him. I didn't even know about Navise. I suppose you'll think I'm naive, but I hoped by driving around the countryside we could talk. Instead of that Tim navigated us straight here.'

'So it would seem he had a purpose?' Metand said quietly.

'I don't know.'

'What did his friends feel about him coming to France? His fellow escapees?'

'They were very much against the idea. They put considerable pressure on me not to force Tim into this. So did their wives,' Lucy added bitterly.

'What are the names of these men?'

'Peter Davis and Martin Latimer.'

'You resisted their pressure.'

'I was determined. Then Martin phoned the hotel. I didn't know Tim had given him the number.'

'A last moment idea?'

'Perhaps.'

'What did he have to say?'

'Martin told me he'd changed his mind, that he thought it *was* a good idea for us to travel out here after all, but I think he was really checking that we'd arrived. I tried to call him later, but all I could get was his wife, May, who said he was in Birmingham. I'm afraid we had a disagreement.' She paused, and then asked the question she had been building up to. 'What about Solange Eclave? Do you think Tim came to see her?'

'Why should he?' asked Metand.

'I've no idea. He never mentioned her before. If he had I'd tell you. I've nothing to hide.'

'Maybe *he* had.'

'But what?' There *must* be some rational explanation. Was amnesia a possibility? Could Tim have tripped and fallen in some wood or field? He didn't *have* any motive for disappearing. Please God, he didn't.

'Was there some reason why your husband couldn't confide in you?'

'They – he and Peter and Martin – always said they couldn't talk because they'd signed the Official Secrets Act.' The fear began to creep back and Lucy had such a dry mouth that she could hardly finish her sentence. 'Monique – Madame Dedoir – says you've mounted a search.'

'Nothing full scale.' Metand was cautious. 'But I would like a more detailed description, the exact clothes he was wearing, and if you've got a photograph I'd be grateful.'

She pulled a fairly recent one out of her bag which showed Tim in his cricket flannels walking out to the wicket. 'He was wearing a brown sports jacket, open-necked checked shirt and grey corduroy trousers with brown brogues. Is that enough?'

Metand nodded. He took out a small leather notebook and scribbled down what she had said, attaching the snapshot to the page.

'This business about the collaborators that the Dedoirs mentioned,' asked Lucy hesitantly. 'Can you tell me about them?' Could there be something there? She looked closely at Metand and wondered if he was also searching for a connection.

'All I know is that three alleged collaborators were executed by local people. One of them was Claude Eclave – Solange's husband.'

'Do you know her?'

'I first met Solange when she asked my advice about security for the ruins of the château. She comes to see us occasionally – just as she does the Dedoirs. She's come to rely on outsiders.'

'Has she ever mentioned my husband's name?'

'No.'

'Would you say she was mentally ill?'

'She needs help, but she has not reached the stage where she is prepared to ask for it.'

Lucy sipped at her coffee, but it was cold and bitter. She glanced at Metand and saw he was patiently waiting. Was this some technique of his? Provoking questions?

'Is there any remote possibility that my husband is with this woman?'

'That is what we have to discover. You're obviously worried that your husband's disappearance may have something to do with his activities in Occupied France. In my experience, much of what happens in wartime can't be forgotten but gets pushed into a corner of the mind where it goes rotten. Like a sore, or a boil which continues to ache until it bursts.' He paused, letting the silence stretch a little too far. 'I hope you won't think I'm being intrusive, but I need to know more about your marriage, about your relationship with your husband.'

'You mean he might have left me? Or I might have killed him?' She spoke flatly, letting the momentous words seem unassuming and unimportant.

Metand looked at her slightly anxiously, and she guessed that he was wondering if she was still drunk. Well, she was. Lucy knew she would never have come out with such dramatic statements if she had been sober. Then he nodded, as if recognising her situation. He's perceptive, Lucy thought, and was encouraged. Metand was more like a reassuring country doctor than a policeman.

'We loved each other.' She felt a stab of betrayal. Why in God's name had she used the past tense?

Metand stood up and Lucy started, for she had been expecting more questions. 'I'll phone you immediately there's news.'

'The search will continue through the night?'

'Of course.'

'And this Solange. You'll find out where she is?'

'We're doing that now.'

Lucy went reluctantly upstairs with a smaller glass of brandy. Not the knockout drops this time. But she hardly even sipped at it, for when she lay down on the empty double bed she slept at once. Lucy woke, trembling, the mellow morning sunlight on the crumpled bedclothes. For a moment she was confused and then the pain returned with a savage intensity. Tim. Where are you? For God's sake make it all right again.

Looking at her watch she saw that it was after nine. How could she have slept this late at a time of such crisis? She dragged herself out of bed, stiff and cold despite the sun, and began to search in one of the suitcases for her dressing gown.

For a while she couldn't find it and then, cursing, she wrenched it out and thrust her arms into the sleeves. Lucy unlocked her door and padded down the uncarpeted corridor towards the galleried staircase.

She looked down into the hall, where Monique was sitting behind the reception desk, reading *Le Figaro*. There was no sign of Louis. Why was she so damned idle at a time like this, Lucy wondered. Didn't she care? More importantly, why hadn't she woken her?

'Any news?'

'I'm afraid not.' Monique got up with a slight start and turned stiffly to gaze up at her. The white face was puffy-looking this morning with mauve marks under her eyes. She looked as if she hadn't slept.

'Metand was going to phone me.'

'I took the call. He had nothing to report.'

Lucy felt welcome anger beginning to fill her, temporarily submerging her acute anxiety. She wanted to make her temper felt. 'You should have woken me.'

'He had nothing to – '

'And told me what he had said. Even if it was nothing.'

Monique flushed and looked for a moment as if she was going to argue. Then she decided against it. 'You needed sleep,' she said wearily.

'You don't look as if *you* had any.' Lucy tried to be more reasonable but her temper was boiling. What was the matter with her? She was usually so passive, always having to build up to being assertive. Now she wanted, demanded, a confrontation.

'No. I didn't. Louis joined the search. He was out all night and I get worried about him. He has angina.'

'I'm sorry.' But almost immediately her rage returned. 'Did Metand find Solange?'

'She got back home late.'

'What about Tim?'

'I don't – '

'Was he with her, for God's sake?' Why was Monique so stupid?

'Of course not. I'd have told you straight away if he was. She hadn't seen your husband at all.'

'Are you sure about that? Why wasn't I told all this? Immediately!' Lucy's voice was shrill. 'You think he's left me, don't you?' she shouted over the bannisters. Monique looked up at her calmly, appealingly. She thinks she's got a hysterical woman on her hands, thought Lucy. Well, she has.

Suddenly her temper went flat. 'I'm sorry.'

'It doesn't matter. Come down. We can't talk like this.'

'Why didn't you tell me he called?'

'It was an error of judgement. Louis will tell you I often make them. He will also tell you I like to manage situations. *Please* come down.'

'I'm not dressed.'

'Let me bring breakfast up to you.'

Lucy began to weep silently. At the same time she thought how fortunate it was there were no other guests at the Hôtel des Arbres.

Monique ran up the stairs and took Lucy's arm, leading her back to the sunlit bedroom. She didn't resist.

'Is Metand coming?' she whispered, as she sank down on the side of the bed.

'Later this morning.'

'So there's no news?' She knew she must sound like a child in need of reassurance.

'He says the search is being redoubled. He will take you out there.'

Lucy nodded. That seemed a good idea. At least she would have something to do. She wouldn't be isolated and left out any longer, as if she was awaiting a doctor's round in hospital.

'When you've had some coffee, don't you think you should ring your friends in England and tell them what's happening? Perhaps they could come out – '

'You've stopped saying it,' said Lucy emptily.

'What do you mean?'

'You've stopped saying there could be a perfectly reasonable explanation.'

'I'm sorry. Of course there must be.' Monique's face was whiter than ever under the heavy powder and Lucy decided not to press her any further. 'They'll find him. I'm sure they will. There's every hope.'

Lucy nodded again. 'Perhaps I could use the phone now?'

'Have some coffee first.' Monique was being managing again.

'Could I use the phone? *Now*, please?'

As she dialled Peter's number Lucy could see the square through the half-open door. It was Saturday and a market had been set up, stalls crowded tightly together under an awning. A small crowd of people were buying fruit and vegetables and turning over the leather goods and bric-à-brac. Navise had come to rather lacklustre life.

A police officer stood talking to a young man a few metres from the front of the hotel and Lucy wondered whether they were discussing the Englishman's disappearance.

'Yes?' Peter's voice was clipped, neutral, reassuringly home counties. She had never been so pleased to hear it before. It was as if she knew him after all.

'Lucy.'

'Thank God. May was so upset. Why did you hang up on her?'

'I couldn't cope.'

'She's been terribly worried and so have I. Where did Tim get to?'

'I don't know.' Wilfully she didn't tell him he was still missing.

'What did he say?'

'Nothing – because he hasn't come back. The police are still searching.' Her voice broke.

'*Christ!*' He was surprised, more than surprised. He was deeply shocked.

'Did you know someone called Solange Eclave when you were in Navise?'

'She was the caretaker of the château where we hid for a few days. The Château Pavilly. Why do you ask?'

'I wondered if Tim had gone to see her.'

'Not a chance. He wouldn't have wanted to spend five minutes in her company. What little we knew of Madame Eclave we utterly despised. She was a real bad egg.'

'Peter – you've got to tell me what happened in the war. It could have some connection with Tim's disappearance, so don't throw your bloody Official Secrets Act at me.'

'I'm not going to.'

'Don't keep anything back.'

'I'll tell you what I know. We had a contact who got us a room at the Hôtel des Arbres. We spent a night there and then went on to the château for a couple more. We were in Navise for three days in all.'

'And then?'

'We moved on. We couldn't stay anywhere long.'

'Was it Solange who allowed you to hide in the château?'

'Yes. But a German patrol arrived while we were there. It was

91

a nasty moment, but Solange had the initiative to move us into the wine cellar. Look, could I speak to the French police officer who's in charge of all this?'

'What for?'

'To support you, of course. I can't get hold of Martin. He's away on a business trip.'

'What about Solange's husband being executed by the locals for collaborating with the Nazis?'

'That was later. When we were gone. Lucy, I – '

'I've been finding out a lot of things.' She didn't invent the menace in her voice deliberately. It seemed to be there naturally.

Peter continued with a quiet authority. 'I gather Claude was a collaborator. There were others, but Solange was not involved. Or, at least, we didn't think so.'

'How do you know all this?'

'I was told by the War Office who got it from the French.' His voice was as clipped and confident as ever. Peter was still very much in charge. In the background she could hear Sally asking questions and being told to go away. When she had gone he cleared his throat and continued, 'They told me some young Frenchmen provided the German patrol with some local girls. Claude took photographs and sold them to the Nazis for them to use as propaganda.'

'What did you make of him?'

'He was just a local peasant who seized an opportunity. His wife had got the job as caretaker of the château and moved up some social notches which hadn't exactly pleased him so he exploited her position. Claude wanted to make some money and arranged to set up the little frolic in the château itself. Possibly he hoped Solange would lose her job. But she didn't.'

'Tim was never involved with her, was he?' Lucy asked abruptly, feeling the flush travel up her neck and over her face.

'Of course not. You're getting things way out of proportion, Lucy. All Tim wanted was to get home. As we did.' He sounded reproving.

Lucy felt acutely self-conscious, aware that Monique was probably lurking near by, wondering how she was going to handle this hysterical British woman.

'Is there anything else you know, Peter, that you should tell me?'

'No. We want to look after you. The hiding, the tension, the

German patrols, the fact that we might be given away at any moment – that's what broke Tim. There was nothing else.' He paused and she waited for his patronage. But it didn't come. Instead she felt unexpected warmth. Then he ruined it all by saying, 'We *did* warn you not to go.'

'Martin changed his mind. He said I was right.'

'He was anxious about you. I think he must have phoned to make sure you were both coping. He didn't want to be dampening.'

'How did he get this number?'

'Tim gave it to him. No harm done, is there? Look – would you like me to get the next flight out?'

'No!'

'I'm sorry?' Peter sounded incredulous.

'I want to handle this myself.'

'But I don't think – '

'You *have* to leave me alone. At least, just for a while.' Suddenly Lucy felt more confident, enjoying staving him off.

'I know you're fluent in the language,' he began. 'But I still feel I could be of use.'

'Please. I'm fine,' she said, beating a tactical retreat.

'You must promise to keep in touch,' he demanded. 'Ring me this evening. I'll be waiting for your call. Say, about six.'

'I don't know if I'll be here. But I'll contact you somehow if there's any news.'

'Very well. But listen, Lucy – '

'Try not to worry,' she interrupted him and put the phone down gently.

'Breakfast.' Monique was hovering in the doorway. 'Come into the dining room. I've put out some croissants and I'll go and make fresh coffee.'

'And then?'

'Metand is on his way. Is that an inducement to eat?'

Lucy had to admit that it was.

As she followed Monique, Lucy felt a sudden homesickness as she remembered the warmth in Peter's voice. She suddenly remembered them all sitting on the riverbank at Walton-on-Thames. The men were lounging with the Sunday papers, the women breaking stale bread to feed the ducks. An austerity picnic followed – but not austere enough to leave out some good Médoc – and this was followed by snoozing and chatting and then a game of French cricket in which the women had been allowed to join. The ball had gone in the river and Tim dived in, followed by Peter and Martin. They had wrestled for it. Then Peter had thrown the ball on the grass and Sally ran away with it screaming, hotly pursued. That had been just after the men had moved into Shrub Lane, the honeymoon period before Tim had gone down so badly.

When Metand arrived in the dining room, he was wearing the same clothes as last night. He took his glasses off and began to rub at the lenses with his handkerchief.

Once again, he was reassuringly direct. Lucy had the strange feeling of having known him for a long time.

'We haven't found your husband yet. But I got hold of Solange. She'd been for a walk but hadn't seen him.'

'Do you believe her?'

'I have no reason not to.' He paused. 'She says she would like to meet you – if that might help.'

'Is there any point? I understand she's ill.' Lucy was alarmed.

'She can still do her job. She can still communicate.' Metand was defensive. 'But you don't have to see her.'

'No – I want to. I'm sorry.'

'You are in a very difficult position, Mrs Groves. I am here to try to alleviate that.' Metand put his glasses back on and tucked his handkerchief away.

Lucy sat down at a table. The croissants were in a basket and jam and butter and honey was laid out on a white cloth. Some of the other tables were also laid. Obviously market day brought the Hôtel des Arbres a little passing trade.

'The search has been widened.' Metand paused as she poured coffee, offering him some. He took the cup and sipped at it as the silence between them lengthened. 'Did you recollect anything more last night? Anything that could help us?'

'Nothing of any use. Have you organized this kind of search before?' Again, Lucy detected an unfortunate patronage in her voice.

'Two years ago. A woman was murdered by her husband. He hid her in the woods.'

'How long did it take you?'

'A week.'

'That's a long time,' she said, breaking up a croissant and putting a small piece in her mouth. It tasted like cardboard.

'The woods are thick.'

'Do you think Tim's dead?' she asked abruptly.

'No. We have other possibilities. He could be ill.'

'Or?' Lucy asked ominously.

'Had a purpose we don't as yet understand.'

'Do you think I killed him?' she asked, knowing she had to repeat the painful question now that she was sober.

He gave her an apologetic smile and shrugged. 'We need to talk.'

Lucy tried to eat another piece of croissant but it stuck in her throat. Dislodging the obstruction with a draught of coffee, she choked.

'The search party are sweeping the countryside towards the Tour des Oiseaux,' said Metand. 'It's a folly in the woods. Solange said she would wait for you there.' He paused. 'You may find her a little strange. She's not particularly well.'

95

5

The heat was sullen and the sky an overcast steel. Above the engine noise of Metand's Renault Lucy could occasionally hear the sound of a tractor, the cawing of a rook, the distant barking of a dog.

Gradually the landscape became more undulating. Glimpses of buildings, the banks of a stream, an old man fishing by a bridge, the sudden shouts of children, all gave hints of the hidden community that had become a fixation in her mind. They were all concealed, just like Tim. Was he amongst them? What had she launched him on? A flight into a past that was a sprung trap?

Metand drew off on to a bumpy track where a dozen or so small trucks and a couple of battered ex-army jeeps were parked.

'Now we walk.'

'How long have they been searching?' she asked.

'Since early this morning.'

Lucy felt guilty, as if she was a privileged visitor, Lady Muck, about to review the toiling peasantry.

As they began to walk up through the dark woods, she caught a glimpse of the Tour des Oiseaux through a gap left by a couple of storm-blasted trees. The dark, ivy-hung monolith, at the top of a steep hill, had round windows.

'We might have a storm,' said Metand, as he led Lucy up a narrow path through the wood which was largely comprised of ancient oaks. Many of the trunks were being slowly strangled by ivy and there was an acrid, musty smell of vegetation.

'Who owns all this?'

'A bankrupt landowner who left the area before the war. It needs clearing. People don't even take a Sunday walk here.' Metand paused and gazed irritably around him. 'With a bit more money, this countryside could flourish. The soil is good. But there's not enough capital – ' He began to talk about regional government but Lucy wasn't listening.

She was gazing around her apprehensively, seeing Tim's body under each tree, just like Baverstock with his throat slit on the Clump.

Police uniforms only made up about a quarter of the search party. The others were largely middle-aged to elderly men, strung out in a long line through the dense woodland, heads down, searching slowly and diligently. To Lucy, they looked as if they were in a painting, carefully planting a crop. All they needed was the tolling of the Angelus bell.

'I didn't realize you'd have so many civilians,' she said hesitantly. 'And some of them are quite old.'

'Since the war – nothing happens. We almost had too many volunteers to search for your husband.'

'It's not personal warmth? Compassion?' suggested Lucy.

'No,' said Metand. 'Pure curiosity. But, as you can see, they are thorough.'

They walked on, the ground rougher now and the path only a hint of its former self, leading uphill, beyond the conscientious searchers. A chaffinch sang, sweet and clear, and a couple of rabbits scampered away from them through dense undergrowth. There was a pungent smell of wild garlic.

'Does the folly have a history?' asked Lucy, needing distraction now, still trying to keep the morbid image of Tim's body out of her mind.

Metand launched into an explanation and she listened with increasing interest, soon finding him an eloquent storyteller. 'The tower was built in the sixteenth century to house a malicious wife. The Goutins were a little less civilized than they are now. Thérèse Goutin was only in her early twenties but she nagged her husband day and night to expand his estates, to buy neighbouring farms. In the end, Thérèse became so ambitious that she had an affair with another landowner and persuaded him to try and kill her husband so she could inherit his land. Then the joint estates of Thérèse and her lover would stretch as far as the eye could see. But the plot failed and the landowner was executed. The tower was built on top of the hill to imprison Thérèse so that she could *see* as far as the distant horizon but could never own the land or visit it. A servant brought her one meal a day. She was given no books, no comforts of any kind, so that she could brood upon her greed. Thérèse's only diversion was to feed the birds, to befriend them.' Metand paused. 'Do you really want me to go on? The story is pure folklore.'

'Tell me more,' Lucy pleaded. Directly he stopped talking, she saw a huddled shape under each bush. If only she hadn't come. If only she had stayed with Monique.

'Apparently Thérèse used to stand on that turreted roof with birds perched on her arms. Then, one day, she attempted to fly. Naturally, she fell to earth. Her grave is in the cemetery.'

'Despite Thérèse's power complex, her husband's vengeance was just a little cruel, don't you think?' observed Lucy, trying to be arch, trying to stop imagining and only succeeding in sounding gauche.

'Look at the fate of those young collaborators only a few years ago. I'm sure there are men in this search party today who were responsible for that.' As they struggled up the last part of the rise, Metand paused for breath. 'Vengeance is the most primitive of all the impulses.'

Solange Eclave was standing in the shadow of the tower in the dull midday heat, staring intently into a hollow. For a dreadful moment Lucy wondered if she had found Tim.

'Solange?' Metand's voice was quiet, almost gentle, as if he didn't want to surprise or frighten her.

'*Oui?*' She turned round and Lucy received an immense shock. Solange Eclave was tall but also extremely broad. Her face seemed enormous, as if she had been taking steroids, the smooth skin stretched tight across her cheekbones, her nose looking as if it had been broken and badly reset. Long, ragged blonde hair swept her large, fleshy shoulders and she wore a smock-like dress of faded blue linen which covered her legs, exposing thick white ankles and feet in sandals. Yet despite all this, there was still a hint of beauty in her full sensual lips and the large cornflower blue eyes that were fixed on Lucy. Brazen was the wrong word for her. Pagan was overblown. Blowzy was better, but it didn't do her justice. Lucy had the strange feeling that Solange had deliberately let herself go as an act of defiance. Then she shrugged off the idea. How could she make up her mind about the woman at first sight?

'This is Mrs Groves. Madame Eclave.'

'Tim's wife.' Her voice was light and delicate with a slight sibilance. She might be bizarre, thought Lucy, but she certainly radiates charisma. Then she was forcibly reminded of her dream of the big red-headed woman straddling the boy-like Tim.

'I'm sorry.' Solange moved towards her with surprising grace and Lucy saw that she wasn't in the least clumsy. In fact she was statuesque, almost majestic.

'I'm going to leave you alone to talk,' said Metand. 'I'll go back and see how my search party is coping.'

The woodland goddess. The earth mother. Lucy felt slightly dazed, regretting Metand's sudden and rather traitorous withdrawal. Was it deliberate? Did he think something might develop between them that his presence could inhibit?

'Let's go up to the tower.' Solange laid a hand on Lucy's arm and the intimate gesture made her want to recoil. 'I am sorry about Tim. Where do you think he might have gone?'

'I've no idea.' The heat seemed to close in as they walked up the hill. Crows were fluttering soundlessly around the battlements and for a wild moment she imagined Thérèse up there, the birds on her arms.

There was no track now, just ridges with only a scattering of trees, and they were able to walk alongside each other, picking their way up the uneven ground.

'I only knew Tim for three days, but I admired him. He did not have the same rank as the other two soldiers, although he was very much their leader.'

Lucy was considerably surprised at the unexpected information.

'Monsieur Metand was telling me about the tragedy of your husband's death.'

'Tragedy? I don't think that's the right word. He deserved what he got. My husband was an opportunist. Shall I give you my version of the events?'

'Only if you would like to.' Lucy was startled by her frankness.

'It's common knowledge round here.' Solange paused. 'You look tired. Are you sure you want to listen to all this?'

'Please.'

'A German patrol came to the château and got drunk. Then Claude brought in a couple of girls from the village. It was not a wise move. Next evening he brought in some friends, Philippe and Robert, who brought more girls with them. They didn't stop to think what the repercussions would be.' She paused, looking closely at Lucy. Then Solange hurried on. 'The Gestapo wanted to requisition the château as an interrogation centre. My strategy was to point out that Pavilly was far too big and uncomfortable for such an enterprise and that a smaller house just outside Honfleur would be more practical.' She paused again, and then continued. 'I kept Pavilly safe from the Germans – but I was never safe from my husband. What he did made the French destroy Pavilly. Ironic, wasn't it?'

'Did you *want* to stay after the war?'

'The locals could go to hell and back for all I cared. I knew the Goutins would restore Pavilly and this is what they plan to do. The family knew what a good job I'd done. They didn't blame me for what Claude and his friends did.' She paused and gazed at Lucy with a cautious smile. 'The rebuilding will take years and it's not even scheduled to start yet. For the moment I'm quite happy to be a ruin amongst the ruins. I've learnt to enjoy my own company and now I have Anna.' Solange was staring at Lucy again, but in a rather different way. Her eyes seemed slightly dilated and for the first time there was sweat on her fleshy upper lip. 'I've only been afraid since you brought Tim back.'

The extraordinary and completely unexpected sentence hung on the air like the expected storm. Lucy was so stunned that she simply gaped at Solange. 'What did you say?'

'I've only been afraid since you brought Tim back.'

The shock waves made Lucy feel faint and she swayed slightly. The folly seemed to lean towards her and then re-settle on its foundations.

'You were afraid of Tim?' She was incredulous.

'Metand knows nothing of this. I suggest we go up the tower so we can speak privately. The stairs are steep and he suffers from asthma.' She laughed and Lucy tried to keep calm. Everyone knew Solange was mentally ill. Everyone. She had simply fooled her, that's all.

A solitary rook wheeled above the battlements. Was it safe to go up with her? A light wind blew, rustling the ivy that clung tenaciously to the crumbling stone.

'All right,' said Lucy, much against her instincts.

She's definitely batty, she told herself. I shouldn't be climbing towers with this crazy woman. Nevertheless, Lucy meekly followed the bulky figure as if she was under a spell. She had the instinctive notion that Solange had been waiting a long time to have this conversation. Just as long, in fact, as she herself had been waiting for Tim to recover.

Lucy noticed that a large key was already in place in the lock of the heavy wooden door.

'I often come here,' Solange explained. 'I associate myself with Thérèse. Have you heard the legend?'

Lucy nodded.

'She cheers me up.'

'I gather she tried to fly.'

'I admire Thérèse for that. I don't have the courage. Not yet.'

The stone steps that led up the tower were steep and the handrail was made of rusty iron. The climb was tiring and Lucy's leg muscles were soon aching.

'There are three floors, each with an identical room off the stairwell.' Despite her weight, she didn't seem to be out of breath. Solange took out a set of keys from the pocket of her voluminous smock and opened a door, revealing a dim, empty space that smelt musty.

'Were the rooms furnished?' asked Lucy, feeling increasingly uneasy. Nevertheless, she drove herself on, hoping that Solange would say more about Tim, however absurd.

'We've only got four pieces at the château that I *know* were in the tower. Three *chaises longues* – all identical – that must have been placed one in each room. Then there was a table with her name carved on it.'

They climbed on up to the top of the tower, passing the two

other identical iron doors and eventually arriving at a smaller and even steeper staircase that led up to a trapdoor.

'It's sometimes a bit sticky,' said Solange casually as she inched it jerkily across. 'Do you get vertigo?' Her face seemed like that of an ageing clown. Lucy had always been frightened of clowns.

The guard rail around the parapet had rusted away in places and the sheer drop to the ground below was unsettling.

Turning round, looking back to the woodlands, she could see the search party conscientiously moving up the valley, slowly checking the terrain.

In front of her, with the road in between, lay the ruins of the Château de Pavilly. The view must once have been spectacular, but now it was simply desolate. The gates fronted a long straight drive with plane trees on either side, leading to the front steps of what had been the château. But now the walls were blackened, the roof had fallen in and only one wing was intact although its windows had been boarded up.

To the right of the ruins lay overgrown parkland, with a lake, a landing stage and a solidly built stone summerhouse. The neatly trimmed lawn was a striking contrast to the surrounding wilderness.

'As far as the eye can see,' said Solange. 'I will be queen bee.'

'Did Thérèse make that up?'

'No. I did. Just now,' said Solange with a careless smile.

Lucy glanced down and wished she hadn't, experiencing an unpleasant drawing sensation. 'How could she *ever* have imagined she could fly?'

Solange didn't reply. Then she turned slowly to Lucy, fixing her with her large, wide eyes. 'I do have a story to tell you. A true story that Metand doesn't know.' She paused. 'When I heard you had arrived – and Tim had disappeared – I thought you should hear it.'

'Why didn't you tell Metand?'

Solange's eyes were on hers, locked tight, ignoring the question.

'Because Tim killed my husband,' she said quietly, as if she was stating a well-known fact. Lucy was sure she was right: Solange had been waiting a long time for this moment.

6

'Is this is a bad joke?' asked Lucy. She felt as if Solange had physically attacked her and the shock waves churned hot and cold. 'Why are you telling me this crazy nonsense?' She wanted outrage to sweep her; instead she was aghast. The wretched woman shouldn't be roaming about like this. She ought to be in an asylum.

'Tim shot Claude because he was in love with me.'

What really happened to make her like this, wondered Lucy. 'You're very cruel,' she said slowly, trying to exert control. 'At a time like this, when I'm out of my mind with worry, you drag me up here and tell me lies.'

Solange suddenly grabbed Lucy's shoulders in such a tight grip that it hurt, but she forced herself not to struggle. Suppose she pushed her over the broken balustrade? She was gripping her shoulders even more tightly now, but still Lucy didn't move. Then Solange let her go, turning away, gazing back at the château. The sultry heat seemed to have increased.

'I haven't seen him. I promise you that.' Solange stood close to the parapet and Lucy felt her fear mount. Somehow she had to get away, back down to the ground. 'The reason he's disappeared is that he's looking for me. Your husband is a violent man.'

Lucy forced herself to speak. 'Tell me what really happened.'

'I'm telling you what happened. Don't you understand? Isn't it simple enough for you?'

Lucy decided to try and humour her, but it was an instinct rather than a reaction. 'Did Peter and Martin know?'

'Of course.'

'So why should my husband search for you? Want to harm you after all these years?'

'Because I have something he needs, something they all need. If I want to, I can destroy them.'

'How?'

Solange gazed blankly at her without replying.

'Tim would never hurt you. He would never hurt anyone.'

Again, Solange didn't reply.

'Why didn't you tell Metand?'

The air of unreality increased. Solange. Thérèse. These lies. Lucy suddenly felt giddy and clung to the parapet for support, while the dense woods seemed to come sweeping up to her. Then her head cleared.

Solange opened the trapdoor. 'I'm going back now,' she said casually.

'Is that all?'

'Isn't it enough?'

'It's a slander. I'll report you.'

'As long as Metand protects me from your husband, I don't give a shit what you say.'

Lucy followed her silently down the steep steps, stumbling once or twice, wanting to explode with fury and indignation but feeling curiously weak and powerless, as if she had to retain what little strength she had for the climb.

As they both stepped out into the heat, Solange said slowly, as if she was speaking to a stupid child, 'I realize what I said must have been painful. But believe me, it's true.'

'Tell Metand,' said Lucy brusquely. 'That's all you have to do.'

She stumbled down the hill towards the search party, conscious that Solange was watching her, statuesque, grotesque and completely out of her mind. As she began to run towards Metand she felt safer. He would protect her.

'That woman is stark, staring, raving mad. And you let me climb that damn tower with her.'

'I've never considered her in the least violent.'

'She accused Tim of murdering her husband.'

There was a long silence during which Metand looked almost comically horrified. It was the first time she had seen him disconcerted. And so he should be, she told herself, reality slowly gathering about her. Lucy had touched madness before, when she had met a woman on a train whose bag was full of torn-up scraps of paper and who had told Lucy she had been swindled out of a fortune by her husband. She could see her now, with the same big staring eyes as Solange, the same clown's face.

'I told you she was ill.' Metand had recovered his composure.

'Claude, like the others, was executed by local people. It would have been common knowledge if he had been killed by an escaping British officer. I should never have left you alone with her. It was a mistake.'

'Were these self-appointed executioners identified?'

'No.'

'Has Solange ever made this allegation before?'

'Not as far as I know.'

'So why make it now? Not that I believe her for a moment.'

'Of course not.'

'It was terrifying.'

There was a distant rumble of thunder but the overcast sky had grown a little lighter and pale sunlight struggled to get through.

'Solange told me that she and Tim were lovers and he had shot Claude in a jealous rage. I had no idea my husband was capable of a *crime passionnel*.' Lucy gave an angry little bark of laughter.

Metand looked increasingly embarrassed. 'Solange once told me she was the illegitimate daughter of an Austrian princess. She informed Louis Dedoir that she was born on a ranch in Argentina and was brought up by her cattle-driving father who raped her. She claims to have shot him at fourteen. I wish I could force her to seek help but the law doesn't allow it. At this stage.'

'She ought to be locked up. Put away!'

Gradually, however, Lucy was getting the bizarre situation into perspective. It had been an unpleasant experience but also one she should dismiss – a mere blip in the search for Tim. She wanted to forget, to concentrate on finding him.

She suddenly thought of Solange, huge and crazy, sitting in Caves Café ordering coffee, or sipping a sherry at a cocktail party in Drakes Close, telling May and Sally about murder and mayhem. They would be engrossed.

'Solange is to be pitied.' Lucy was working her way through the gamut of shock, trying to find a calm acceptance of the spiteful but crazy accusations. Oh yes, Solange should be pitied all right.

Metand was watching a small patch of blue appearing in the dark sky. 'The storm's passing over,' he muttered. Then he said, 'What would you have done, madame, if your husband had been executed and you were never spoken to again by your neighbours?'

'She's mad,' Lucy said firmly, ignoring Metand's plea for compassion. 'Not worth getting worked up about. I'd like to join the search party now. Make my own contribution.' She paused. 'You must ensure I don't see that demented woman again.'

At lunchtime a short rest was declared and surprisingly large quantities of food and wine were laid out.

'Do you think Tim's dead?' she asked Metand again, the despair, never far away, resurfacing.

They were sitting at a distance from the others as he uncorked a bottle of red wine and poured some into a glass for her.

'There can be a simple explanation.'

'I can't imagine what it could be.'

'Have some pâté. It's good.'

She took a portion unwillingly and found it delicious.

'What would you prefer to do now? Stay with us, or return to the hotel?'

'I'd rather stay,' said Lucy. 'Back there I'll just wait for the telephone.'

'Very well. We shall keep going until sundown.' Metand paused. 'While you were with Solange, one of the search party, a young man called Henri Tissot, approached me.'

'Well?' There was something in his voice that made her tense again. What was he proposing now?

'It's nothing to do with the investigation, but he says he knew your husband slightly during the war and would like to tell you what a brave man he was. Apparently he rescued his son. You don't have to meet him, of course. I haven't had much luck with my introductions recently. But I can assure you Henri has all his faculties.'

Lucy tried to fall in with Metand's mood, to banish the Solange encounter with irony. 'As long as he doesn't accuse Tim of murdering his mother, I'd be pleased to talk to him.' She broke off, wanting to come a little cleaner, even become something of a martyr. 'It was equally my fault about Solange. I was curious to know what she knew of Tim. Now I'm curious again.'

'I'll go and fetch Tissot,' said Metand briskly. He didn't sound as if he believed her.

*

106

He was away some time. Lucy sank back on the blanket he had courteously spread out and closed her eyes against the oppressive woods with their sticky heat. She was sure the search party were enjoying their task. No doubt there was some kind of incentive or reward for the first man to find the body. How wonderful it would be if Tim could confound them all and suddenly stride out of the densely packed trees with the 'simple' explanation that they had all hoped for and now seemed so elusive.

'Sorry, Lucy. I was so tired I went into the woods and slept and do you know I've only just woken up.'

'Sorry, Lucy. I went and twisted this damned ankle and had to sit around and wait for someone to come. Shadows of the war, old thing!'

'Sorry, Lucy. I came over faint and – '

Would the search party be relieved or disappointed? If human nature was anything to go by, Lucy was sure they would be disappointed. It would be something to remember if they found a corpse. A corpse in the woods. A corpse on the Clump, you chump!

Lucy opened her eyes and saw the patch of blue was spreading over the Tour des Oiseaux, giving the ivy a lighter, less ominous colour.

Then a figure hovered above her, late thirties, clean-shaven oval face, fair hair. Lucy must have been half asleep because, for a fraction of a second, she had the illusion that she was gazing up at Tim. She rose, staggering a little as Metand made the introductions.

'Mrs Groves. This is Henri Tissot. He has an anecdote he thought you would like to hear about your husband. You may find it comforting. If you want me, I'll be with the search party.'

'Excuse me.' Tissot spoke softly and nervously. 'I hope you don't mind – '

'Of course not.' She wondered if he was regretting his initiative and tried to be as warm as possible. 'I gather you met Tim during the war.'

'I've every reason to be grateful to him. My son, André, fell off his bike near your husband who was hiding out in the woods. Apparently a Nazi jeep suddenly appeared on a right-hand bend and gave André such a scare that he lost control. The bastard didn't stop and the kid fell into a ditch and was knocked unconscious. Anyway, your husband not only revived him but had the courage to bring André home.'

'Brought him home?' said Lucy in amazement. 'That was a risk in the circumstances, wasn't it?'

'The bike was a wreck, but André couldn't have cycled back anyway. He was too groggy to walk. Yes – of course it was an amazing risk and we could easily have been the types to give all three of them away. Your husband told us he was on his own. To protect the others.'

'Thank you,' said Lucy. 'I feel very proud of him.' She had thought that Tim's mental state might have deteriorated so much that he would be incapable of such an act of bravery. Obviously that was not the case. It was an instinct with him.

'You have good reason to be proud, madame. Your husband saved André's life. The doctor told us he had severe concussion.' There was a slightly awkward pause. 'I must be getting back. I do hope we find him safe and well soon. There is every chance that we will and then I can thank your husband in person.'

Lucy's adrenalin was now running so high that she decided to risk a second opinion. 'I wonder if you could help me.'

'I'd be delighted to if I can.'

'I had a brief conversation with Solange Eclave earlier. She made some – wild accusations about Tim. I'm quite sure she's absolutely demented. Would you be of the same opinion, monsieur?'

Tissot was silent. Then to her amazement and dismay he said, 'She's cunning, I think. Many people believe her to be mentally ill. But I have my doubts.'

'You think her behaviour is that of a sane woman?'

'She has made herself like that.'

'Why?' asked Lucy baldly.

'To take her revenge on Navise.'

'How do you mean?'

'I knew her when she was younger. Claude and Solange were very much in love and she was an extremely beautiful woman. I think Solange wants the village to believe that she has been driven mad.'

'Are you sorry for her?'

'In some ways.'

'She told me – terrible things about my husband.'

'Then you mustn't believe her. She would like to use his disappearance as another opportunity to get back at the community for what they did. I can never work out whether she was more outraged that they burnt Pavilly or that they executed her husband. I remember that a couple of years after the war she stopped me when I was cycling past the château and begged me to talk to her. I weakened, but I was seen by a friend who told on me. I got beaten up. Solange is to be pitied rather than feared. I think that she is partly a desperately lonely woman who longs for attention. She also wants to hurt. I believe she's been waiting a long time to do that.'

When he had gone, Lucy wondered where Henri Tissot's theory left her. But in her heart of hearts she knew. Suppose Tissot was right? Suppose Solange *was* sane?

She climbed the hill to find Metand, not wanting to think any more. The heat had diminished slightly and a light breeze stirred the leaves so they rasped together. She poured out the story, considerably alarmed but also utterly exhausted. Metand, however, was yet again his usual reassuring self.

'I understand what Tissot means,' he said calmly. 'But I don't agree with him. Solange is mentally ill. Far more than your husband ever was. There is no doubt about that. And as for waiting to exact revenge – ' He paused. 'I can't comment on that because I don't know.'

'Suppose he's right?' Lucy was not to be mollified and a wave of hysteria swept her. It was as if she was being deliberately misled. The story about Tim and André seemed to count for nothing in her confusion. 'What should I believe?'

'Look, you are getting yourself in a bad state. Tissot is wrong. Solange is mad. I've already apologized for my part in this. Don't you think it would be easier if you had your English friends here. To support you?'

'No,' said Lucy firmly. 'And you have made a wrong assumption, monsieur. They are *not* my friends.'

*

The search party moved inexorably on, and then split into two, one group taking a route on to the top of the hill and the other to a steep valley below. Lucy and Metand took the latter.

Solange's malicious words repeated themselves, until they became a mocking rhythm in Lucy's exhausted mind. Tim? A violent lover who killed? Tim a violent . . .

Then she suddenly remembered his dream and realized that this was something she had forgotten to tell Metand.

'Can we stop? You asked me to rack my brains and I've come up with some more information.'

He motioned her over to a dead oak tree and leant wearily against the trunk.

'Just before we left England, Tim had a nightmare.'

'He often had these?'

'Yes. But he never told me what he dreamt. That night he did. Tim was half awake and I grabbed his hand and he said, without really knowing what he was saying, "The angels are dying".'

'The angels are dying,' repeated Metand. He looked straight ahead, as if he was trying to remember something but so far not succeeding.

'Then he said, "Don't make me". And that was it.'

Metand seemed to refocus. 'I think I know where his angels were dying,' he said at last. 'There was a painting on the ceiling of the chapel at the château, but most of it was destroyed by the fire. A few small pieces remain. The painting is entitled Armageddon and depicts the final battle between the angels and the dark host. I would not say it was outstanding, but it's a pity it was destroyed. I wonder if your husband was dreaming about the chapel?'

'"Don't make me"?' Lucy asked. 'What could that mean?'

Metand shrugged and was about to reply when they both heard the roar of a motorbike. There was an unnerving urgency to the sound.

Metand hurried to meet the policeman, leaving her alone, and the search party stopped work, turning round to watch the encounter curiously.

Lucy suddenly felt as if she was in a lift that was plunging down a high building, and her heartbeats were like hammer blows. What in God's name was going on?

She glanced towards an old man in blue dungarees. He smiled and shrugged and then smiled again. She knew he was trying to reassure her.

Lucy watched Metand walking back towards her, his face expressionless. It's Tim, she said to herself over and over again, the terrible chill creeping over her together with a feeling of desolate finality. 'That's it, old thing,' came his voice. 'Got to go. Pip-pip. Cheerio.' You *are* dead, aren't you? My darling, you've gone and died on me, haven't you?

'It's Tim,' she gasped, as Metand came up, his face set. One hand fluttered up to her neck, the other plucked at small red berries on a bush near by, scattering dozens of them.

'It's Solange.'

'Solange?' Lucy stared at him, not able to make sense of what he was saying. 'Solange says he's dead?'

'It's *Solange* who is dead.'

'She can't be. I only saw – ' Lucy almost laughed. This must be another of her lies, another mad joke. She was playing a trick. She was –

'Solange was found by the gardener at Pavilly. She had fallen from the fourth floor.' He was silent for a few moments and then said abruptly, 'The strange thing is that she was holding something.'

'What do you mean?'

'My colleague tells me it's a scrap of cloth.'

'Yes?'

'It looks as if it could have been torn from a shirt. A check shirt. I'm going to have to ask you to come with me and make an identification. I'll make it as painless as I can. We'd better go now.'

He turned away and began to walk back so fast that Lucy had difficulty in keeping up with him. A check shirt? A shirt that was checked? Checking a shirt? The phrases beat banally but painfully in her head. Then they were replaced by a terrible and deep-seated sense of foreboding that sent Lucy's mind shooting back into a traumatic moment of the past.

*

A crow flapped its wings over her head and from somewhere deep in the wood there was the sound of cawing. Surely the trees were denser? Why were they so familiar? Then Lucy realized they were a reminder of times past that she hadn't thought about in years. Twice she had got lost in the woods at the back of Claygate Common. Twice she had been sure she would not be able to get home. And, on the second occasion, she had seen the boy walking towards her, his penis hanging out of his trousers. She had run and run until she was lost, dashing about in a breathless panic. The boy had been about her own age and there was a look in his eyes that she had known was dangerous.

Eventually Lucy had emerged from the woods on to the main road. She went home the long way round, but when she arrived her father was not there. In fact he returned a few minutes later, having gone to buy some cigarettes, but in her panicky mind he had gone for good, leaving her to the boy with his penis hanging out.

Lucy had never walked in those woods again, but whenever she looked at them she didn't think so much of the boy but her terror of being left alone.

Now the worst had happened. Her father was dead. Tim was missing. She *was* alone. Instead of the sex-hungry boy there was Solange. And she apparently still held a fragment of check shirt. But Tim had one of those.

7

29–30 July

A couple of police cars were already parked outside the gates of Pavilly as Metand drove through. Lucy sat in the passenger seat, dreading what she might witness.

In her mind's eye, she could see Solange now, on the top of the tower, her saucer eyes fixed hypnotically on her own. 'As far as the eye can see, I will be queen bee.' The phrase beat idiotically in Lucy's head but only to mask the other phrases – 'He killed my husband. Tim shot Claude because he was in love with me.'

Desperately, Lucy tried to rationalize the situation. Solange had driven herself mad with her bitter fantasies that were designed to shock and hurt. She had already been moving inexorably towards destruction.

'The reason he's disappeared is that he's looking for me. Your husband is a violent man.'

Lucy knew she should instantly dismiss the crazy, malicious words. Metand believed Solange to be mad. He was bound to be right. Tissot was wrong.

As they drove alongside the banks of the still lake she tried to adjust to some coherent pattern of thinking but found it impossible.

Metand also seemed stunned by the sudden turn of events, but he eventually slowed down and came to a halt by a jetty that had partly collapsed into the water.

'Let's give ourselves a little time in which to collect our thoughts. My colleague can cope for a few moments.'

Lucy became even more unsettled. 'What you're really saying is that you think Tim had something to do with this – and that I'm covering up for him. This shirt – I don't – '

'There's no point in jumping to conclusions, Mrs Groves. I just wondered if you'd remembered *anything* else that might help us, or you felt able to confide in me.'

They sat in silence, the water stirred by a breeze lapping at the algae-covered wood. Strangely, rather than resenting Metand's

113

request she found it had calmed her. She had to think. Remember.

There seemed to be two ways of looking at the horror of what had happened. The first was straightforward. She had inveigled Tim into the journey, he had wandered off somewhere, his memories had made him ill and he had got lost in the woods. The alternative was much more disturbing. Could Tim possibly have been mixed up in this collaboration business?

Then Metand gently asked, 'Did anything happen in England before you left? Did you notice any difference in your husband's behaviour patterns?'

Then Lucy remembered Graham Baverstock. Of course his death had nothing to do with –

'There was a local murder.' She spoke hurriedly and dismissively. 'The gardener employed by Peter Davis had his throat cut. I believe the police thought it might be a – a homosexual killing.'

'That's something else you haven't told me,' Metand said irritably.

'I hardly thought it was relevant,' she snapped.

'How did Tim react?'

'He was appalled. Then he brushed it aside. Something unpleasant from Hersham.'

'Hersham? Where is that?'

'A working-class district near Esher.'

'So murderers and homosexuals only come from the working classes in England?'

Lucy shrugged. 'I can only tell you what little I know.' There was a long silence between them while Metand gazed out over the lake, watching a heron swoop low over the water, plunging suddenly after a fish.

'I'm afraid I can't think of anything else that would be helpful. I'm genuinely sorry.'

'At the moment everything is circumstantial. We've got to be careful. Let's leave the gardener out of the picture for the time being. Did you notice anything in your husband's behaviour over the last few days that might make you think *he* was in charge and not you?'

'That he capitalized on my ultimatum?'

'Possibly.'

'He was going down badly. Dreaming more. But then he'd

114

been a nervous wreck for such a long time it would be difficult to say how much worse he was getting.' She paused. 'He was definitely feeling the pressure of Martin and Peter.' She frowned. 'It wasn't like a normal friendship.'

'They had never met before the war?'

'No. They were bonded together by their experiences.'

'Experiences you know little about.'

Lucy gave an angry shrug. 'I should have been more forceful, but I was afraid they would close ranks and shut me out completely. I suppose they did that anyway.'

'Was your husband afraid of them?'

'He was afraid of something.'

'Suppose Tim had *wanted* to come to France, rather than being dragged here by your threat of leaving him – presumably Martin and Peter would have tried to stop him as much as they tried to stop you.'

'And their wives. They put pressure on too. All four of them were obviously terrified of what might happen if we came. Of course they said it would be bad for Tim. Then Martin phoned and gave us his blessing. It doesn't make sense.'

'Presumably that was before he knew Tim was missing – '

'Yes.' She turned to face him, needing support. 'Are you saying that if there was a plan, then Martin and Peter were in it too?'

'It's another way of thinking about the problem.'

The heron dived again and came up with a small fish struggling in his beak.

'Even while I'm talking,' said Lucy, 'I'm thinking of the normality of Esher. Everyone has got back to their routines after the interruption of the war. They're going up on the train to the Festival, playing cricket, attending Evensong; the women are doing what the women do, the men are doing what the men do. The war's over. It's been banished into history. But in Tim's case it was still being fought in a way I couldn't understand.'

'Instincts are inhibited in peacetime. War unchains the wild beasts. The combatants usually have God on their side, but war allows a kind of undercover freedom. While it rages away some masks can be removed, can't they?'

'What are you saying?'

'Suppose your husband *did* come here with a purpose? Perhaps he thought he might be able to achieve his goal quickly and decisively in a short space of time? Even an hour. Suppose

115

coincidence had brought together the escaping English soldiers with Solange and Claude and Philippe and Robert? What about the Germans who were investigating Château Pavilly as a possible venue for a Gestapo regional headquarters and who Solange was trying to fob off? Now we have the English, the French, the Germans. All together for a while. Later we have the execution of three Frenchmen by an outraged local community, Frenchmen who apparently procured local girls for the Germans.' Metand paused. 'Solange's role appears ambiguous, but so does everybody else's. Suppose the English and the Germans and the French had been up to something much more damaging than procuring? Suppose your husband took his opportunity to come back here and face out whatever was still bothering him?'

Despair swept Lucy. Metand was putting forward the worst scenario of all.

'Do you think Tim killed Solange? I thought you'd dismissed her accusations? I thought you said she was mentally ill.'

'She was. And at this stage I'm not saying anything of the kind.' Metand switched on the ignition again. 'This is going to be very difficult for you, Mrs Groves, and that's why I'm glad we've had this talk first.'

'Wait a minute. I've remembered something else, but it may be insignificant.'

'Well?'

'We were talking about Thérèse and her attempted flight from the tower. Solange said, "I admire Thérèse for that. I don't have the courage. Not yet." '

Metand nodded. 'I'll bear that in mind.'

He drove away from the lake towards the ruins of the château, its windows blind gaps in a blackened stonework shell. The classical façade was surmounted at each end by two medieval towers, and it had been built in four storeys, the walls decorated with coats of arms.

The front entrance had collapsed and was masked by more galvanized sheeting. A section of the roof had fallen into the stone hall below and the wall bulged outwards, shored up by scaffolding. On the left-hand side, a small part of one wing had remained intact and was hardly blackened. Just underneath, a

116

small bell tent had been erected on the lawn. A police car was drawn up beside it and an officer stood outside.

'I must ask you to remain in the car for the moment,' said Metand. 'The pathologist hasn't arrived yet so it might be some time before I need you.' He got stiffly out of the car and slammed the door. Then he came round to Lucy's half-open window. 'While you are waiting, please keep thinking.'

Lucy's encounter with Solange at the Tour des Oiseaux had taken on a dream-like quality that was beginning to give her acute anxiety. Again and again she saw her monstrous bulk, the terrible accusations, the crumbling balustrade, the ground seeming to claw at her from below. Solange was ill, she told herself determinedly. Mentally ill. Mad. Crazy. Deluded. Demented. She couldn't touch Tim. Not in any possible way. She should be locked up. But now she was dead. And did she really have something of Tim's?

Metand quietly opened the door of the car, startling her.

'I'm afraid I need you now.'

Lucy gazed up at him fearfully. 'Do I have to go in there?'

'The pathologist still hasn't arrived and I can't disturb her body. I'm sorry I'm having to ask you to do this.'

'Let's get it over with then.'

He tried to take her arm as she reluctantly climbed out of the car, but she impatiently shook him off.

Metand led Lucy into the stuffy tent where there were more police officers and a young man with owlish spectacles, tall and slim, in plain clothes. He gave Lucy an apologetic smile.

'This is my colleague, Gerard Villet,' said Metand.

The heat was intense and there was a heavy smell of faeces that immediately made her want to choke. The body was covered with a tarpaulin, but some dark stains had leaked through.

'Turn away for a moment, madame, please,' said Villet.

Lucy faced the canvas wall, the smell of shit filling her nostrils. She wondered if she was going to faint.

'If you'll turn back.' Villet sounded even more apologetic.

She saw a wide, wooden bracelet clamped round thick white flesh. There were no abrasions of any kind. Only one fingernail was broken – a half-moon that had been jaggedly torn away, revealing a little blood underneath that was dried and caked.

Between the two middle fingers was a scrap of material that was instantly familiar. For a moment she couldn't speak and a feeling of utter, unbelieving horror filled her mind.

It couldn't be. There was a mistake. An explanation. A coincidence. A misunderstanding. Again she heard Solange's voice and again she pushed away the words.

'I think that *is* a piece of my husband's shirt,' Lucy said as if she was confirming personal information to her doctor in Esher.

The nausea finally choked her and she ran outside, just reaching the long grass before she was violently sick.

The shirt had had a particularly memorable pattern with its houndstooth check in red and blue. She had bought it with him last Christmas and she remembered how upset Tim had been when he found the collar size had been too large. Lucy had forgotten how thin his neck had become.

Nevertheless, he had worn the shirt stubbornly and she had wished he hadn't for it had made his now pronounced Adam's apple far too obvious. He had even worn it when they set out yesterday, with his sports coat and corduroys.

'Are you sure?' asked Metand gently, emerging from the tent.

Lucy nodded. What have you done, Tim, she asked him. In God's name, what have you done? Despair swept her.

'What has he done?' she asked aloud, trembling violently, and Metand steadied her, putting an arm around her shoulders. 'Do you think he's here? Somewhere in the château? Or the grounds?'

'They're searching now,' he said quietly. 'I'm going to have you driven back to the hotel. I'm sure you don't want to go but I still have to stay here and wait for the pathologist. I think you should phone your friends and tell them what has happened. Then I'll interview them in England. Villet can take over here.'

'In England?' Lucy was completely thrown. 'You're going to speak to them there?' she asked in amazement. 'What about Tim? What about the search?'

118

'That will continue. Villet is very capable and knows exactly what to do.'

'Perhaps it would be easier if Peter and Martin *did* come.' Then she thought of them in the Hôtel des Arbres and winced. They would take her over.

'No,' said Metand, and she was surprised by his vehemence. 'If I'm going to get anywhere in this case I need to see both sides of it.'

'I don't understand what you mean.'

'I'm sure that these two men, Peter Davis and Martin Latimer, hold the key to all this. If your husband can't tell me what is going on, then I'm hoping they can. If they won't co-operate, I may need to liaise with the British police.'

'You really think they know what's going on?'

'I hope so.'

'Do you think she killed herself?'

Metand gazed at Lucy with some curiosity, unsettling her even more. 'It's the shirt – '

'Yes. I'm getting muddled.'

'I would like to interview these two men in their own homes. If they come here I'm concerned they'll feel under too much scrutiny. Back home they might be more receptive.'

'And I'm to wait here? Liaise with your colleague? Sit in that damned room until – '

'On the contrary, Mrs Groves. I was hoping you would join me. We could travel together and talk some more.'

'You think I'm still holding back?'

'Not intentionally, I'm sure. But consider your husband and Solange Eclave. A young and heroic army officer makes a remarkable escape. A young and beautiful farmer's wife betters herself and becomes a valued employee of a distinguished French family. Look at them a few years after the war. Timothy Groves has become a neurotic wreck. Solange Eclave is mentally ill. What caused all that? Not some kind of shell shock. Not a brutal husband. Not vigilante executioners. No – there *has* to be something else. Something that happened here – when they were together. I know Solange but I don't know your husband and if I'm to do that I have to travel to England. I can assure you it will be a very short trip – little more than twenty-four hours. No doubt you will wish to return with me. I can get official clearance.'

'I'll come,' said Lucy. 'I certainly don't want to stay here.' She felt utterly confused and still a little faint.

Looking up she saw a tall, elegant woman walking up the overgrown drive, dressed in a white linen suit. Her auburn hair was cut short, almost severely so, and her eyes squinted slightly in the sun.

As she came closer, Lucy could see the long languid walk was deceptive; she was barely able to control herself, her hands shaking and mouth working without any sound emerging.

'Anna.' Metand seemed flummoxed.

'I want to see her.' She had the most striking face. It was almost boyish, with a delicate complexion and high cheekbones, but the dark eyes were bleak and on closer inspection Lucy saw her skin was blemished.

Metand stepped between Anna and the tent.

'You can't go in there.'

She came to a halt, gazing at him, her eyes glazed. Her shoulders heaved slightly but no tears came. 'They wouldn't let me bring the car in. So I walked.' The prosaic little statement was incredibly pathetic.

Metand still seemed flustered.

'She fell but I can't tell you the precise cause of death. I'm waiting for the pathologist.'

'Do you think someone killed her? This man they're looking for? The Englishman who disappeared. She knew him, you know.'

'This is his wife,' said Metand bleakly.

For the first time Anna's eyes rested on Lucy's. 'Solange had an affair with your husband during the war. She said he'd shot her husband Claude and that she was frightened he would come back one day.' She spoke decisively and with considerable authority.

Lucy was determined to keep calm, but the panic rose. It was all happening again. The impossible nightmare was back. Solange was ill, she told herself. Mentally ill. You shouldn't have believed her.

For a moment it looked as if Metand was going to intercede. But he said nothing.

Anna Ribault gave a sharp intake of breath and then a half-sob. 'For God's sake. I must see her.'

'That's impossible.'

She rounded on Lucy. 'Do you know why your husband did this?' she demanded.

'He didn't. Surely you knew Solange well enough to realize how ill she was. You couldn't believe a word she said.'

'We can't have this conversation here,' said Metand. 'Mrs Groves, I'll arrange for you to be taken back to the hotel. I'll come and see you later.'

'Tell me about your husband,' said Anna threateningly, ignoring him. 'Tell me why he's done this. After all these years. Why did he have to come back?'

'You mustn't say that,' Lucy yelled at her, the hysteria rising into her throat like bile.

'Solange was my closest friend. Your husband – your filthy pig of a husband – '

Lucy ran forward, not knowing what she was going to do, her hand instinctively rising as if to slap her and then failing to follow through. Anna Ribault stepped back, dropping her briefcase, somehow managing to keep on her feet.

'Nothing's proven against Tim,' yelled Lucy as one of the police officers grabbed her round the waist and pulled her back towards the car, kicking and struggling. 'When you find him, he'll be able to explain everything. I promise he'll tell you what we all want to know – that he didn't do it, couldn't do it. Your friend Solange was ill. Why don't you accept that?'

'She was afraid,' said Anna, picking up her briefcase. 'Solange was afraid for a long time. She told me about your husband. She told me over and over again.'

The police officer pulled Lucy towards the back door of the car while one of his colleagues opened it and helped her in. She was shaking all over now.

Metand came and poked his head through the window. 'I'm alerting Monique. You need looking after.'

When Lucy arrived back in the dusty square at Navise, the dog with the cut paw came snuffling up to her and the officer swore, driving him limping back to his usual position under the trees.

There was no sign of his companions and the dog crouched down, whining slightly.

The police officer took her arm gently and led her to the front door of the hotel and rang the bell. After a while Louis opened it and stood there while the officer told him how upset Lucy was. Then he went back to the car, looking relieved that he had delivered his awkward charge.

Louis steered her inside and towards the sitting room. 'Sit down,' he said gently, and she collapsed in the old armchair.

'Solange has been found dead.'

Louis looked as if he didn't believe her, that she was making it all up. 'What in God's name happened?'

Lucy was in the middle of a stumbling explanation when Monique arrived. After that a good deal of brandy was poured. Only dimly did she remember the Dedoirs helping her up the stairs between them.

She slept through until four next morning, waking in confusion, not knowing where she was or what had happened to her. A dim recollection of Monique's comforting arms slid into her mind, and then she remembered drinking a little soup, eating some bread, drinking some more brandy and talking, talking, talking.

When the memory of the terrible events of the previous day surfaced, she sought protection in sleep again. But this time it was shallow, and Lucy dreamt fractured nightmares.

She woke to Monique's hand in hers.

'You were screaming,' she said. 'I came as fast as I could.'

I was screaming like Tim, thought Lucy, the sweat pouring off her again. The sheets on the bed were soaked. 'What was I saying?' she whispered.

'The angels are dying,' said Monique. 'You kept saying the angels are dying.'

'Solange – '

'Don't talk now.' She began to rock Lucy to and fro like a baby. 'Don't talk now, my darling. Sleep. Sleep in my arms. I'll keep you safe.'

After a while, Lucy drifted off again.

*

When she woke, Monique was back in the room. A tray of coffee and croissants and orange juice had been placed on the small table.

'Shall I draw the curtains?'

Lucy nodded. She felt light-headed.

Monique let the early sunlight dapple the room, enriching its faded wallpaper. Lucy glanced at her watch. It was only eight, yet she felt she had slept for days.

'You are very good to look after me like this,' she said as Monique poured out coffee and brought it across. Lucy sipped at it gratefully, needing its comfort. Everything was still mercifully remote.

'Poor Solange,' said Monique. 'I never really thought she'd take her own life.'

The horrendous news of her violent death returned, as if Lucy had stepped out into freezing fog. 'I saw her earlier. Solange told me she and Tim had an affair and he shot her husband. *My* Tim? Do all that?'

'You told us last night. And I told *you* she wasn't accountable for what she said. You know how ill she was.'

'But *something* happened out here that involved her and Tim,' said Lucy. 'It must have been something terrible – no wonder he suffered so much.'

'And so did she,' said Monique almost defensively.

'I spoke to a man called Henri Tissot about her. Do you know him?'

'Not at all.'

'He said she wasn't that ill – that her madness was a revenge. She wanted to hurt people. For all she'd lost.'

'What *had* she lost? Claude's execution did her a favour and the Goutins kept her on. She was lucky. This Tissot is talking nonsense.'

'Did you feel you ever knew Solange?'

'No. Not really.' Monique admitted.

'That's how I felt about Tim. Not when we first met, but when he came back. I just didn't know him. Like I didn't know the Men.'

'What do we ever know about other people – even those who are closest to us? I see Louis in a very different light from the way he actually is.'

Her answer was so surprising that Lucy splashed her coffee on the bed and set it down on the table with a shaking hand.

'What are you saying?' As with May, she had expected total support. The remark seemed like another betrayal.

'I'm saying that everyone has some mystery about them and once you take them for granted, you push them into doing something unexpected. I remember, in America, that Louis had an affair with a woman, a waitress in our restaurant, almost entirely because I was sure he wouldn't. He didn't even enjoy it.'

'He did it on purpose? To spite you?'

'To remind me not to take him for granted. But your situation is different.' Monique suddenly looked as if she realized she was saying absolutely the wrong thing.

'You told me not to believe Solange.'

'And I told you correctly. But if you want to find out what has happened to your husband, you must keep an open mind.'

'What *am* I to believe?' The comfort had gone. The wallpaper was no longer enriched by the sunlight but made to look even more tawdry than it actually was. The table had a patina of dust and the curtains needed washing. Monique's face was more sallow than before. Why wasn't she being reassuring? Why had she questioned her need to believe in Tim?

'You shouldn't have listened to Solange. But neither should you simply accept what you know of your husband.' Monique sounded anxious, wanting to make her point clearer.

'So he *could* have been the jealous lover? He *could* have shot Claude? What are you saying?' Lucy was confused and a feeling of injustice swept her. It wasn't fair. She only wanted reassurance.

'No. There is no doubt in my mind that Claude, Philippe and Robert were executed by their own countrymen. We shall never know who they were, particularly as we're outsiders, but if a British soldier had shot Claude – we would all know. It would be public knowledge.'

Lucy felt a little more reassured. That was exactly what Metand had said. But then the fear came back. Because she wasn't sure, she almost wanted to accept the worst. 'How can I know for certain that Tim didn't have an affair with her?'

Monique didn't reply and Lucy plunged on.

'He was in such a terrible state for so many years in England.'

'There were many reasons for that, I'm sure.'

'What if Solange was one of them?'

'You mean she could have had some kind of grip on him? Even if they did have an affair, I don't think that's much of a hold, do you? I mean – what would you have done if you discovered your husband had had an affair in wartime? Ask for a divorce? Or do you have some special – '

'No. It's not against my religion either. I don't have one.'

'You might have been devastated,' said Monique, 'but you would also have recognized that men can be unfaithful. And as you obviously love him, you would have made excuses, particularly to yourself.'

'That's right.'

'Then what else?'

'I don't know,' said Lucy miserably. 'I just don't know. But isn't it too much of a coincidence. He disappears. She dies.'

'It may be a coincidence, but I wouldn't count on the connections. The main thing is to find your husband. That's what the police are trying to do now.'

'There's more.' Lucy felt that she was testing Monique's loyalty to her in a singularly pathetic way. But she needed it so much. Now, however, she was about to be her own saboteur, to shoot herself in the foot, as Tim would have said.

'She had a piece of material in her hand. I had to identify it.' Lucy let the damning statement fall into the lake of complacency they had created together. 'It was torn from Tim's shirt. It couldn't have been anyone else's.'

'I don't understand.'

'Neither do I. But it's a fact. Solange was clutching a piece of his shirt.'

'There *has* to be an explanation.' Monique was shaken.

'I hope to God there is,' said Lucy, her eyes filling with tears.

'I feel for you so much. You're in a terrible position. What – '

'Metand wants to go to England and talk to Peter and Martin. He seems to think they will be able to help. I'm going with him.'

Monique clapped a hand to her mouth. 'My God. I forgot to tell you. Peter Davis phoned last night. I keep failing to communicate. Perhaps I'm trying to protect you from them. Anyway, I said you had gone to bed and were asleep and that Tim hadn't been found. I didn't tell him anything else.' She paused, waiting for Lucy to explode with rage as she had done so violently last time, but she simply gazed at her passively and Monique continued. 'I'm sure you should go back. Metand will need to get to the roots of this.'

'And Peter and Martin are the roots?'

'Perhaps they might be a little less reticent if he questions them.'

'If only they'd confided in me before.' She paused. 'Of course I'm coming back.'

'You will be very welcome to stay here again.' Monique smiled at her affectionately.

'I can't thank you enough for what you're doing. I know how badly I've coped with all this. And then there's Anna Ribault – I created a scene. She seemed to believe Solange. Surely *anyone* could see what a consummate liar she was?'

'They were very close. Anna was the only person to really know Solange.' Then she saw how uneasy Lucy was becoming again and hurriedly reassured her. 'But I expect Anna was only reacting out of shock.'

'What kind of person is she?'

'I don't know her well. The Goutins gave her this job a year ago and she's based in the summerhouse by the lake, working on documents that the salvage people rescued. She is restoring them – or trying to. Most are badly damaged.'

'So she and Solange are the only staff at the château?'

'Except for the old gardener.'

'I'd like to go and apologize to her.'

'You'll do no such thing. You have your croissants to eat and Monsieur Davis to phone. I'm sure Metand will be here soon, so you'd better hurry.'

Ten minutes later, Lucy dialled the Davises' number and the phone only rang a couple of times before Peter picked up the receiver.

'Thank God. We've all been out of our minds with worry.' He sounded anxious and slightly indignant. 'You said you'd phone last night. In the end I rang the hotel and spoke to this Monique Dedoir. Is she the proprietor?'

'With her husband.'

'She was very proprietorial over you. She told me there was no news and she couldn't disturb you. So what's the latest?'

'Nothing about Tim. But other – things have happened. I'm coming back to England with the policeman who's in charge of the case. François Metand. He wants to talk to you.'

'Right-ho. Any particular aspect?'

'Solange Eclave.'

'What about her?'

'She's dead.'

At last he didn't seem to have anything to say.

'Did you hear?'

'Yes.'

'Before she died she told me Tim was her lover.'

'Nonsense!' Despite the shock, he was reassuringly angry.

'And that he had become jealous. So much so that he had shot her husband Claude.'

Peter laughed derisively. 'I don't think Tim's capable of a *crime passionnel*, do you?'

'There's something else. Solange fell from a window in the burnt-out château and she had a piece of Tim's shirt between her fingers.'

This time the silence seemed to last for a very long time.

'Don't be absurd.' He sounded taken aback.

'He was wearing that shirt when we started out. That awful check one that made his neck look so horribly thin. I've always hated – '

Peter's voice, rigid with authority, cut through her own. 'Lucy. This is all rubbish. You do understand that, don't you?' She was under orders. 'When they find Tim, all this will be cleared up. There'll be a proper explanation. He'll straighten it all out. Do you see?'

'No,' she said coldly. 'I don't.'

'You're in shock.'

'So was Tim. For years. What do *you* know about this, Peter? What does Martin?'

'I know only one thing, Lucy. I trust Tim.'

'That's about the only point we'll ever agree on,' she replied cuttingly.

'I do wish you wouldn't invent conspiracies.' He sounded pained but understanding, an attitude that infuriated her. But she was determined not to lose her temper again.

127

'When you've heard all the facts, Peter, you won't be able to think of anything else *but* conspiracy. If there's something you know, you must tell me now. Can't you understand how I feel?'

'Yes, I can. I do realize how dreadful it is for you over there. After all, I *did* offer to come out.' He paused, waiting for her to speak, to admit some dependence on him. Deliberately, she didn't reply and eventually he carried on, a little more briskly. 'Let me try to reassure you again. When we arrived in Navise we spent a night at the Hôtel des Arbres. Then we moved into the Château Pavilly for a couple of days, where we were hidden in the cellar by Solange. After that we moved on to Celin, a village about ten miles away.'

'That doesn't tell me anything,' she said.

'Solange's husband, Claude, was a pig-ignorant farmer, the son of a pig-ignorant farmer. He intimidated Solange continually. Beat her up, too. She had rejected the farm for the château. She wanted to make something out of her ill-educated self and I suppose she succeeded. Her husband was extremely jealous.'

'How did you gather all that? Over three days – '

'Solange tried to seduce all of us. One by one. She failed.' For the first time he sounded vulnerable. 'We all had commitments at home. Women we loved. None of us would soil our hands on her. But obviously we were grateful to her for hiding us and at least she eventually had some vestige of honour.'

'Honour?' The boy scout in Peter had surfaced again. A chap's integrity was paramount. But Lucy also thought she could detect an artificiality in his voice. Or was it her imagination?

'She could very easily have given us away to the Germans. They came through Navise every day and made regular visits to the château. And that's before the patrol arrived to review the buildings as a possible Gestapo headquarters.'

'Why didn't you tell me about this?'

'Why on earth should I?'

'I thought you were going to say that you were bound by the Official Secrets Act,' she sneered.

'Solange was ambitious. That's all the information your Frenchman will get out of me because that's all the information there is.' Then his voice softened. 'I'm very anxious about Tim. As to her clutching a piece of his shirt, it's inexplicable. But I'm quite certain he neither slept with her, shot her husband nor killed her. It's a monstrous travesty and I know you don't believe

128

it yourself. There's nothing wrong in being afraid, but don't let it affect your judgement.'

'Some of the evidence is difficult to explain away,' she said flatly.

'If I was there I could sort it out.'

'Don't be so absurd. Of course you couldn't – and you're not to come. Monsieur Metand will be phoning you to arrange a time to talk in England tonight.'

'Hasn't he got an inquiry to run out there?'

'He has a second-in-command.'

Peter sighed. 'If he wants to come we'll talk to him.'

'Tell me one more thing about Solange. Did she lie? Tell you bizarre fantasies?'

'No.' He sounded surprised. 'I thought she was rather self-contained.'

'I must go now.' Lucy wanted to ring off, to think it all out yet again.

'Keep in touch, Lucy,' snapped Peter as if talking to a recalcitrant child. 'Just keep in touch.'

Muttering a conventional farewell, she put the phone down and then had another unsettling thought. If Peter was so forceful, why didn't he disobey her and simply get in his car and drive to the ferry, bringing Martin with him? Why wasn't he being his usual overbearing self?

Gradually she became certain that Peter had beat a tactical retreat, letting the enemy take ground but not too much.

She, of course, was the enemy. Lucy knew she had to make another foray, get another advantage, before she could learn any more.

8

30 July

The graveyard was ornate, despite the simplicity of the Roman-esque church. Monique had suggested the walk. As a result Lucy was now convinced that she was under instruction from Metand to keep her occupied until he arrived. But rather than being annoyed or patronized she felt touched by their concern.

'There were several big houses near Navise, but they were either abandoned or turned into farms years ago. The château was the only fine building that hadn't been spoilt – until it was burnt down.' Monique's tall figure was draped in a dull print dress which, along with her thick stockings, made her look rather matronly. Lucy was wearing the same clothes as yesterday which she had simply dragged on for her telephone call to Peter, vaguely wondering if they smelt.

Most of the graves were neglected, the gravestones rearing out of the long grass and largely made of slate or granite with moss covering up the lettering. The family mausoleums were in much worse condition; nature was gradually taking over, the stonework crumbling and the faces of the saints obscured by strands of ivy.

The graves of the three collaborators, however, were in surprisingly pristine condition.

Reading her thoughts, Monique said, 'They were punished. Now they have to be remembered.'

They had certainly been remembered with considerable devotion. The three graves adjoined each other, their headstones made of white marble, names and dates engraved without comment.

CLAUDE ECLAVE 1916–1941
PHILIPPE GERARD 1916–1941
ROBERT SOUTIN 1915–1941

Stone pots were filled with carnations, while three fresh bouquets of roses lay on the gravel.

'Their mothers come here each week.'

'It must have been terrible,' said Lucy. 'Claude and Philippe were twenty-five and Robert only twenty-six. Did they *have* to be executed? Couldn't there have been some other punishment?'

'Not at that time. The Germans were hated. Surely you can imagine how high feelings ran?' Monique sounded reproving.

'What about the girls?'

'They were horsewhipped. It was all a tragedy. But the reason I've brought you down here was to make something clear to you. Look at these graves. If Claude had been killed by an Englishman, everyone would have known. Can't you understand?'

Lucy didn't feel particularly relieved, simply uncertain. She was grateful, however, for the renewed show of support.

'I gather that Philippe procured his own sister,' Monique continued. 'Madame Gerard has that to bear as well.'

'God!' Lucy shuddered. 'It's just so terrible.'

'There isn't much community around here. People tend to stick to their homes and their farms. Nationalism, yes. Local community, no. But do you not see my point? If your husband had murdered Claude, it would never be forgotten.'

'You're very kind.'

'But you don't believe me – '

'I don't know what to believe. I feel totally confused. It seems years since Tim went. It's as if he's been enchanted, just walking away into nowhere.'

'Let's sit down under the yew tree. It's not time to go back yet.'

They walked over to the wooden seat which was slightly in shadow. A small black cat was basking in the sunlight amongst the long grass.

'To Louis and me, Solange was just a lonely woman who was mentally unstable – and who wouldn't do anything about it. She depended on us for our friendship.'

'And now I'm doing the same. Like Solange, Tim never recovered from the war.' Lucy paused. 'Before he was called up, he was a real adventurer, someone who didn't want to stand still and put down roots in Esher. We were going to travel together.' She paused again, irritated with herself. 'What am I saying? I'm turning him into some kind of stupid cliché.'

'No,' Monique protested.

'That's just *my* particular fantasy.'

'Tim was *not* like that?'

'He was in some ways. It's just so easy to rebuild the past to one's own specification.'

'Obviously I only knew Solange after the war. But I could still feel her despair in her isolation.'

'I thought she was so close to Anna?'

'I think they simply punished each other.' Monique's voice had an edge to it now. 'I told you we didn't know Anna very well and that was true, largely because Solange didn't *want* us to meet her. I just felt – and I could be prejudiced and wrong – that they were bad for each other. That they used each other up. Anna always looks so drained. But it's only an impression.'

'Does Louis agree?'

'No.'

'And Metand?'

'I never asked him. He's not the kind of man who gossips. He and his wife and their two small daughters have their own world. If you knew him better you would realize what a good man he is. He's not some officious bureaucrat. He's got a first-class degree in psychology.'

'Why on earth did he go into the police?' asked Lucy.

'He wouldn't want me to tell you this, but his parents were shot dead in a bank raid in Paris and no one was arrested. François has a strong sense of justice, but he works intuitively. Haven't you noticed?'

'Yes,' said Lucy with conviction. 'I had.'

'His wife is a writer. Dominique Tertois.'

'She writes detective stories?'

Monique smiled. 'No. She's a historian. A military historian. They live on a farm near Saliers. It's their retreat.'

'Have you been there?'

'We've never been invited.'

'But Solange was.'

'She invited herself, but I think she interested him.'

'You make him sound arid.'

'I don't mean to. Solange sought out his company. Maybe he was a mirror to her soul.'

'A confessor?'

'She'd never confess to anyone,' said Monique. 'But then she

132

wouldn't have to with him. I think she found they could talk as equals and that she didn't have to lie or fantasize to him. In fact they would go up the tower together and watch the birds.'

'So they were soulmates?'

'I didn't say that.'

Lucy was suddenly ashamed of herself. Was she jealous of Solange's relationship with him? Metand had been kind to her, that's all. Just like Louis and Monique Dedoir.

'Is he very analytical?' she asked.

'Yes, I think he is. But perhaps what you don't realize is how compassionate he is. François is not a run-of-the-mill detective. He really cares about the human condition. He really cares about you, Lucy. You must bear that in mind. Now, there's one last grave you might like to see.'

Feeling that she was under criticism, that she had said something wrong, Lucy followed Monique to the back of the cemetery where she received a considerable surprise.

'She's magnificent,' she muttered. 'Quite magnificent.'

'Isn't she?' Monique had returned to being warm again.

Thérèse Goutin stood above her tomb. On her outstretched arms were a number of intricately carved birds. Her face was round, almost childlike.

'A martyr?' Monique smiled. 'Or was she simply a manipulator?'

'Either way she lost out,' observed Lucy.

When they returned to the hotel, Metand was sitting in the small dark brown bar drinking Pernod.

'No news, I'm afraid. Will you have a drink?'

'No. I want to keep a clear head.'

'I propose to drive to Dieppe and then to your Esher.'

'It's not *my* Esher. Why don't I take you in the Riley?'

'I'm afraid you'll have to take a risk and have me as your chauffeur.'

'I didn't mean – '

'It would be better to leave your car here – if you are returning.'

'Of course I am!' Lucy was indignant and then she realized what he meant. 'You think Tim might come back to the hotel and be distraught if he doesn't see the Riley.'

'Anything's possible at this stage, Mrs Groves.'

'Could you not bring yourself to call me Lucy as we're going to travel together?'

'I could try.' He smiled and relaxed slightly. 'I've calculated that if we take an early lunch, then we would arrive in Esher at about seven. I will have to return the next day – early in the morning. I'm afraid I haven't had time to phone your – friends.'

'I'll do that,' said Lucy.

'Thank you. I'm sorry the time is so short.'

'I'm not.'

Unfortunately, it was May who answered the phone but she had clearly decided to pretend to forget their previous altercation.

'Martin's not here. He's gone up to The Wheatsheaf with Peter.'

Lucy could visualize the pub's interior with its fake horse-brasses, the pile of pennies in the glass bottle for the Sunshine Homes (give a bob or two for charity, old thing), the beer pumps, the wet counter, the crowded tables, the cricket cartoons on the wall, the cavalry twills and sports jackets of the men and the bright summer prints of the women. Outside, the sports cars would be drawn up, young men sitting on the bonnets, clutching pints in meaty fists, the canvas roofs rolled down.

May was saying something that Lucy hadn't heard, lost in her reverie about The Wheatsheaf. 'What was that?'

'I said, is there any news?'

'No.'

'Peter has been telling us the most dreadful things. A young woman murdered and idiotic rumours about Tim. What's going on?'

'I can't explain now. I've already told Peter. I'm coming back to Esher for a night, accompanied by the detective who's in charge of the case here. He has been very good to me and his name is François Metand.' Lucy stopped talking and listened instead to the disapproving silence at the other end. 'May?'

134

'Yes?' Her voice was expressionless.

'He wants to talk to Peter and Martin.'

'What on earth for?' She was blockish now, negative in a particularly British way. The idea of a French policeman was clearly as hard a concept to May as a nun at her dinner table.

'At our house.' Lucy had almost said 'my'.

'At what time?'

'Seven.'

'For how long?'

'I've no idea.'

'I see.' May sounded as if she was trying to think of an excuse for refusing an invitation to a particularly dull party.

Suddenly, unpredictably, Lucy's temper snapped.

'He insists.'

'Who?'

'Metand. Why are you being so bloody uncooperative?'

'I beg your pardon?'

'I said – why are you being so bloody uncooperative?' That'll jerk her out of her eternal complacency, thought Lucy in real delight, the adrenalin pumping again.

'How *can* you speak to me like that?'

Lucy could sense that she was afraid.

'Don't you understand what's happened to me?'

'Of course, it's dreadful – '

'Then don't you think that the arrival of a policeman is perfectly logical? Even the arrival of a *French* policeman?'

'We've been *besieged* with the police here about that dreadful murder on the Clump. Now we're trying to put the whole ghastly business out of our minds.'

'Tim's disappeared. He's linked with this dreadful death. Perhaps you think he killed the gardener too?'

'You *must* calm down.'

But the prosaic response only drove her to further heights of anger. 'You're all going to have to explain yourselves, tell Monsieur Metand what you know.'

'We don't know anything. You're very upset. That's quite natural. But I have to tell you that abusing me – '

'Abusing you?' Lucy screamed into the phone. 'I'd love to horsewhip you, drown you in sandwich spread, fill your gob with mayonnaise.' Suddenly she ran out of steam and began to shriek with laughter while Metand pushed past the hovering Monique and wrenched the receiver out of Lucy's hand. As he did so, she beat at his chest with her fists.

Monique tried to pull her away but it was not until Louis hurried in from the kitchen, wearing his familiar stained apron, that Lucy could be effectively restrained and taken into the office.

Metand picked up the receiver. 'Madame – '

May could only emit a gasping sound. Then she said, 'Who am I speaking to?'

'François Metand.'

'The French policeman?' asked May, speaking slowly and very clearly for this foreigner.

'Mrs Groves is not well.' He was struggling slightly with his English.

'I've never been spoken to like that. It was such a shock. Especially from her.'

'Her husband is missing and a woman has died violently. It is only natural she is upset. As you will know, I need to speak to Mr Latimer and yourself as well as Mr Davis and his wife. I have questions to ask you. Am I making myself clear?'

'Yes,' May said after a fractional pause.

'The arrangement is that the four of you will arrive at Mrs Groves's house at seven tonight. I have to insist that you break any other engagements you may – '

'We'll be there. But none of us are going to put up with being abused.'

'I will ensure you are not.'

'I don't know what we can tell you – '

'I hope your husband and his friend can tell me a great deal. I have very little time. I must return to France with Mrs Groves early the next morning.'

'I understand. And Monsieur – '

'Metand.'

'Monsieur Metand, I do understand how shocked Lucy is. Please reassure her that all her abuse, although most upsetting, will be forgotten.'

'Thank you.' He put down the phone and opened the office door to find Lucy crying quietly in Monique's arms.

'Have you been consorting with the enemy?' she asked him.

'No,' said Metand. 'Much worse. Like your Neville Chamberlain, I have been negotiating a false peace.'

Lucy found herself standing in almost the exact place on the stern deck as she had stood before, gazing down at Tim and realizing how ill he looked, how unprepared for the stress of such a trip.

François Metand, buttoned up in a huge overcoat, scarf and trilby hat, seemed to have come prepared for arctic exploration rather than a summer voyage over the English Channel. He had also lit a cigarette.

'I haven't seen you smoking before,' she commented.

'I only smoke on water,' he told her. 'It makes me less nervous.'

'Do you have a phobia?'

'I have a phobia about leaving my territory.'

'It's special?'

'I fish. I think. I read.' He suddenly smiled. 'Therefore I am. Elsewhere I am often not. Do you understand me?'

Lucy nodded. Suddenly he had reminded her of her father.

'I have my own patch. My wife and I – we have similar tastes. The girls are different. I'm sure you would find them most outgoing, unlike their parents. Perhaps it's a family gene going far back.'

'I should have been like you and stayed safely at home. Except, unlike you, I don't love my home. I hate it.'

'What would you have felt if your friends had not lived so close to you?'

'They're not my friends. Never were. They were forced on me.'

'That's why I'm taking the unusual step of travelling abroad,' said Metand.

'There's nowhere you want to go?'

'Nowhere but my valley. Solange found our house peaceful. She didn't have to manipulate anybody or make up any lies. She just sat by the stream.'

'At least she didn't have to *live* a lie,' said Lucy bitterly. 'Like Tim.'

'You're sure he was doing that?' Metand spoke gently.

'I know he wasn't capable of killing Claude Eclave. But I'm

equally sure he had to live with something so oppressive that it finally broke him.'

'Much depends on what these men will tell me.'

'You really believe they're holding back? Or are you trying to help me remember something?'

But Metand only shrugged.

He was watching the wake of the boat, just as Tim had done, when Lucy returned from the cafeteria with two black coffees.

'In Esher, we live for cricket.'

He smiled. 'What you really mean is that you are all middle-class people with the same outlook.'

'They enjoy structure. I don't.'

'How would you have liked to live?'

'Tim and I always talked of travelling.'

'Did you want children?'

'Desperately.'

'Both of you?'

'Tim was in no state to even contemplate the idea.'

'But you were?'

'I can't conceive.'

'I'm sorry.'

'Perhaps we could adopt – ' Lucy faltered. 'If he's alive.'

Metand was silent and she was grateful to him for not mouthing clichés.

'Tell me more about Esher. It sounds a social phenomenon.'

'It's not. Much of England is devoted to keeping up a front. Death is a forbidden subject and so is any form of deviation. Sport is vitally important. Rugby in winter. Cricket in summer.'

'The English team games. The playing-fields of Eton. That's how you won your battles.'

'Our men are sportsmen. Inhibited. Jovial. Honourable. Back slappers.'

'Do the women play games?'

'Tennis, perhaps. Maybe golf. But on the whole they are expected to cut up sandwiches.'

'An occupation that you would not have wished to share,' Metand said drily.

'Before the war it was different. But then Tim met Peter and Martin and they moved into Shrub Lane and created a prison;

138

they were the warders and Tim was their prisoner. And yet I was wondering just now when I went to get the coffee if they were frightened of him. Worried that he was going to give them away.' Lucy paused. 'That's right,' she repeated. 'Worried that he was going to give them away.'

'That's an interesting idea,' said Metand. 'Do you have any evidence to back it up?'

'Not a shred.'

Metand lit another cigarette from the butt of his first.

'You doubt me?'

'Not at all. But what *could* your husband give away? Have you thought about that? You dragged him to France. He didn't want to go, but suppose he decided to take an initiative that he should have taken a long time ago.'

'Do you think that's why Martin was pleased? When we'd arrived in Navise? He was checking that we were there. Don't you think that's a possibility?'

'I don't know.'

'And the key to all this is what Peter and Martin are covering up.'

'I think so.'

'Are you confident of finding out what it is?'

'Only with your help, Lucy. But I'm beginning to feel a little more optimistic. That's why I'm so glad we're travelling companions.'

9

Metand drove well and at some speed. Lucy felt much more comfortable with him now. Monique had been right. He did care about her and was attentive in small ways, ensuring she was not too hot and then not too cold as he wound one of the windows half down. He was companionable and cultivated in a way the men – even Tim – could never be.

On the way from Newhaven she had discovered he admired Elizabeth Bowen, while she was able to discuss Cocteau and, in particular, *Les Enfants Terribles*.

'That kind of closeness,' she had told him, 'is almost how the men were. Locked into their own little secrets from which there couldn't be any escape.'

He let her talk about the old Tim a good deal and didn't ask too many questions.

They drove through Esher High Street at about six and, because she was with Metand, because she had suffered such trauma, the place seemed distant, only familiar as a memory. She could hardly believe she lived there and had hauled the trolley up the Cut so many times to the familiar shops. The ABC Bakery, Cullen's the grocers, the International Stores, Denham's Garage, Howards the chemist, Newlands Newsagency – even Caves Café looked different, almost alien after the quiet grey square in Navise.

Metand turned down towards the green and drove past Esher parish church where she and Tim had been married in 1938, well before he had come under the influence of Peter and Martin.

'It's a pretty place,' observed Metand. 'I had imagined much more mock Tudor.'

'I suppose it is. A pretty prison.'

'How did you meet Tim?'

'On a walking holiday. I was with my father. We met by chance.'

'What was he like?'

140

'Restless. Wanted to avoid putting down roots – to travel. I was quite frightened.'

'What of?'

'Pulling up *my* roots. But I loved him. He had a special sort of integrity. That's why I'm glad I met Tissot. That story about his boy is so typical of what Tim would have done.'

'And then he went to war.'

Lucy leant back in the seat and closed her eyes as they drove down Shrub Lane. 'Now if you were pining for mock Tudor, you've got your heart's delight.'

Without Tim, Gables was a stage set on which two people had once led imagined lives.

The evening was clear and mellow, a sickle moon rode a cloudless night sky, and Lucy decided to open up the terrace. She would serve drinks and hope the discussion would end at a reasonable time so that she could make Metand a simple dinner – and they could take the first ferry back to France in the morning. Yet, at the same time, she was in a state of rising excitement.

Could Metand make Peter and Martin co-operate, or would they work a flanker on him?

They all arrived together. Peter and Martin, looking suitably grave and commanding as if they had come to address the troops. Or perhaps the cricket club committee? Peter wore a dark blue blazer, white shirt, regimental tie, grey slacks and highly polished black shoes. Martin wore a linen suit, a coloured shirt, cravat and brogues.

May, going out of her way not to make eye contact with Lucy, wore a blue circular skirt and neat white blouse whilst Sally was wearing one of her little black dresses.

They sat around the large wrought-iron table on the terrace while Lucy fussed with drinks on a trolley and Martin doggedly tried to help her but was firmly repulsed.

The twilight was slow to give way to night and the garden scents were deep and musky. Lucy glanced at the lawn and flower beds with their regimented patches of colour in some amazement. Had she really spent so much time achieving this perfection? What had been the point of it all? Again she had the same feeling of distancing, as if three days had become three years.

She looked down at the garden shed to which Tim had so often retreated, and thought for a moment she could see the familiar shape of his silhouette in the shifting shadows.

When she had poured the last drink, an uncomfortable silence settled around the table and there was a great deal of throat clearing, coughing and scraping of chairs. Lucy was sure that Metand was encouraging social unease and was in no hurry to begin.

She gave him a covert glance but he was staring down into the garden, watching the light fade and the darkness creep over the rose bed.

Then, slowly and rather hesitantly, he began. 'Thank you for coming, ladies and gentlemen. I hope it wasn't inconvenient.'

Lucy noticed that Peter was gazing at Metand, a half-smile on his lips, as if to say, 'So the little frog can speak our lingo, can he?'

'I'm afraid there is no further news to report on Mr Groves's disappearance. But the search continues.'

'You've come all this way to talk to us, Monsieur Metand,' said Martin. Surprisingly he sounded affable, almost grateful. 'On our own territory.'

'It is always preferable.'

'The trouble is, I just don't see how we can help you. I've racked my brains to find an answer to this. Would you mind running over the facts again for us? Then we'll obviously do the same for you.'

The frank, honest approach, thought Lucy. But suppose it happens to be true? She might be prejudiced against Martin and Peter, but wasn't it only because of their custodianship?

Metand nodded. 'Tim Groves disappeared at about 5 p.m. on Friday evening. I was contacted at 9 p.m. that same night and organized a small-scale search. At that stage we presumed he had either got lost or been taken ill. There was no sign of him in the direction he was thought to have taken, and when he didn't reappear I widened the search. We found no trace of him. At 6 p.m. the next evening, Madame Eclave was found dead at the Château Pavilly. She was lying on the ground in front of the building, having fallen from a fourth-floor window. Between her

142

fingers she held a small piece of torn check shirt which Mrs Groves later identified as her husband's. There was still no sign of Mr Groves. Madame Eclave had had a conversation with Mrs Groves a few hours earlier. To paraphrase this conversation, Madame Eclave told Lucy that she had had a brief affair with her husband while he was in hiding at the château, and that he had become so exceedingly jealous that he had murdered her husband Claude.'

Sally raised her eyebrows and May compressed her lips, but Peter was the first to comment. 'Rubbish,' he said. His voice was crisp and authoritative. 'My experience of Solange was not pleasant, but one thing is certain, even then – ten years ago – she was vengeful. Her marriage was a disaster. She had jumped up to what she imagined was a superior social status by caretaking the Château Pavilly in the owners' absence. Her husband resented this and made things exceedingly difficult for her. Tim was an attractive young man who rejected her advances, as we all did. Claude was unofficially executed later, along with the two other French collaborators, by the locals. As a result of all this, the wretched woman became mentally ill, made up a pack of lies and then committed suicide. It all seems a very sad story, monsieur, but one that is over.'

'The only problem is that we haven't found Mr Groves,' Metand pointed out. 'Talking of mental breakdown, wasn't he having one himself?'

'Yes,' said Peter. 'And he was getting worse, poor chap. But his breakdown is connected with war trauma, nothing more.'

'Please explain.'

'We spent three months in France on the run, just a few steps ahead of the Germans. That's what broke him.'

'But neither of you were affected in the same way?'

Martin shrugged. 'We all have different psychological make-ups.'

'Tell me about your journey across France.'

Peter, the ex-commanding officer, became the authoritative spokesman. 'We weren't prepared to surrender to the Nazis on the Havre peninsula so we kept walking, and later cycling. It was a long hike and was largely spent sleeping by day and travelling by night. When we got to Selais, the hamlet before Navise, we met a member of the Resistance called Matthieu Tournon. He was a farmer. Do you know of him?'

Metand shook his head.

'He can be checked, I'm sure. Tournon was extremely helpful to us and got us bikes and some shelter in the cellar of the Hôtel des Arbres, which was then owned by a couple called Philippe and Babette Madol.' Again Peter gazed across at Metand expectantly.

'Yes, I know of them. They have retired now.'

'We spent a night in the cellar, being fed after a long journey during which we nearly starved. Yes, it is possible to starve in a civilized country in wartime. The Madols were marvellous to us, but the area was crawling with German patrols and we didn't want to risk staying too long in any one place; it was too dangerous for us and for our hosts. So, Tournon took us to the Château Pavilly where Solange was caretaker. Once again, we got the cellars. We also got more than we bargained for.' Peter turned to Martin, who took up the story.

'The facts of this unpleasant matter are that Solange tried to – make us have relations with her in exchange for her hospitality. When we refused, she put pressure on us and even threatened to deprive us of food and drink.'

'Was her husband Claude present during this propositioning?' asked Metand.

'No,' replied Peter. 'She spoke to us individually in a very unpleasant and sordid manner. We all refused and conferred about how to handle it. We still needed to rest up – Martin had a badly swollen ankle – and at least she didn't give us away to the Germans. Tournon may have seen to that.'

'Did you tell him about the lady's propositions?'

'Of course,' said Martin. 'He and Solange had a blazing row.'

Sally fidgeted, and May retained a kind of withering silence, looking straight ahead at the wistaria on the wall of Gables.

'And were you propositioned again?'

Martin shook his head. 'Two days later we cycled on. And kept cycling. Solange was a greater challenge than the enemy.' He gave a hearty and dismissive laugh.

'What kind of mental condition was Mr Groves in at this stage?'

'Shaky.'

'Can you be a little specific?'

'He was cracking up,' said Peter.

*

144

A long silence followed his remark. Metand glanced at Lucy, willing her not to interrupt, and she said nothing, inadvertently catching May's eye before she could look away.

'As to Tim having an affair with Solange,' said Martin hurriedly, 'that would be utterly ridiculous. He was in no state for anything like that.'

'Had he been deteriorating *before* this – incident?' asked Metand.

'He was losing his nerve. I don't blame him.' Peter was magnanimous now, giving Lucy a straight look. 'This isn't meant as a criticism. It's a fact. We were just as scared, just as apprehensive about what we were trying to do. His nerve went first, that's all.'

'It was bad luck,' volunteered Martin.

'There was no trigger point?' asked Metand.

'None at all as far as we could see,' said Peter.

'Nothing connected with Solange?'

'It would be ludicrous to even consider the idea.'

'And there's something else,' said Peter.

'Yes?' Metand was encouraging.

'You say she plunged to her death and that in her hand Solange appeared to have grasped a piece of Tim's shirt.'

'Mrs Groves has identified it.'

'Of course. But you shouldn't jump to conclusions,' broke in Martin.

'How do you mean?'

'Because I believe she could simply be taking a nasty revenge while the balance of her mind was disturbed.'

'I don't understand,' said Metand.

'While we were at the château,' said Peter slowly, 'Solange had a row with Claude and later, as I have said, with Tournon.'

'Yes?'

'Each time she threatened to kill herself.'

Lucy was listening intently now. She turned to Metand.

'Wouldn't you agree that she was suicidal? You'll remember what she told me. About not having the courage to kill herself. Then she added the word "yet".'

Metand paused and then spoke slowly and a little reluctantly. 'It is true that she has told me she would like to take her own life.'

145

Peter's face was expressionless as he said slowly, 'Suppose she deliberately threw herself from the window of the château?'

'What about the shirt?' asked Sally, needing to assert herself, to contribute in some way.

'That could have been part of the trick.' Peter was even more authoritative now. 'Suppose Solange *did* meet Tim for some reason or even by chance, and enticed him into the château and ripped his shirt. She could have wanted to punish him for continuing to reject her, so when she jumped she could have taken the fragment of shirt with her to incriminate him.'

'It's a theory,' said Metand without much enthusiasm. 'But what has happened to Mr Groves? Where is he?'

As he spoke Lucy knew that it was all too glib and her false hopes faded.

'Have you thoroughly searched the château?' Peter sounded incredibly patronizing, but Metand's face remained inscrutable.

'Of course.' He gazed at a moth flickering over one of the coach-house lamps that lit the terrace. 'I still don't see why he should have vanished.'

'I'm not implying anything,' said Peter cautiously, 'but of the three of us, Solange was definitely most interested in Tim. If she tried to proposition him again, as I've suggested, in his state he might just have wandered off.'

'For so long?'

Lucy knew that Peter and Martin were clutching at straws, but she was suddenly grateful to them.

'I'm not satisfied,' said Metand, and let the comment spread as a ripple into the pool of silence.

'We've done our best,' said Martin brusquely. 'I assure you that there's nothing more we can tell you.'

'What about Baverstock?'

For the very first time he looked taken aback and even Peter seemed startled. 'I don't see the connection. That's a completely separate issue.'

'How well did you know your gardener, Mrs Davis?'

Sally was obviously surprised to be drawn into the discussion. 'Hardly at all.'

'We've already talked to the British police about this.' Peter somehow made them sound a superior force, but Metand didn't seem to notice.

'Now you can talk to me.'

Sally looked awkward. 'There's very little to say. Old Mr Tanner – that's our previous gardener – was getting past it but Peter didn't want to pension him off until the last moment. Then he had a heart attack and of course we *had* to look round for someone else. I went to see the old boy in hospital and he recommended his cousin's boy.'

'Graham Baverstock.'

'Yes.'

'And he was satisfactory?'

'Yes. Quite a refreshing change after Mr T. who could be very idiosyncratic *and* obnoxious as he got older.'

'I had a word with an Inspector Frasier on the telephone before I came here,' Metand said quietly, and Lucy looked at him in amazement. Why hadn't he told her? It was almost as if he had deceived her.

'What on earth for?' Peter now looked distinctly rattled.

'I wanted to hear more about this case.'

'How many times do we have to tell you?' Martin said sharply. 'This Baverstock affair has nothing to do with what we are talking about.'

'Can I be the judge of that? Frasier told me that Baverstock had been arrested last year for soliciting outside a public toilet.'

'In Esher?' gasped May, as if Metand had seriously blasphemed.

'In a place called Kingston-on-Thames which is apparently just a few miles away. He was put on probation.'

'So?' Peter was impatient. 'It's a pity we employed him, I grant you, but how were we to know?'

'Frasier told me that Baverstock mixed with other homosexuals.'

'In Hersham,' May was heard to mutter amidst the spreading silence.

'Rather wider than that, I gather.' Metand was patient with her. 'Frasier has been looking at some possessions found in Baverstock's room – '

'You don't mean my lighter, do you?' asked Peter quietly. He seemed more confident now.

He turned to Sally. 'We've been turning the house upside down looking for it, haven't we?'

'Yes. It belonged to Peter's father. He was really upset when he couldn't find it.'

'I expect you will have it returned,' Metand said casually.

Sally got up. 'I'm tired,' she complained. 'Are we finished? Is there any more?'

Peter and Martin remained sitting.

'What were you trying to imply, Monsieur Metand?' asked May icily. 'That there's some link between Baverstock's murder and what is happening in France?'

'Not necessarily. It just seems a bit of a coincidence – one I thought I should explore.'

'And have you finished exploring?'

'For the time being.'

'I'm so terribly sorry about all this.' Sally gazed down at Lucy. 'It's just so awful. I've been praying for you every day. The world's so violent now. May and I were thinking – would it be a help if *we* came back with you? I know Peter and Martin would like to – ' Her voice faded as she waited for the inevitable rejection.

Lucy made it as gentle as she could. She was still wondering why Metand had got hold of Frasier without confiding in her. 'It's sweet of you, but I can cope. The people at the hotel are supportive and Monsieur Metand has been wonderful. I'll be all right.'

'Could I at least have a word with you?' asked May. 'A private word.' She sounded severe again, every inch the fair but stern-minded schoolmistress.

'Of course.' Lucy was all cold courtesy. 'Why don't you help me with the glasses?' She knew that she should offer them all coffee, but that would prolong their visit too painfully.

While she and May reloaded the trolley, an awkward silence spread.

'And how's French rugby?' Peter asked brightly.

'I know nothing of French rugby,' replied Metand.

The men proceeded to enlighten him while Sally openly yawned.

'I'm sorry for shouting at you down the phone,' said Lucy once she and May were in the kitchen.

'You weren't yourself.'

Or I was more myself than ever I was in England, despite all the terrible things that have happened, she thought rebelliously, but she didn't want to argue with May again.

'It was quite understandable. But I wish you wouldn't be so hostile to Martin – and to Peter. They're only trying to help. They've always been trying to help.'

So that's it, thought Lucy. She wants them involved. She glanced at May and realized that she was nervous, almost afraid.

'I know.' Suddenly all she wanted to do was to crawl into bed, pull the covers over her head and seek oblivion. Instead, she knew she had to try and talk to an unsettled May. 'I'm grateful. Really I am.'

'The shock's been dreadful for you. You need help.'

'I've got it.'

'All they wanted to do was to protect you and Tim.'

Despite her best intentions, Lucy felt a flash of irritation. 'They always seemed like jailors.'

'That wasn't their intention.'

'I know they're trying to help.' She struggled to be more gracious, and then realized that if Tim was found they might both end up in Gables, watched over again. She had to assert herself now. 'But I've found the situation very claustrophobic, unhealthy.'

'And why is that, may I ask?' May had quickly reverted to hostility.

'For the reasons I've just stated. And I've made up my mind about something. If, please God, Tim is found alive we'll up sticks and live in France.' Her voice was too bright, too light, but at least it masked her anger.

'In Navise?'

'No.'

'Where then?'

'I don't know. In the south perhaps.'

'But what would you both *do*?'

'I don't know about Tim. But I could teach English.'

May was silent. Then she said, 'Well – on your own head be it. Naturally I pray he's alive. But I still feel you're behaving – very brutally to Peter and Martin. I don't think Tim would approve.'

He probably wouldn't, thought Lucy. 'I've always felt excluded and Peter and Martin were patronizing, don't you think?'

May's lips were compressed again. 'We always wanted to help. Martin has been deeply concerned for Tim over a long period of years. Their experiences brought the men together quite naturally. We were never a part of that.'

'The three musketeers?' Lucy couldn't prevent herself from being destructive. 'All for one and one for all?'

May was determined to plod on. 'If you like – although I know you're being cynical. I don't think I should say any more at a time like this. I'm sorry if mistakes have been made and I'm even more sorry that you feel the way you do. Please continue to call on us if we're needed.'

May was close to tears but Lucy was determined to bring the intimate chat, the 'private word', to an abrupt conclusion.

She kissed her on the cheek and received a watery smile. May was a good sort. But Lucy knew that having sought protection for so long she actually needed protection from good sorts.

When they had gone, she ransacked the refrigerator and, with apologies, made herself and Metand eggs Florentine followed by unripe camembert washed down with whisky.

Then she confronted him, still nettled by his surprise disclosure. 'Why did you bring up Baverstock? And you didn't tell me you'd spoken to Frasier.'

'That's because I'm conducting the investigation, Lucy.'

'Ouch!'

'I'm sorry. But we are very far from getting anywhere. And you are not a privileged confidante, despite the fact that I'm staying in your delightful home.'

'Ouch again.'

Metand gave her a slow smile. 'As to Baverstock, I just wanted to gauge their reaction.'

'And did you?'

'They didn't give much away. And I find it difficult to believe that Solange went to all that trouble to take such a revenge.'

'Yes,' said Lucy, 'but you did agree she was suicidal.' For the first time she wondered if it might be possible to take the men's theory seriously. 'Peter and Martin said she was attracted to Tim. The fact that he came to see her, after all these years, might have pushed her over the edge literally. She played her games

150

with me and then threw herself off the roof, trying to incriminate Tim.'

Metand didn't reply directly. 'There are two essential questions unanswered. Why did he go to see her – if he *did* go to see her – and where is he now?'

Lucy was determined to hang on to the men's scenario for just a little longer, however unlikely it sounded. 'Maybe he's still wandering or even hiding, in some kind of state of shock – '

Metand took a long pull on his whisky and shrugged. 'I see no point in this speculation.' He sounded so final that she hurriedly changed the subject.

'What did you think of the men?'

'They were afraid.'

Lucy felt a new sense of shock. Was he acting on a hunch again. 'What of?'

'Something they won't tell me about. That they *can't* tell me about.' Metand closed his eyes.

'How do you know?'

'They both try too hard. It's so glib, so obvious. But I can't undermine them. Not yet. Lucy – ' he continued, blinking his eyes to keep awake – 'you have to appreciate that going to France was your *only* course of action. But Tim may well have taken the opportunity to put something right.'

'I don't understand – '

'Suppose, just suppose we revert to your theory on the ferry which, as I told you, is very interesting. The men, as you call them, weren't protecting Tim at all; he was protecting them. All the time, all these years, they could have been dependent on *him*.'

'But how?'

'That I don't know. But we must look at each possibility. Could your husband have had his breakdown because of the burden of protecting the others?'

'That's just another theory. First we have Solange's revenge suicide. Now we have Tim protecting Peter and Martin. Then there's other scenarios – Solange's, for instance. The one I *don't* want to believe in.' She paused. 'And of course you've raised this mysterious Baverstock connection.'

151

'We have to eliminate each one. I shall increase the scale of the hunt. Tim's our first priority.'

'Would it be better if the men *did* come?'

'No,' said Metand. 'I don't want them in France, and neither do you. The situation is complicated enough.'

10

Lucy lay in the double bed and failed to sleep. Instead, her mind raced, the images coming and going like steel grinding across the inside of her head. The warm night now seemed to have become humid, enclosing her in a moist cocoon from which she couldn't escape.

Sleep had never been a problem to her in the past. Before they had set off for France, despite all her worries about Tim, she had been able to drop off almost immediately, often finding release from the building tensions at Gables.

She got up and went to the window, drawing the curtains aside and gazing out into a dense blackness that, as her eyes became accustomed to it, revealed the chestnut trees rustling in a darting night breeze.

Where are you, Tim? Are you dead? Or are you hiding? Did I force you into something you couldn't stop?

Lucy closed her eyes against the self-interrogation. She wandered around the bedroom, not sure what to do, wondering if she should quietly slip downstairs and pour herself a Scotch.

In the end she gave in, blundering into the sitting room, almost knocking over a vase. It was ludicrous. She had always been able to find her way about the house in the dark, yet after her three traumatic days in France, it had become alien territory.

Eventually she turned on a small lamp by the sofa, poured herself a huge Scotch from the cocktail cabinet, and then went into the kitchen. Lucy giggled foolishly at May's outrage, indignation and sense of injustice. Restlessly, she returned to the sitting room and let her eyes rove around the familiar/unfamiliar room until she came to what she had always termed 'Tim's side of the bookcase'.

They had always had very different reading habits. She preferred 'literature', he detective fiction, both gently scoffing at the other's taste. Now the memory made her wince and Lucy sat down on the sofa, feeling vaguely sick as despair gripped her.

To compensate she drank more Scotch, rose, topped up her glass and returned to the sofa. Feeling comforted, Lucy resumed her scanning of the room, noting each object as if she had not seen it before.

Restlessly, she got up again and walked over to Tim's books. She had never examined them in such detail before. Peter Cheyney, Agatha Christie, Dorothy L. Sayers. Idly she picked up *The Nine Tailors* and flicked through its pages. As she put it back she saw the envelope behind the books, next to Agatha Christie's *The Murder of Roger Ackroyd*. Inside the envelope were photographs and she took them out, flicking over prints of their wedding and a few that were taken earlier in Swanage and Canterbury. The last one was instantly familiar.

The three men. On bicycles. Riding down a road with poplars on each side. A traditional French view. It was the same photograph she had seen in the Hôtel des Arbres. Lucy went to the sofa with it and sat down, gazing at Peter, Martin and Tim. Why hadn't he told her he'd got this? Had he hidden it from her? To discover the photograph now was discomforting, as if the house had been invaded. Why hadn't Tim shown it to her? Why hadn't Metand admitted to contacting Frasier? Why were secrets kept? From her?

All three men were smiling. They're saying cheese, she thought and giggled again, realizing with some satisfaction she was now drunk.

'He loved me,' she could hear Solange saying. 'We had an affair. He was jealous. He killed my husband. He was jealous. He killed my husband.' The statements became a rhythm and she filled up her glass yet again.

At last oblivion was coming. It was like a dark cloak, wrapping itself around her, taking away the pain.

Lucy lay back on the sofa, her empty glass falling on to the Axminster.

'*Bonjour.*'

Lucy jerked awake, her mouth dry and her head aching. A stooped man she didn't recognize at first was standing rather self-consciously beside her. He had a cup of black coffee in his hand.

'Tim?'

'Metand.' He passed her the coffee and the present abruptly returned.

'I'm sorry,' she muttered.

'What for?'

'I got drunk.'

'You probably couldn't sleep. I'll leave you to – '

'No. I've got something to show you.' Lucy held up the photograph of the three men on their bicycles.

Metand took it, squinting slightly. 'This is the same as the picture at the hotel.'

'I found it behind a book.'

'Last night?'

'Before I got drunk – or while I got drunk. You know Solange took it? Tim told me.'

Metand passed the photograph back to her without comment.

'We must leave soon. If you are still returning with me?'

'You know I am.' Lucy was immediately alarmed, like a child threatened with being abandoned.

'I'm afraid I don't take much breakfast.'

'I'm afraid I can't.'

They smiled uneasily at each other.

'What could Tim have meant by saying "Don't make me do it"?' asked Metand as they drove back to Newhaven.

Lucy's headache was better. She was glad to be returning to France, leaving Shrub Lane behind. She knew that she didn't belong there any more.

'And the angels are dying. Maybe they were just a nightmare.'

'Even fragments of dreams can have significance, particularly as we already know the angels were painted on the ceiling of the chapel at Pavilly.'

'Do you think Villet would have phoned if anything had happened?'

'Of course.'

'So I'm meant to go back to the hotel and start waiting all over again? I just *can't* do that.'

'I've got to be briefed on what's been happening in my absence. I'm sorry.'

'Then I'd like to go to the château and apologize to Anna Ribault.'

Metand shrugged ungraciously. 'If you would prefer.'

'I *do* prefer,' said Lucy gratefully. 'Thank you.' She realized now how heavily dependent she had become on him.

The Channel crossing was rough and Metand spent all his time in a deckchair on the aft deck with his eyes closed, opening them only to light another cigarette.

Lucy, who was not in the least afraid of the sea, was concerned for him as spray came over the side and the ferry rolled in the dips between the waves.

'Wouldn't you be better below?' she asked, but Metand merely shook his head mournfully.

'I don't want to go down,' he mumbled. 'I want to get to the lifeboats first.'

Eventually Lucy went to the rail, watching the grey waves of the English Channel lash and foam, the swell running towards the French coast, seagulls mewing in the face of the wind. This is an adventure, she thought. A wild, wet adventure on the sea, and Lucy wanted to share it with Tim. The old Tim. The one who was lost in France.

She gazed at the dim outline of the French coastline through the rain mist. Please, Tim. Whatever happened. Come back to me. If you love me.

François Metand seemed to undergo a miracle recovery as they sped along the long, straight roads that she and Tim had taken until they came to the secret, hedged-in countryside that surrounded Navise. Lucy was forcibly reminded of how he had begun to haltingly confide in her.

'I can guess how painful this journey is for you. Returning without him.' Metand was as perceptive as ever and Lucy was grateful.

'He's here. Somewhere,' she said resolutely. 'Are you feeling better?'

'From *mal de mer*? I am always thankful to be returning. It's travelling that makes me ill. Not just the sea.'

'And that is the *only* time you smoke?'

'The only time. I expect I more than make up for my abstinence.' There was silence as fine rain spread gently on the windscreen, broken by the sudden hum of the wipers. 'And you still wish to go to Pavilly?' He sounded uncertain.

'You think I'll create a scene?'

'Anna is not easy.'

'I've got to *do* something.'

He sighed.

Metand dropped Lucy at the Hôtel des Arbres. It was comforting to be back in the quiet, grey square, to push open the by now familiar door and to stand for a moment where she and Tim had stood on the worn tree-patterned tiles.

Louis came out almost immediately when she pressed the bell on the reception desk. For once he was without his bloodied apron, and wore instead a voluminous boiler suit.

'How was the journey?'

'Tiring.' She suddenly kissed him on his unshaven cheek. He was an old friend now. A friend who made no demands. The best kind of friend.

He looked slightly abashed. 'And the interview?'

'I don't think Metand got very far.'

'I'm sorry.'

'No news?'

Louis shook his head and then said, 'Navise is buzzing – at least as much as it will ever buzz. Solange's death is on everyone's lips.'

'And what is the popular vote? Suicide or murder?'

'If your husband had not gone missing it would be suicide while the balance of mind was disturbed.'

'But as it is?'

'The missing Englishman? The fall? They add up to – '

'Murder?'

'I'm sorry.'

'Have they mentioned the shirt?'

'The police have kept that quiet.'

'What have you been doing?' Lucy asked, desperate now to change the subject, gazing curiously at his boiler suit.

'Working in my garden. The antidote to boredom.'

'Where's Monique?'

'She is not so well this morning. I'm afraid the whole business has started her up again. But she'll recover.'

'I didn't realize – '

'That she had a drink problem? Don't be polite, madame. It's a little obvious, isn't it?'

Lucy nodded, ashamed of herself.

'What are you going to do? Take a rest? Is there anything I can get you?'

'No. I don't want a rest. I'm going up to the château to see Anna Ribault. I owe her an apology.'

'I wonder if that's wise?'

'You sound like Metand. I need to fill my time. I can't keep waiting.'

'Would you like to help me in the garden? There's a lot to do.'

'I'm sorry. I need to get away.'

'Anna may not be pleased to see you.' Clearly Louis wasn't going to give up as quickly as Metand. 'She will be devastated.'

'I really do need to apologize,' Lucy said briskly. 'I'll take the Riley.'

This was the first time she had driven the car since Tim's disappearance. Lucy condemned herself for being a coward. She should have been using the Riley to search for him, but she also knew – had always known – that she would soon get lost in the lanes. Or was that just a cheap excuse?

As Lucy drove towards Pavilly she could feel Tim's presence in the passenger seat and she had the strange impression she was nearer to him than she had ever been over the last few days. She kept glancing down beside her.

'Tim,' she whispered. 'Find me, Tim.'

Very soon, perhaps too soon, she arrived at the château gates. When she told the police officer who she was he let her through at once.

*

'You were distraught, Mrs Groves,' replied Anna Ribault after Lucy had made her apology. She was calm and completely detached, her boyish face expressionless. It was difficult to work out whether she was hostile or merely neutral. She looked exhausted and her pale skin was waxy and slightly discoloured. Lucy wondered if she was ill.

'I was out of control.'

'I've felt much the same myself.'

Lucy gazed around her. The summerhouse was a much more substantial building inside than she had imagined, with long windows overlooking the lake.

'Am I in your way?'

'You're welcome to stay and take a look at the archives.' There was marginal warmth in Anna's voice. 'You must be tired of counting the hours.'

The large room was on two well-lit levels, with trestle tables running down each side and a large circular one in the middle on which was heaped a pile of singed and in some cases burnt paper.

Labelled boxes were distributed along the side tables, and for a moment Lucy was reminded of the cricket pavilion at Esher, seeing ghostly May making sandwiches, Sally pushing her blonde hair out of her eyes and little old invalid Tim dozing in a deckchair outside.

'Would you like a drink?' Anna was watching her curiously, as if she was calculating something.

Lucy shook her head. 'I got drunk last night in England and fell asleep on the sofa. Metand found me and I felt a fool.'

'Do you want to talk?' She sat down on a stool at one of the tables. 'Would that help?'

Lucy was surprised at her generosity, wondering how intrusive she was being.

'I was wrong to come here. I'm just being selfish. I'm not even thinking about how you feel.'

'I also got drunk last night.' Anna smiled ironically. 'So we are both hung over. Sit down and let's talk for a while. It would probably do us good. Then I shall start work but you're very welcome to stay until – until you've had enough. The archive is interesting, and although it won't enlighten you about your husband's brief stay here, it will give you a picture of an ancient French aristocratic family.'

159

Lucy sat down, suddenly not knowing how to begin. Then she decided to plunge straight in. 'Solange told me that she had an affair with Tim and that he shot her husband Claude. Isn't that exactly what you repeated to me?'

Anna stared at her in silence for a while and then said, 'Yes.'

'You believed her?'

'She generally told me the truth. As you will appreciate, that was not her usual style.'

'Were you close?' Lucy asked tentatively, the despair sweeping her. Anna seemed to be so reasonable, so convincing.

'We had become friends. After all, we were the only two women working at Pavilly. It would not have been a good idea to quarrel.'

'Why did she fantasize?'

'Solange was ill. I tried as hard as I could to persuade her to get help. But she was stubborn.' Anna shrugged. 'She was ill in her head and I'm ill in my body. We made a good pair.'

Lucy realized that she had been right. 'I'm sorry,' she said uncertainly. 'Really sorry.'

'Solange was saving up to send me to America for treatment. There is a clinic in California that has a new regime for cancer. But who knows if it would work. Anyway, it's naturally very expensive and Solange was not paid that well. So it will remain a dream.'

Lucy didn't know how to react and sought safety in her next question. 'Perhaps you were the only person she had a genuine relationship with?'

'I hope so.'

There was an awkward pause, during which Lucy wondered whether she should leave or go for a walk in the grounds, or even force herself to go back to the hotel. Nevertheless, she pressed on. 'How did she feel about Claude?'

'She hated the bastard. He used to beat her. Solange told me she was overjoyed when she got the caretaker's job.'

'And Claude?'

'I get the impression he bided his time until he thought he was in with a chance.'

'In what way?'

'To make money. Especially in the war. Especially with the Germans. So he went into local prostitution for lonely Nazi boys. And if Solange objected, he would beat her again.'

160

'Why was she afraid of my husband?'

'I don't know.'

There was a long pause. Then Lucy blurted out the impossible question, 'Do you think Tim killed her?'

'Obviously I was jumping to conclusions when I said that. Now I don't know what to think.'

'Has Metand spoken to you?'

'Yes. He questioned me closely. It was painful and I'd rather not have to go through that again.'

They had reached an impasse and Lucy felt a surge of anger. Why had she led her on, seeming to be sympathetic when she was not?

'I'm sorry. I *must* ask you one other question. Do you think Solange could have killed herself and tried to incriminate Tim at the same time?'

Anna sighed. It was as if she had started with the best of intentions but now knew she couldn't fulfil them. Lucy felt distraught. The conversation had been like wading in cold shallows before plunging into a freezing ocean. She was out of her depth.

'I don't *know* the answers to your questions.' Anna paused, as if she was making a considerable effort to be amenable. 'Something inexplicable happened in the war. As a result, your husband and Solange are linked in a way we don't understand. You must realize that her death is as deeply painful to me as your husband's disappearance is to you.'

'I'm sorry.' Lucy was guilty at her clumsiness yet deeply depressed by Anna's refusal to help her. Could she be protecting Solange? Looking at her shut-in expression Lucy realized she would never know.

'Would you like me to show you the archive?' Anna asked wearily.

Lucy nodded. She still had to pass an eternity of time and she didn't want to be ordered out into the rain, to drive the lonely roads.

Anna got up and went over to one of the trestle tables. 'Boxes F to H contain the material relating to the proposed German occupation of Pavilly, the one that Solange staved off. It's badly damaged, but you might be interested in having a look.'

'Have you been through all this?' asked Lucy.

'In detail.'

'What were they?'

'Mainly letters and documents. French and German bureau-cracy at its most overbearing.'

'And what's that pile of stuff on the central table?'

'That's where I do the analysis. I comb the parts of the building I can get into and anything – everything – I bring back here, photograph and file it. I'm a slow worker – but conscientious.' She bent over the documents with a magnifying glass. 'Why don't you have a look?' Anna was casually dismissive.

Lucy dragged a canvas chair over to the table and opened a box at random. Like the summerhouse, it smelt strongly of charcoal.

The German correspondence between the relevant army departments and the Goutin family were simply scraps of burnt paper stuck in brown folders and barely recognizable for what they once were. Idly she sifted through them. Then something dropped out of one of them and fell on to the floor, rolling under the table.

Lucy extricated the cylinder. 'Sorry,' she muttered.

Anna looked up impatiently. Then she said sharply, 'I've never seen that before.' She put on her glasses and came over to the trestle table. 'It's a roll of film.' She looked increasingly bewildered. 'I don't understand how this got here.'

'There was something wrapped round it,' said Lucy, holding up a small blue envelope. 'It's addressed to you.'

Anna tore it open, her hands shaking. She pulled out a sheet of notepaper which she gazed at for a long time.

'What does it say?'

'"Dearest," ' Anna read. '"This film is for Lucy Groves. Two of the men are French. The others are British. All my love. S."'

'I don't understand.'

'Neither do I. It could only have been put in here yesterday. I would have seen it otherwise.'

Lucy was sweating, the fear crawling. 'What would I want this for?'

'I've no idea, but I've got a dark room here and I could develop it for you.' Anna was clearly shaken.

'Why didn't Solange leave the film on your work table?'

'I'd told her I was going to add some material to those boxes this week.'

'How did she know I'd go through it? It was just chance I came here. She wouldn't – couldn't – have guessed.'

'I suppose she guessed I'd be dealing with the material today. She knew how methodical I am. Perhaps she meant me to be the messenger.' Anna looked intently at Lucy as if gauging her reaction. 'I'll develop the film. We'll soon find out what's on it.' She sounded even colder now, her voice distant, and Lucy began to wonder if she had actually planted the film in the box for her to find, if it had nothing to do with Solange at all. But what about the envelope and the note it contained? Surely Anna wouldn't pretend it was from Solange when it wasn't? She would be so easily found out.

She led Lucy towards the rear of the summerhouse. To the left was a small, neat bedroom with an elephant nightdress case lying on a gingham quilt. There were Tin-Tin prints around the walls, a Bakelite radio, and a chest of drawers with a photograph of Solange on top, dressed in a cloak and a hat trimmed with artificial fruit. There was also a miniature grandfather clock and a table with a teddy-bear.

The room gave Lucy an uncomfortable feeling, as if she had invaded a special privacy. Solange and Anna. How close were they? How much did they need each other? She thought about them both being ill in their different, terrible ways.

For some time Lucy could see nothing under the fluid in the developing tray. Then she saw the image begin to form and, for a few seconds, gazed down in utter mystification. It didn't make sense. Couldn't make sense. The men were playing a game – a game that she couldn't begin to understand.

'Dear God,' breathed Anna.

Lucy ran to the dark room door, the bile rising in her throat, rattling for a moment at the handle and then opening it, rushing to the bathroom and retching, but bringing nothing up. This was as bad as smelling Solange's shit, seeing that white, waxy wrist.

She seemed to go on heaving for a long time as she thought about the game that she was now slowly beginning to understand. Lucy saw May's face as she told Sally and her her suspicions about Baverstock. She remembered Sally's evasion – and her own.

'You'd better not come back in.'

Lucy stood at the door of the dark room. Anna had taken the photographs out of the tray and placed them on the bench.

But she was already there, gazing down at the unbelievable, unspeakable images.

'Who took them?'

'I don't know,' replied Anna woodenly.

Lucy couldn't take her eyes off what the men were doing.

'They're in the chapel. You can see the angels dying above them.' Anna sounded distanced, as if the vile scene was not worthy of her attention, and Lucy could think of nothing to say, still unable to believe what she was seeing. Did May know? What about Sally?

'Maybe these were meant to be Nazi propaganda.' She spoke crisply now, with academic detachment. 'I think the film is German. As you may know, the collaborators were executed because they procured French girls for the Germans and licentious photographs of them were passed around the region to demoralize the community. This could be the same. But different. If you know what I mean. After all, local French boys don't play such fun and games with escaping British army officers every day of the week, do they? This would be a real propaganda coup for the Germans that could be distributed in England as well as France.' She paused. 'You know the Nazis condemned this? They regarded homosexuals as perverts. They would execute them.'

'But it wasn't distributed,' said Lucy.

'How do you know? There could have been other films showing much the same.'

'Obviously they were all compelled to – do this terrible thing.'

May's voice came back into Lucy's mind. 'It was a homosexual thing. Some kind of homosexual thing.' 'I phoned Frasier about Baverstock,' Metand had told the men. Then she forced herself to glance at the prints again.

Martin and Peter were astride the young men's backs. They were naked. Their expressions were ecstatic, absorbed.

'The angels are dying,' said Tim. 'Don't make me do it.'

'Looks like buggery,' observed Anna viciously. 'They all seem to be having fun, don't they?'

'My husband isn't there.' But Lucy knew that this wasn't the answer, that she couldn't so glibly accept his lack of involvement. Maybe there were other photos in existence showing Tim – She broke off the speculation, unable to bear the horror of it all.

'Perhaps Tim took the photographs,' suggested Anna. There was no expression in her voice.

11

31 July

'They were compelled,' stated Lucy doggedly. 'By the Germans.'

Anna didn't reply. 'Homosexual acts between British officers and French peasants. Just imagine how the British War Office would react to that? Or even the Free French?'

'Could Tim have decided to get hold of the film and destroy it?' Lucy needed reassurance but knew she wasn't going to get any.

'Who from?' Anna chose to be obtuse.

'Solange. Perhaps she'd been blackmailing him.'

'Solange wouldn't do that.'

'How can you be so sure?'

'I knew her.'

'Did you? I thought I knew Tim. I thought I knew Peter and Martin. But I didn't. So why did she give the film to me?'

Anna ignored the question. 'Solange wouldn't blackmail anyone. She had no real need for money and she just wasn't that sort of person. Please remember how well I knew her. And if Tim's not in the pictures there's no disgrace for you. Who's to know or care now who took the film. What are you worrying about?'

'I'm worrying there might be more.' Again May's and Sally's faces swam into her mind. Could they know? Would they have known all this time without telling her?

Anna took over half an hour checking through the cardboard boxes on the trestle tables. She came up with nothing, but Lucy felt mentally drained and deeply relieved when she had finished. If Peter and Martin had known about the film's existence, then it must have been a time-bomb ticking away, always ready to confront them. Lucy remembered how the men had *seemed* to guard Tim. Had he been the weak link, or was he really the strongest of the three? 'I need to talk to Metand.'

Anna walked across to the phone, her face once again set and expressionless. 'I'll ring his office. They'll find him.'

As she dialled, Lucy went to the window. The sky was overcast, bulbous with rain, and even as she watched the first drops began to fall, rippling the surface of the lake, slowly at first and then in a torrential downpour. Soon, the sound began to penetrate the windows of the summerhouse and she saw that one of them leaked slightly, water dripping down the inside of the pane. The horrendous detail in the photographs hammered away in her mind.

She listened to Anna talking and wondered about her. What did she know? Was she an accomplice? Had all this been prearranged? But the adrenalin was once again flowing and Lucy grimly realized she had made a breakthrough. Or had Solange made it for her? If only she had never insisted on Tim's journey back into such a past.

'Metand's already on his way out here,' said Anna. 'They wouldn't say why.'

Lucy's mind reeled. Events were moving so quickly now that she felt punch-drunk. She was reminded of unpeeling an onion, layer by layer. Again and again the dreadful images recurred.

Anna joined her, gazing out at the rain.

They had nothing more to say to each other.

The wait was interminable. The minutes ticked past with a hollow resonance and Lucy drank pale tea that Anna made with Elephant teabags. They still didn't speak, preoccupied with their own thoughts.

Eventually Lucy was relieved to see Metand arrive. Like Anna, the expression on his face gave nothing away as he hurried up the path to the summerhouse. When he came in, however, he was his usual immediate self. 'They've found your husband's shirt. I need you to identify it.'

Lucy didn't immediately take the information in. She felt in too great a state of shock.

'Where's Tim?'

'We only found the shirt. It's a step forward, don't you think?'

But she didn't know what to think and Metand seemed tense.

'Where is it?' Lucy managed to ask.

'On the derelict farm that once belonged to Claude Eclave.'

'Hadn't the place been searched?' She found shelter in indignation.

'There are extensive woods at the back of the buildings. I ordered another, more concentrated search this morning. The shirt was under a bush, torn into small pieces. Will you come and make an identification now?'

Lucy nodded, but then she saw something in Metand's face that made her realize there was more.

'I'm afraid the shirt is bloodstained.'

She gazed at him hopelessly, her heart pounding.

Anna intervened. 'Before you go, we've got something very unfortunate to show you.' She went away into the darkroom.

While she was gone, Lucy forced herself into a stumbling explanation, although she was thinking about Tim's shirt at the same time. The ominous discovery only slightly overlaid the impossible images.

'I found the film in one of these document boxes but Anna says it couldn't have been there long. There was a note from Solange. She wanted the film to be given to me and then Anna developed it. She'll show you. I can't.' Her words were falling over each other at a ridiculously fast pace until she came to a grinding halt as Anna returned with one of the prints. She gave it to Metand who scrutinized it carefully while Lucy watched the revulsion spread across his face.

'Dear God,' he muttered. 'This is dreadful. I had no idea that – ' He broke off.

'They're Martin and Peter,' said Lucy woodenly.

'You'll remember the Nazi propaganda photographs that began those executions?' Anna prompted.

He nodded.

'Could these be for the same purpose?'

Metand didn't reply and the rain pattered at the glass.

'Very likely. This must have been the most appalling shock for you both.' Then he turned to Lucy. 'But at least Tim wasn't involved.' Immediately Metand looked as if he shouldn't have made the statement.

She replied slowly and haltingly. 'I was afraid there could be another film, but we didn't find one.'

Metand seemed to be trying to work something out. 'If Solange left the film for Anna to find and pass on to you, maybe she really *did* feel threatened. Otherwise she would have given it to you herself.'

'But Tim wasn't involved. Thank God,' Lucy repeated. She was hanging on to his absence like a talisman, but she also knew how wrong she might be.

'Suppose he seized that opportunity we've been talking about so much? Could he have come here to persuade Solange to give up the film?'

'And she refused? Why then did she suddenly decide to leave it out for me?'

Metand hesitated, but Lucy was sure she knew what he was thinking. Solange had arranged for her to have the film because she knew Tim was already dead.

The silence lengthened. Then he said, 'Let's go and see if you can identify the shirt.'

But Lucy was still struggling to come to terms with the dreadful possibilities. 'What was Tim going to do with the film if he *did* manage to get Solange to hand it over? Destroy it?'

'I don't know,' said Metand. 'And neither do you. There's no time for this sort of speculation now.' He was unusually agitated which made Lucy feel doubly anxious.

'I shall need to take the prints.' Metand turned to Anna. 'All of them.'

As they drove down narrow lanes between flat fields and great swathes of forest, Lucy asked a now familiar question, 'Do you think he's dead?' Again, the images in the photos assaulted her.

'The fact that the shirt has now been found so far away from the château might mean he could still be alive.'

'So there *is* hope?'

'Always.' Metand replied with some fervour. 'There is *always* hope.' But she already knew how despairing he was. This was the first time he had tried to falsely cheer her. Then he continued rather more convincingly, 'Solange decided you would be the best person to give the film to. I'm sure she was right, whatever motive she had.'

'What are you going to do with the prints?' Lucy had hardly been able to ask the question which had so many dreadful ramifications. Peter and Martin would be condemned by the photographs as criminals. They would be ruined by their arrests and subsequent trial. As to May and Sally – their suffering didn't bear thinking about. Lucy tried to block out of her mind the conversations that would rattle the roof of Caves Café and failed to do so.

'Eventually I'm going to show them to a propaganda expert,' said Metand. 'But for the moment I need to think. Think hard.'

The woods were dense and looked as if they hadn't been entered in years. Brambles were everywhere and the trees were tightly packed together, many of them slowly being strangled by ivy.

There was no birdsong and a heavy stillness hung in the musty air. It was as if the undergrowth and foliage were too acidic, too arid to support life. Wild garlic and fennel pervaded the atmosphere and Lucy now understood the difficult terrain the police were up against.

An officer was standing by a thicket about fifty yards into the wilderness. Then she saw the all too familiar shirt entangled in some brambles.

She remembered buying it at Horne's near Waterloo Bridge.

'I say, old girl. It's a bit loud, isn't it?' Tim had said.

'It's stylish,' she had told him firmly. 'Nicely tailored. It'll go with your sports jacket.'

'What about the cavalry twill?' he had asked, substituting one worry for another.

The first time he had worn the shirt Tim had been embarrassed. 'Do you really think – ' he had begun.

'I think it's lovely,' she had said lightly. 'Matches your eyes.'

He had laughed doubtfully at the time. But then he had got used to the shirt and, as with everything, it became a habit. In the end she had had to practically tear the shirt off him. Now someone had torn it up. What a waste.

'It's his,' she said reluctantly. 'That's Tim's shirt.'

'Do you have the slightest doubt?'

'None.' The misery swept her as she looked round at the

170

tangled thickets, the too closely packed trees, the dense brambles that shrouded the wood. Where are you, Tim? Are you hiding somewhere? Lucy tried to keep the images of the photographs out of her mind, but they kept coming back. Then she started as something stirred amongst the ferns and then ran through a tunnel of dead bracken.

'What was that?'

'A rabbit,' said Metand discouragingly.

'Do you think he's around?'

'The shirt has been here some time. It's soaked with dew and there are animal droppings on it. Probably badger.'

'How long could it have been here?'

'A couple of days. Maybe three.'

'He'll be cold,' Lucy muttered. 'Especially at night. But he has his coat,' she added, trying to comfort herself.

'I'll take you back.'

'To Anna?' She sounded confused.

'To Louis.'

'Very well. I mustn't get in your way. I tried not to get in hers.'

'It's not that – '

'It's just that you think I'll get too upset.'

They walked silently back to the car. Then Metand stumbled and would have fallen if Lucy hadn't grabbed his arm.

'Thank you.' He looked slightly embarrassed, and despite all her own preoccupations her heart went out to him.

'You must be exhausted,' she said anxiously, aware again of how much she had come to rely on him.

'The possibility of a result keeps me going. I like to believe I might one day understand human behaviour. But as the years pass that seems an increasingly unlikely goal. The trouble is that human motives are so self-protective. But then I am the same. My home is my fortress, as the British say. Have you discovered the garden at the hotel? Louis's garden?'

'It's a delight.' She tried to remember its glory but only saw the men in the chapel.

'Yes. It's been a real refuge. He's worked so hard on it. Do you have a refuge, Lucy?'

She had to think carefully and then told him about her father and the willow tree that bent over the pond.

171

'You didn't have such a place with Tim?'

'We never found one. But we will. After all this is cleared up. We'll find one somewhere.' Then she asked him the question that had been on her mind for some time. 'Do you think Anna knew Solange had left that film for me?'

'It's possible. They were very close.'

'How close?'

'Two women on their own cut off in a ruined château? I hardly know Anna, but Solange told me she was the only person she could trust to be with for a long time.' He paused and added, 'I should perhaps tell you that Anna is sick. She has cancer.'

'She told me. She also said Solange had been hoping to get her to America for some kind of special treatment.'

'Yes,' said Metand. Then he came to an abrupt halt.

'What's the matter?'

'The photographs,' he muttered.

'What about them?'

He looked at her in an abstracted way and then began to hurry on again. 'It doesn't matter for the moment.'

Lucy stared at him blankly, suddenly needing to be put to bed, to sleep and to remain sleeping. The only place where this could happen was the Hôtel des Arbres. Her mind was so tired that it hurt.

'Who would have done that to his shirt?' she muttered, hardly knowing what she was saying. 'It cost a fortune at Horne Brothers.'

Then she saw a policeman pushing his way through the brambles towards them. Lucy noticed that one of his wrists was badly scratched and he was breathing heavily.

A feeling of leaden despair filled her as she turned, her eyes sweeping the wild-wood, like a lost child, waiting for her tormentor.

172

12

Metand hurried over to his colleague and for some reason Lucy waited, watching them conferring. Then he began to follow the policeman through the wilderness, now seemingly oblivious of her existence. Why had he deserted her?

'I'll be back in a minute.' Metand sounded agitated.

'I don't understand.'

'Why don't you go to the car?'

'Where are you going?'

'Over the hill. I'll be back. I just need to – check something.'

'I want to come with you.' Lucy began a stumbling run, like a younger child left out of a game, desperate to follow her older siblings, determined to force them to wait for her. To include her. 'I want to come with you.'

Reluctantly, Metand hesitated and so did his colleague. She felt an unwanted appendage.

'What's going on?'

'It could be nothing. I'd much rather you waited by the car.'

But Lucy was already at his side, already fearing the worst. Something scurried amongst a cluster of ivy-covered oak trees. More rabbits? 'You won't get away, Tim,' she said aloud, and then felt a fool as she stumbled after them, nettles scraping at her stockings and a thorny bramble catching her skirt. Lucy wanted her father. She wasn't dressed for this.

Now they were walking on an overgrown path, striding uphill through the mulch of last year's leaves. They came to a ridge and she gazed down into a small valley. The ruins of a stone farmhouse rose above the scattered remains of collapsed out-buildings; the roof had fallen in, the doors and windows had long since disappeared and a chimney stack was resting against a huge oak, branches weaving around the masonry.

Beyond the farmhouse, at the bottom of another overgrown track, was the crumbling brick base of a well.

A group of men were heaving at a couple of ropes they had made into a primitive pulley while a police officer gave instructions. When they saw the three of them hurrying down the hill, the strenuous group activity ceased.

Metand stopped and grabbed Lucy's arm. His colleague strode on, anxious to confer. 'For the moment I would like you to stay where you are.'

'I *have* to see.' She forced herself from his grip. Then she came to a halt.

Metand spoke to the men by the improvised pulley for what seemed an inordinate length of time. As he did so, Lucy was conscious of the stillness of the woods wrapping itself around her. But this time the sensation wasn't threatening. It was as if there was a membrane across her mind, mercifully stopping her thinking.

Eventually Metand turned back to Lucy. 'There is a heavy object down there.' He looked as if he was under an impossible strain. He also seemed extremely apprehensive.

'Who alerted them?'

'A dog. The – object is about eight metres down.'

Lucy didn't want Metand to stop talking. She had to procrastinate as long as she could.

'What is it?'

'We don't know.'

'Can't they see?'

'Not at the moment.' He turned away, gave a signal, and the men – she counted eight of them – began to pull on the improvised winch. Slowly the body appeared.

'For Christ's sake,' she screamed. 'You'll hurt him.'

Metand gripped her arm, but she shook him off again and ran the last few paces to the top of the well. The men were looking at her in distaste, as if she was a voyeur. Then Lucy realized it wasn't distaste, but shock.

Still the body rose up. Now she could see the ripped and gory corduroy around the thighs. Then the ropes gave a jerk and a torso appeared, naked and covered in mud. An arm cracked against the well head, twig-like in rigor mortis, and then the chest and head. She saw the other arm was bent at an extraordinary angle.

Lucy felt encased in stone.

But then, when she saw the blackened turnip that had once been Tim's head, she began to run in hopeless little circles, her mouth open, the scream silent at first and then emerging as a thin wail.

As the turnip hit the top of the well she could see Tim's wide-open eyes staring at her. The nose was gone and the mouth was only a ragged tear. Above the eyes was a section of matted brown hair. He looked as if he had been scalped and a blackbird sang as if in triumph. The nursery rhyme beat in Lucy's head like crackling feathers.

> Who tolled the bell?
> All the birds of the air
> Fell a-sighing and a-sobbing
> When they heard of the death
> Of poor Cock Robin.

She looked up and saw birds soaring. She'd known, hadn't she? She'd known she'd tolled the bell. I drove him to this, she said. I drove him here.

Lucy fell to her knees as she watched the body rise, flies buzzing about its charnel hulk, winched up to whirl a sombre dance and then down to the ground where it lay as stiff as a board, rigid at every impossible angle.

Metand pulled Lucy to her feet, smothering her face against the thick wool of his jacket.

'Let me help you.' He let her go and she leant against him while he unscrewed the top of the brandy flask. 'Drink.'

She did, eventually spluttering and then taking another long draught.

She gave the flask back to him and moved towards the well. 'I want to see him,' she said.

'Animals have been down there. They have – they have interfered with him.'

'Tim!' She screamed out his name over and over again. 'I've found you. You got lost. It's going to be all right now, my darling. It's going to be all right.'

Metand pulled her against him and pushed the flask to her lips again. This time Lucy drank until she choked.

'I'm sorry.' He was patting her back like her father had done when she'd swallowed something the wrong way. 'I'm so sorry.'

More birds flew overhead, rustling the trees at the edge of the woodlands until the sound filled her ears, blocking out everything else except one stabbing thought. *I killed him.*

The afternoon sunlight sent long, low, dust swirling beams through the half-closed shutters of her bedroom in the Hôtel des Arbres.

Metand had driven her back and she had sat beside him in the front seat, unresponsive to his attempts to comfort her.

It was over. He was dead. There had never been any hope from the start.

Lucy could not associate the thing in the well with Tim but, at the same time, she now had to accept that it was all over.

Suddenly she was thinking more clearly. Tim killed Claude. Tim killed Solange. But who killed Tim?

Overall, Lucy knew it was all her fault. The men had tried to stop this happening, tried to protect them both. So had poor May. But she wouldn't listen, hadn't been able to listen. Then there were the prints. Those obscene, unbelievably vile photographs.

She bore the blame.

She had driven Tim to his death.

It was all plain, unvarnished fact.

Tim had killed Claude. But surely it hadn't been because of Solange? It must be to do with the prints. No wonder he had become a nervous wreck. No wonder the men had moved into Shrub Lane to guard him.

But why had he agreed to go? Was it just because she had threatened to leave him? Or was he glad to be prompted to face his unfinished business, glad to confront Solange over the roll of film. Just as Tim had been driven to breakdown, she been driven mad.

Yet there were so many loose ends, so many things Lucy didn't understand. Nevertheless, all she now wanted was the safety of Esher, even the safety of the men. Peter and Martin would look after her. They would forgive her. For she was, after all, only a misguided little woman who should never have left her mock Tudor home. She was no good on her own.

Some hours later, Lucy leapt out of bed and rang the bell that Monique had so thoughtfully left on the table. Another possibility had crept into her mind. Why hadn't she realized? Why hadn't she been able to deduce such a simple fact? She realized that Metand would have tried to shield her. But why had she been so blindly foolish?

Monique came running breathlessly up the stairs and Lucy knew she had to tell her, to gauge her reaction at once.

'Would you say that Solange was capable of murder?' Lucy gabbled. 'You see, I've just realized that if he – if Tim has been dead all this time, then she might have killed him. Must have killed him.'

Monique sat down on the edge of the bed and took her hands in hers. 'I don't think she would be capable of doing that.'

'How do you know?'

'And why should it be Solange? The killer could be anyone.'

Lucy sprang her trump card. She wanted to shock Monique into agreeing with her. Then it would all be over and she could start trying to cope with the fact that Tim was the turnip head in the well. That Tim was dead. That he would never call her 'old thing' again.

Lucy spoke slowly, concisely. 'Solange left a note and roll of film for me in the archive at Pavilly.'

'Does Metand know? You're not – '

'I told him. Anna was sure the film had only been placed there the previous day, just before Solange died. The photographs are of Martin and Peter. Tim wasn't in them. They were engaged in something unspeakable. A homosexual act. I don't know the law in France, but in England homosexuality is a criminal offence. No one even mentions the word. If it ever came out – Martin and

Peter would be ruined. But I'm certain they were forced to do this by the Nazis for propaganda. I gather that's how Claude Eclave and his friends were found out. The girls they supplied were caught on film and that was bad enough, except their activities were rather more orthodox.'

Monique's expression didn't change. 'You say Solange left the film for *you*?'

'Yes.'

'I don't see the purpose of that. If Tim wasn't in the photograph.'

They gazed at each other in silence.

'Then why did she do it?' demanded Lucy.

'I don't know. Does Metand?'

'We didn't discuss it.'

'Where are these prints now?'

'Metand has them. He said he'd give them careful thought and maybe show them to a propaganda – '

'Lucy.' Monique was now determined to cut off the flow of words. 'You've had the most terrible shock. You can't talk about all this now. You've got to give your mind a rest – or you'll go mad.'

'Like Solange? Like Tim?'

'Let me ring our local doctor. He's very good. He can prescribe some sleeping pills, or a sedative.'

'No.' Lucy was insistent. 'I've got to talk to someone. I don't want you to be soothing.'

'Very well.' Monique resigned herself. 'I won't be soothing.'

'Martin and Peter were obviously compelled to do that horrible – ' Lucy's voice died away. 'I'm sure Tim went to get that film.'

'But then at least his task has been completed. The photographs are safely with Metand.'

'Peter and Martin wouldn't have wanted to have got involved in something like that.'

'No,' said Monique. 'I'm sure they wouldn't.'

But Lucy knew that despite all her pleading there was no point in trying to discuss it with her. She could only be soothing, however much she tried not to.

Suddenly Lucy began to cry and Monique put her arms around her, holding her as tightly as Metand had. Eventually the tears were replaced by dry, hard sobs and a great bleakness spread inside. Tim was dead. The hope had gone.

'I killed him. No one else. He would have been safe if we'd stayed at home.'

'You can't go on destroying yourself. You did what you had to do. What would have happened if Tim had stayed in England? What sort of state would he have ended up in?'

Lucy's sobs lessened. 'I can't bear him to be dead.'

Monique stroked her hair gently. 'None of us can bear it for you.'

She was silent, feeling as if she was stranded on some fog-bound island, unable to see which way to go. 'I want to go back to England in the morning. I'm sure that they won't release Tim's body until there's been a post mortem. That could be days – or even weeks.'

Monique said nothing, which she immediately took as a negative response.

'Does he suspect *me*? Does he think *I* killed him?'

'Lucy. If you won't see the doctor and let him prescribe sedatives, at least let me bring you up a stiff drink. A brandy or – '

'Metand gave me some.'

'Let me get you another. You *have* to sleep. I want you to sleep. You must do what I say.'

Lucy gave in.

In fact she didn't need the brandy. While Monique was down-stairs she slipped into exhausted sleep to find herself cycling over the Clump with Tim. They were racing each other up a hill which was steep and covered in long grass, puffing and groan-ing, standing up on their pedals, shouting and jeering at each other until Tim's bike flipped over and he fell off, fortunately rolling clear of the machine and coming to rest, scratched and breathless, in a blackberry bush.

He was lying there, mock dead. At last he opened his eyes. Tim gazed up at her as they had done when he was hauled from the well. He looked blind. Then she knew he was dead.

But still Lucy didn't wake. Instead, the first nightmare merged into the second.

Peter and Martin were mounted on the backs of the young Frenchmen, frozen in a tableau-like stance, an exhibit around which she and Tim were walking slowly, as if in admiration of a

179

particularly good piece of sculpture that they had come a long way to see and which had cost them a good deal of entrance money.

Lucy struggled to wake. Someone was gripping her shoulder. 'It's propaganda,' she said over and over again. 'Only propaganda.'

'You were dreaming,' said her father. Then she saw it was Metand. Lucy found nothing strange in him being in her room, sitting by her bed. In fact she was delighted to see him for she knew that he would help her to surface from the night's horrors.

'I want to go home.'

He smiled. 'Shall we both go?' Metand paused and then said, 'Please don't think I'm only interested in solving this investigation. You've already been through a series of terrible ordeals and this is the worst.'

'But it's not the last, is it?'

'I lost my parents. They met violent deaths and I never recovered and neither will you. But the pain will lessen until the grief becomes part of you. That's what happened to me. Also, I believe that you will eventually find Tim was not a hero once, but a hero twice.'

'Do you know something I don't?'

'I can't talk about it now. But trust me.'

'Are you coming to a conclusion?'

'Yes. But it lies in Shrub Lane.'

'How did he die?'

'He was stabbed.'

'Where is he now?'

'At the mortuary in Honfleur.'

'Is Solange's body there too?'

He nodded.

'Together again?'

'Don't, Lucy.'

'I want it over.'

'We must leave in an hour or so. You must have some breakfast and I'll make some calls. Then we shall be back on our commuters' journey on the ferry. They'll be getting used to us.'

'You think the photographs are crucial to all this?'

'Yes.' Metand got up. 'I'm with you, Lucy. Please remember that.'

'Thank God,' she replied.

Monique and Louis Dedoir stood on the cracked and faded tree-patterned tiles in the foyer of the Hôtel des Arbres. They were both looking tired and Louis had his boiler suit on again.

'I don't want to say goodbye. And I'll be back. If you'll have me, after all this.' Lucy was tearful but controlled.

Monique was not. She gripped her tightly and kissed Lucy several times on each cheek, the alcohol strong on her breath. 'Come back,' she said. 'Come back to us.'

Louis looked embarrassed and shuffled, wanting to return to his garden. It was he who brought Lucy the greatest comfort.

13

This time, Metand sat on the lounge deck, a cigarette between his teeth and the packet in front of him on the table. Lucy pretended to read *The Times*, aware that, whatever happened, she couldn't escape the deadly reality of being alone. No father. No Tim. Just a long life to lead.

'Do you *know* what's going to happen?' Lucy asked Metand. The sea was glassy calm, the ferry only a quarter full and they had the row of seats to themselves.

'I have some theories.' He reluctantly put down a novel. 'They need to be put to the test.'

'You won't tell me what kind of conclusion you're coming to?'

'Not yet.'

'You're not going to eventually tell me Tim killed Solange, are you?' she pleaded.

'Remember what I told you. He will emerge heroically. I'm sure of that.'

'You have evidence?'

'I know it. As strongly as you do.'

'What a peculiar detective you are.'

'Thank you. I must tell my boss.'

'Do many policemen act on intuition?'

Metand abruptly returned to his book and Lucy got up and prowled the decks of the ferry.

The sun was high in the sky and there was a mist on the sea. She gazed into the heat haze and muttered to herself, 'You're not out there any more, are you? You've gone, left me. Just when we might have got going.' She began to cry.

When Lucy returned to Metand he had put down his book and was gazing at a poster proclaiming the delights of St Malo.

'Tell me what Peter said when you phoned him.'

'I've already told you.'

182

'Tell me again.'

'He was horrified.'

'Didn't he ask any questions?'

'He asked after you with very great concern. He wanted to know if Tim's death was connected with Solange's and I said I couldn't make any comment but I had to see both of them urgently.'

'They didn't ask you why?'

'No.'

As he spoke, Metand gave Lucy a glancing look that seemed so full of tenderness and regret that she bent over and kissed him on the forehead. He looked up in such genuine surprise and bewilderment that, despite everything, she laughed.

'What was that for?' he asked, blushing.

'For you.'

The evening was grey and cold as Metand drove down Shrub Lane towards the cricket pitch. They were early and Lucy had suggested they caught the Men at nets practice which was held with unbreakable routine on a Tuesday evening.

'I don't want to go back to the house. Not yet anyway.'

They passed the coal yard that now inhabited the ruins of an old brewery. Next door was a village shop and a butcher.

'This is still Esher?'

'It's called West End. The original village.'

'Prettier than Navise.'

'Yes, but it's got such bad memories.'

'Cricket?'

'Man's domination. Women's subjugation. Sandwich-making,' she added.

'A local industry?'

'Practically.'

'Why didn't you fit in, Lucy? Surely most women do?'

'It was my father.' She began to tell Metand about him, and as she did so the village green came into view with the pavilion, the pitch and the nets where a number of men in whites were standing watching someone bowling.

'He sounds interesting,' Metand pronounced when she had finished. 'He gave you quite different expectations.'

'So did Tim. Until he got sucked under.'

183

'And now? What will you do when this tragedy is resolved?'

'I shan't stay here. I shall travel. I shall travel without him.' Her voice shook, and when they had pulled up on the verge Metand gently took her hand. To Lucy's surprise, she realized she hadn't thought about the prints for some time.

Peter embraced Lucy with a bear-hug, drawing her to him, holding her in a strong grip that was meant to be reassuring but was, in fact, merely uncomfortable.

'You're safe now,' he said, the dark mat of hair blooming at his cricket shirt collar.

Martin, his face drawn, also took her in his arms, but his touch was gentle, more tentative. 'It's awful,' he said. 'So awful for you. We're both here to help.'

She wanted one of them to say, 'It was your fault,' so she could fight back, but neither of them did. Then the detail in the photographs sharply returned.

'We're early. I knew it would be nets practice tonight so why not finish and we'll just sit here for a while and take a break.'

'You can't do that,' Peter began.

'Please do as Mrs Groves suggests.' Metand spoke abruptly.

Peter and Martin had walked slowly back to the nets looking rebuffed and Lucy wondered what they were thinking.

They sat together on an uncomfortable wooden seat on the edge of the village green.

'Are you sure you're going to be up to this?' asked Metand as Peter hit the ball back to the bowler while Martin stood silently gazing across the village green to the church.

She nodded. 'When will you want me to come back to France?'

'I don't know. It depends on how things go.'

'Here?'

'And there.' He was vague. 'Your husband's body won't be released for some time, I'm afraid.'

'Will you need to question me again?'

'Of course.' He tried to distract her. 'Can you tell me about the temperament that drives these men?'

Lucy thought carefully before she answered. 'The English believe in king and country, and that's why they went to war.

184

They also believe in home in a very special way, as a kind of bastion. The Englishman's castle and all that, protected by privet hedges and a gravelled drive. The lawn is the shrine. They see normality as the pivot of their lives; they want an unruffled surface. Their men are protective and have a certain concept of honour. They like to say they believe in God and uphold the Ten Commandments. But they don't want to show their feelings. They need to conform to a certain pattern, to their chosen way of life.'

'I didn't realize you were such a cynic.'

'I was bred to be one.'

'You never talk – husband and wife – on an equal basis?'

'There's a tendency, in our class, for the men to manage.'

'You weave, paint, arrange flowers? You are not meant to take a job?'

'Martin's wife is a teacher. A good one.'

'And you and Tim? That was so different?'

'We weren't going to fit into the system. We were going to travel.' Lucy's voice shook. 'If he had come home from the war in any way whole, we'd never have lived in Esher.'

'As it is – '

'He became an invalid and I had to try and help him without knowing what was wrong. Peter and Martin, they kept an eye on him. Their relationship with him never changed.'

'This might be a difficult question to answer, but I have to ask it. Did you feel they feared him?'

'Perhaps. Tim was ashamed of himself. He didn't believe in psychiatry or even medication for bad nerves. He wanted to recover. Peter and Martin wanted him to recover too. But instead he got worse.'

'Why do you think he couldn't confide in you? He must have known how much you loved him, longed for the relief of sharing it all.'

'How *could* he have confided in me? Given the kind of person he was? Given the pressure he was under?' Lucy paused and then asked, 'Do you think he went to Solange to ask her to give him the film? Ask her to be merciful? Do you think she could have been blackmailing Peter and Martin?'

'Wouldn't you have known? Wouldn't there be tension you would have picked up from their wives?'

'Frankly,' said Lucy, 'it all goes round and round. But it

185

doesn't come out anywhere, does it? But then, of course, you are keeping your own counsel, aren't you?' she added bitterly.

'I'm afraid I have to,' he said regretfully. 'Just for a while longer.'

Peter walked slowly across the grass towards them from the pavilion. He looked wary.

'The other chaps are going home,' he said apprehensively, his cricket jersey round his shoulders, although the dull evening was not cold. 'There's only Martin in the pavilion. Would you like to talk in there? It's not particularly comfortable but there's wine in the fridge.'

Lucy watched Metand get up stiffly. He looked tired and rather frail. Why had he stopped confiding in her, she wondered.

14

Directly she was inside the pavilion again Lucy remembered the sandwich-making of last weekend, with May so conscientiously filling the thin slices and Sally coming through the door to talk about the murder of Graham Baverstock.

Sunlight no longer played on the sandwich-makers. Instead, the atmosphere was dark and gloomy. Nevertheless, Lucy still had total recall. The team was batting outside and Tim, just run out, was watching from the deckchair, his thin, invalid's frame defeated.

Peter brought up chairs and she sat down heavily.

'Are you all right?' Martin asked quietly.

She nodded, her heart pounding as she gazed around her. Her anxiety had dispersed a little, but raw fear had taken over. The chairs were placed in a semicircle at the back of the pavilion which smelt unappetizingly of linseed oil and stale food.

Martin poured out wine into smeared glasses. Lucy noticed his hands were shaking. She took a sip, only to discover it was slightly bitter.

'I have something to show you,' said Metand.

He seemed to take a very long time foraging in his briefcase for the envelope containing the photograph, and then an equally long time taking it out.

He passed it to Martin, who was sitting next to Peter. They studied the print together and, for a while, betrayed not the slightest emotion. Neither did they exchange a glance. Lucy watched them in mounting amazement. Why didn't they react?

Then Peter looked up at Metand, only just meeting his eyes, while Martin gazed down at the cracked and discoloured lino on the floor. There was embarrassment, certainly, but not the extreme reaction Lucy had expected. Why were they so controlled? Had they expected this? Had plans been made?

'I don't think we should be looking at this kind of stuff with Mrs Groves here,' Peter said eventually. He sounded, as ever, briskly protective.

'She has already seen it.'

'How?' asked Martin. His voice was expressionless.

'Solange arranged for the film to be handed to her.'

Peter's eyes met Lucy's for only a few seconds before they moved away again.

'It's disgusting,' he muttered, but once again she had the impression that he was acting.

'I – it's – yes, it is.' Lucy could barely get the words out.

'But you did it,' said Metand.

'We had to. But I don't want to talk about this in front of Mrs Groves.' He sounded like a prep school headmaster, faced by juvenile pornography.

'Regrettably you must.'

'Why?' asked Peter a little more uncertainly.

Metand ignored the question. 'Can you tell me when this photograph was taken and in what circumstances?'

'Has it been publicly circulated?' asked Martin tentatively. He still seemed unexpectedly calm, but Lucy could see the beads of sweat on his brow.

'No. It was developed yesterday.'

'We were forced to – do that disgusting thing. At least we were drunk.' Peter gave a little bark of a laugh.

'We should have owned up to all this a long time ago, but you must admit, monsieur, that it's embarrassing – to say the least.' Martin undid a button on his cricket shirt and pulled at the small folds of skin at his neck.

'Did Tim know?' asked Lucy.

'Yes. It was because of him that we did it. I'd better explain what happened.' Martin continued, speaking quickly, as if wanting to get it all over.

As he did so, Lucy became increasingly tense. The Men were so reasonable, so frank, so neatly controlled. Had they actually rehearsed?

'As we told you before, we were given shelter in the cellars of the château. On the second night, Solange got drunk and started making advances to us and in particular to Tim. Naturally she was told where to go. Then the German patrol arrived. A couple of Gestapo officers were with them.' Martin paused. 'To our horror, Solange gave us away to them. It was unbelievable and she did it out of pure vindictiveness. At first I thought we would either be executed or taken away to a prison camp. Then I realized that the Gestapo officers had visited Pavilly before. We were told that local French girls had been photographed having intercourse with German soldiers as a propaganda exercise to demoralize the French, and that Solange and her husband Claude had been paid to organize the event. Now they were being paid again and I'm sure very highly. This time the Nazis thought they would demoralize the English. We were told to go through with this obscene act and at first we refused. But we were forced to drink a considerable quantity of alcohol and told that if we didn't – co-operate – Tim would be shot. Then Claude and his two friends arrived. Do I have to go on?'

'Why was Tim let off?' asked Metand.

'Solange. She intervened on his behalf.'

'And they let you go afterwards?' he asked in astonishment.

'One of the German officers felt sorry for us and they helped us get across the border. I can tell you how nauseated we were by all this and how terrible it's been living in its shadow. Peter and I could have cracked just as much as Tim did. Even gone mad like Solange. But we didn't. We sweated it out. If the photographs *had* come to light we would have been prosecuted.'

'You never thought to try and get them back?'

'It would have been too risky. We let sleeping dogs lie.'

The hounds of hell, thought Lucy. Woken at last by Tim.

Martin's explanation was received in a forbidding silence.

'You mean you were escorted through France by the Germans?' asked Metand.

'In a truck.'

Peter was looking out of the window at a dog chasing a ball across the cricket pitch.

'That must have shortened your "escape" considerably.'

'It was still unpleasant,' said Peter.

'But it didn't take three months.' Lucy was gazing at Martin who returned her stare blankly. 'And you didn't escape. The Germans did it for you.'

189

Metand paused and then continued. 'They took you to the border in exchange for the photographs. Are you sure that wasn't always the bargain?'

'No,' said Peter quietly. 'Of course it wasn't. You must appreciate how honest we are being with you. We were drunk when we were ordered to be involved in that obscene farce. If we hadn't agreed, Tim would have been shot. We've explained all that.'

'You realize the seriousness of this investigation,' said Metand testily. 'Why didn't you give us this information earlier?'

'Could we have saved Tim's life?' snapped Peter. 'I don't think so. What happened is not something you confess unless you absolutely have to. Bearing in mind the law and our reputations.'

Metand sighed. 'Let me fully understand what you are saying. Solange Eclave betrayed you to the Germans. The Gestapo then seized a propaganda opportunity, based on a demoralization plan they had for the British troops. Am I correct so far?'

The Men, thought Lucy. Are these really the men who commanded my life and Sally's and May's? The men who set the standards?

'How many Germans were there?'

'Half a dozen uncommissioned officers, an Oberleutnant and two plainclothes members of the Gestapo,' said Peter briskly.

'That's a very accurate memory for one who had been forced to drink considerable quantities of alcohol.'

'I can tell you we soon sobered up,' said Martin bitterly.

'But you said you were still drunk.'

'We knew enough to realize we were in a very difficult situation.'

'Did you fully understand the reason for the photographs being taken?' asked Metand.

For the first time Peter and Martin exchanged glances.

'Were you aware at the time that the photographs would be used for propaganda purposes? In other words they would be distributed to British troops, clearly illustrating British officers indulging in homosexual acts with French citizens.'

'That was the implication,' said Peter.

'Implication?'

'They never told us directly. But I think it was obvious.'

190

Martin's face was neutral but Peter was beginning to betray more agitation now.

'Did they tell Claude, Robert and Philippe?'

'God knows what they were told.'

'Look,' Peter broke in. 'I don't see why Mrs Groves should continue to sit through this. Surely there's no need to – '

'I want to stay.' For the first time Lucy was able to make her own decisions and the knowledge gave her a heady feeling of satisfaction.

'Very well.' Peter's gaze once again returned to the dog playing on the green outside.

'You've spent years judging me and Tim. Now it's my turn.'

'Judging?' Martin met her eyes. 'That's unfair. We were trying to protect him – and you.' He sounded awkward, as if he was disputing an umpire's decision.

'Rubbish!' Lucy's anger boiled over. 'You were trying to protect yourselves.'

'I think it would be best,' said Metand, 'if I asked the questions.' He paused. 'Did you know of the previous propaganda?'

'Yes.'

'How?'

'Claude told us.'

'Did he receive money from the Germans?'

'I'm sure both he and Solange did just that.'

'What then?'

'We were told we were to be given an escort across the border.'

'You are quite sure that this wasn't the bargain?'

'I've told you before. *No.*' Martin was on his feet, his face a dull red.

'Nevertheless, you took advantage of the offer.'

'Of course.'

'I find that unacceptable.' Metand's voice hardened. 'You aided German propaganda and then let them help you out of the country. Surely you could have been court-martialled if this had leaked out? Apart from having to face criminal prosecution.'

'I've no doubt of that,' said Martin crisply.

'You told your commanding officer the truth when you returned?'

'No.'

The silence that followed was profound. Lucy could hardly take it in. The Men. The men of honour. They had done this? Then she realized that Tim had done it too. Metand's next question was the very one she wanted answered.

'And Tim accepted all this?'

Martin glanced at Peter again, but he was rigidly staring out of the window of the pavilion.

'No. He didn't. He felt that we had behaved dishonourably. Not so much in going through the obscene ritual in the château but by taking German assistance and not reporting it to our commanding officer afterwards.'

'You put pressure on him?'

'He would never have given us away.'

'Were you aware that the propaganda would soon be in circulation?'

'We were hopeful that it wouldn't.'

'Why?'

'Solange told us she had managed to hide the film. That she regretted setting it all up.'

There was a long silence during which Lucy was sure both men were beginning to panic and were clutching at invention.

'When did she tell you that?'

'Before we were driven away.'

'You trusted her?'

'Hardly. But when we heard nothing we began to wonder if she *had* protected us.'

'And what about the Germans? How did Solange manage to get their valuable propaganda away from them?'

'They had also been drinking heavily and she claimed she'd managed to take the film without them noticing and conceal it.'

'That sounds unlikely.'

'It's what she told us,' said Peter.

'You never heard from her again?'

'You mean – did she try and blackmail us? No. She didn't. In the end,' Peter abruptly turned to face them, 'she was more of a decent person than we had imagined.' He was beginning to sound increasingly artificial. The men's gathering lack of credibility fascinated Lucy, and, at the same time, appalled her. Their fortress had been invincible for so long. Now it was in ruins.

'When you got back,' Metand continued. 'You were treated as heroes?'

'No.'

Metand turned to Lucy. 'Is this true?'

She nodded. 'I always thought it odd that there were no medals, so little fuss made.'

'Why was that?' asked Metand.

'We told our commanding officer a half-truth. That we had bribed a German driver to get us to the border.'

'What with?'

'We'd collected some francs before we left the Havre peninsula.'

'Yet you said you were starving?'

'We could hardly go into a shop and buy food, could we?' snapped Peter. 'We had about two thousand francs between us and we claimed he accepted that.'

'And you were believed?'

'The C.O. *wanted* to believe us,' said Martin. 'We were closely questioned, but we got away with it.'

'Is that why Tim broke?' asked Lucy suddenly, and Metand frowned at her interruption.

'Probably.' Martin lit a cigarette. He didn't offer one to Peter.

'You never thought you could tell me any of this? To help Tim get better?' demanded Lucy.

'How could we?' asked Peter savagely. 'It would have meant telling May and Sally.'

'So you pretended that it was just Tim's nerves, left him to rot in case it all came out and your army careers were ruined.'

'More than that,' said Martin. 'It wouldn't just have been our army careers, would it? Our whole way of life was at stake. We'd have been disgraced.'

'And now you admit it all so readily.'

'Not readily,' replied Peter.

Something's badly wrong, thought Lucy. She had the feeling that there was more, that once again the men had beaten a tactical retreat. At the same time she could imagine the sheer horror and disgrace of the headlines in the *Esher News*, let alone those in the nationals.

'So why were you trying to prevent Tim from going to France?' Metand asked quietly.

'He would never have gone.' Martin was confident. 'It was only when Lucy intervened that he had this dangerous idea.'

'I don't understand.'

'Tim seized his opportunity,' said Peter. 'He wanted to try to get the film back.'

'So *he* was protecting you?'

'By this stage we were both sure that Solange never had the film, that she was lying when she told us she'd hidden it. Martin and I were absolutely certain that the Gestapo had taken their precious propaganda away but, for some reason, not used it.'

'Why did you tell Lucy she had been right to go to France – and that you had been wrong in trying to prevent her?'

'Once she was there, I wanted to know what was going on,' said Martin briskly. 'It was better to be on good terms.'

'Tim gave you the telephone number of the Hôtel des Arbres?'

'I told him to. Just in case.'

'In case of what?'

'We didn't want to be out of touch.'

'Did Tim have an affair with Solange?'

'I've told you. No.'

'He didn't shoot Claude?'

'Of course not.'

'So Solange had no reason to kill him.'

'Not that I know of,' said Peter. 'We had a good deal to lose, but circumstances forced us to be honest with you – and we have been. We've got no more to tell you.'

'Does all this have to come out?' Martin was sitting down again now, his legs in the carefully creased flannels crossed, his arms folded against his chest. He looked defeated.

Metand was silent.

Peter's voice shook as he tried to negotiate. 'Can't our wives at least be shielded? I mean, are the photographs really relevant to this murder investigation?'

'They might be.' Metand stood up. 'The problem is that you still haven't told me the truth, have you? Either of you.' He didn't raise his voice and there was a long silence during which Lucy began to feel she couldn't cope with much more.

'How do you make that out?' asked Peter. He seemed genuinely surprised, while Martin raised his eyebrows derisively.

Does he have any hard facts, or was he just trying to unsettle them, Lucy wondered. Yet she knew instinctively that Metand was right.

'There is still the question of the burning shed.'

'What shed?' demanded Martin.

'The one in Mr Davis's garden. The one that Inspector Frasier of your local police told me about. Do you remember, Lucy? You didn't tell me, did you? Despite the fact I kept asking you to try and remember.'

'I didn't think it was of any significance.' She was considerably shaken. William Tell launched himself into her mind, apple and all.

'I believe Lucy discovered the fire and then Sally came to help her. But there wasn't much they could do, was there? It was too well alight. Lucky it didn't set fire to anything else. I mean the trees were very dry, weren't they? And so was the grass.'

Lucy gazed at Metand in amazement. What had the shed got to do with anything?

'What possible link could that have?' asked Martin irritably. Yet there was something behind the irritability – a hint of caution, possibly even fear.

Metand turned to Lucy. 'When you looked inside, you told a local policeman that you thought someone had spilled some paint, didn't you?'

'It was everywhere. But it was hard to see how much because of the smoke and the flames.'

'Did you notice anything else?'

Lucy was watching Peter. He had begun to sweat and there was a strange unfocused expression in his eyes.

'Yes. On the bench and up the walls were paint splashes. Then I wondered if they could be words and someone had thrown paint at them – so they couldn't be read. It was as if a nasty act of vandalism had been covered up. Sally agreed. She said something about teenagers from Hersham.'

'That's a familiar name in this case, isn't it?' said Metand quietly. 'Hersham. Where all the evil comes from. Local teenagers on the prowl. A young gardener who had been arrested for indecency.'

Lucy continued. 'I told Sally I thought the words spelt WILL TELL. She was angry and told me that she'd stopped this bunch of louts from Hersham bullying a child on the green. A child called William Tell. While she was remonstrating with them the local bobby had turned up and gave all those young louts a dressing down. So they got their own back on her by vandalizing the garden shed and then burning it.'

There was a long uncomfortable silence. Then Metand said,

'Forgive me, but I've been thinking. Suppose William Tell never existed. Suppose Sally Davis had never broken up this gang from the dark underworld of Hersham. Suppose she invented the whole story?'

'Why on earth should my wife do that?' Peter seemed to have recovered and was back to his usual decisive self. But his eyes kept blinking.

'Because I don't believe the words spelt a name. They formed part of a message, a very threatening message. Something will tell. How about I will tell? I suggest, Mr Davis, that you saw the damage and the threat written up in paint. I also suggest you didn't have the time or the patience or maybe even the paint to remove the entire message, so you burnt the shed.'

'What utter nonsense!' Peter blustered. 'It was pure vandalism.'

Martin laughed in amusement. 'And who do you think was the vandal?'

'How about Graham Baverstock?' suggested Metand quietly. 'I shall keep Inspector Frasier briefed, and I'd like you both to come to Mrs Groves's home with your wives at about seven.'

Peter and Martin gazed back at him blankly. They've got their backs to the wall, thought Lucy. Maybe that's when they're at their best.

'I just can't accept any of this,' said Peter slowly and reasonably. 'It's a lot of tommy-rot.'

'I'm sorry.' Metand was confident. 'I need you to think over your denial. I do suggest you do that, Mr Davis. Think it over very carefully indeed.'

After the traumatic discussion in the pavilion Lucy and Metand went to The Prince of Wales, the pub near the cricket ground, where they each drank a couple of glasses of dry white wine.

She hoped Metand would discuss tactics for tonight's meeting; instead he was gloomily silent. Puzzled, Lucy sought contact.

'The British disease has rubbed off on you. Don't you want to tell me?'

'Tell you what?'

'What you think. What they haven't told you.'

'I should have moved faster. Not left this *entr'acte*.'

'I'm still not clear about this Baverstock connection.' The

possible permutations whirled round in her mind. 'You're saying that he was going to tell on Peter. Tell what? Was he blackmailing him? And why *didn't* you bring it all to a conclusion?'

'I want to see whether they will finally decide to tell the truth. We lack concrete evidence. I need a confession.'

'Aren't you just allowing them to fall back on another strategy?'

'I'm hoping they'll think their options have run out.'

'You have no more evidence, no more facts to throw at them?'

'I have nothing.'

'And you're worried?'

'I'm worried I could have overplayed my hand.'

Lucy dreaded returning to Gables. Last time there had been hope that Tim was alive. She didn't know how to cope with the intimacy of the place, his presence in every nook and cranny.

To gain a little more time, she took Metand the long way back, strolling across the recreation ground by the river. It was chilly and she kept shivering, while he had buttoned his coat up to the neck and stuck his hands deep into the pockets.

Lucy could feel his anxiety and the tension growing between them. Had he set off a chain of events that was running out of control? Her heart pounded with the uncertainty of it all.

Then Metand took a decision. 'Look. I'm sorry. I'll have to go and see Peter Davis again. There are things we need to talk about before tonight. I'm not satisfied with the way I handled the final part of that interview.'

'Of course. I'll take you to – '

Suddenly, Sally was running across the grass towards them, waving frantically, a twisted look on her face that Lucy had never seen before.

Metand watched her and, for the first time, Lucy could see that he was afraid.

'I've been looking for Peter,' Sally burst out as soon as she was within earshot, trying to walk normally now but only succeeding in making little scampering movements. 'I can't find him any-where.' Her skin was chalk white and there were sweat stains under the arms of her crisply laundered cotton dress.

'We were talking to Mr Davis in the pavilion.' Metand's voice was strained, apprehensive.

'He hasn't come home.'

'I expect the men – I expect they've gone off for a drink somewhere,' suggested Lucy.

'Martin said Peter went to get some cigarettes. He's been away a long time.'

What could have frightened Sally so much that she could forget to mention Tim's death, wondered Lucy. Was it because she was terrified that something had happened to Peter? She glanced at Metand. He started to say something and then stopped.

'I need some help,' began Sally. Her voice was shaking so much now that she could hardly get the words out. 'He should have come home.'

'Where do you think he has gone?'

'I don't know. How can I tell you if I don't know?'

'You may not know where he's gone.' Metand spoke reluctantly. 'But you know what he's done, don't you?'

She nodded, as if she was relieved that he knew, wanting his protection.

'How long have you known?' Metand asked gently.

'Ever since Peter came back from the war.' Sally gazed at them, her voice a monotone. 'But when the shed was burnt, when I saw Baverstock's pathetic blackmail, I was sure.' She paused. 'But I suppose I was always wondering. When Peter and I were making love I knew he didn't want me.'

'Some film has been developed in France. The prints show your husband and Martin Latimer in compromising positions with a couple of young Frenchmen. Originally I thought that the shots had been taken for German propaganda purposes – but then I began to think of another possibility. Suppose the Germans were not present when the photographs were taken?'

'What are you trying to say?' She had Tim's old look of evasion.

'What has worried me was the enjoyment in the men's eyes. The pleasure.'

Sally turned to Lucy as if she had suddenly snapped. As if she was pleased to have snapped. The words were torrential. 'I know about Peter. I wish I didn't, but I do. I should have faced up to it. He isn't interested in me physically and never has been.' She paused, but there were no tears and little emotion – just a hardness that had been building for a long time, the grim knowledge that she took shelter from in her so-called illnesses. 'When May saw Baverstock with a man she fortunately couldn't identify, I knew it was Peter.' She paused and glanced at Lucy. 'I'm fed up with them being in charge. Now we're in charge. Aren't we?' Her voice shook but somehow Sally just managed to remain in control. Lucy knew the men were no longer able to do that. Their regime was over.

The elderly woman with her equally elderly spaniel was on them before they saw her.

'Mrs Davis – ' she began excitedly – 'I'm afraid those Eyeties are up to it again.'

'What are you talking about, Sheila?' Sally sounded remarkably calm.

'Mrs Groves. I hear you've been out of the country. Did you have a pleasant holiday?'

Lucy couldn't bring herself to reply, and after a decent interval Sheila returned to more fertile ground.

'They've been shooting rabbits on the Clump again. I'm sure of it. They've been told time and time again that this is illegal. But I heard at least six shots when I was taking Barney for a walk.'

Lucy watched Sally's expression change from strained social interest to the realization of what must have happened. She seemed to go limp and then stiffen again, her lips working but no sound emerging. Then she turned and began to run athletically back up the lane. She didn't even glance round to see if Lucy and Metand were following.

'I hope she's not going to go up the Clump single-handed,' said Sheila, relishing the drama. 'The Eyeties are very temperamental you know.'

'Shall I get the car?' asked Metand.

'There's no access for vehicles.' Sheila was delighted to be negative. 'There's only the path.'

While she watched with rising curiosity, Metand and Lucy set off at a brisk pace. After a while they too began to run.

'I'm glad you feel like me,' Sheila shouted after them. 'They shouldn't be allowed to get away with it. After all – we won the war!'

Hurrying back past the coal yard and on down West End Lane in the gathering twilight, they eventually took a footpath that at first crossed a field and then climbed a fenced hill through dense woodland.

Unlike Normandy, Lucy thought, the British countryside felt over-populated. A couple of sweet wrappers and a soft drink bottle confirmed the problem and she saw Metand glancing at an abandoned mangle half buried in the bracken. With fearful trepidation she remembered the indignity of Tim's body being winched out of the well, the snapped arm splayed behind him.

Panic welled up in Lucy and she wanted to run back home, go to bed like Sally and pull the sheets tight over her head, just as she had at the Hôtel des Arbres. But she knew she couldn't. Not now.

The keening seemed to soar out of the ground itself, pulsing, changing rhythm until it was a shrill wailing.

When they arrived in the glade, Lucy saw Sally sitting beside Peter, his shattered head in her lap, the raw hole seeping blood and bone and brains.

He had shot himself in the mouth and his service revolver was still clasped in his right hand. Sally was rocking him gently, like a mother with a child, the strange keening still on her lips.

Lucy ran over to her, stroking her damp hair, aware that her print dress was spattered. She saw the matted hair on Peter's chest, protruding from his shirt. The blood had flowed copiously, but now it had crusted around the hole where his mouth and part of his nose had once been.

You won't need to go to bed now, Lucy told Sally in her mind. You won't have to feign illness ever again.

Sally rose awkwardly to her feet, letting Peter slide away from her. 'I loved him. But not enough. I just let him run out of control.'

She led the way down the path, without even glancing back at her husband's body. Lucy came next, failing to match her stride and Metand brought up the rear, stumbling, finding the pace difficult. He was wheezing slightly.

Once back on the main road they met Sheila and her spaniel again.

'You're covered in blood, Mrs Davis,' she began, alarm and curiosity competing with each other.

'Yes,' said Sally at her most sweepingly competent. 'There's been an accident.'

'The Eyeties? Well, all I can say is that they've cried wolf with those guns once too often.'

'I'll ring Frasier. Make the necessary arrangements,' said Metand. 'There's a telephone box over there.' He glanced helplessly at them. 'I may need assistance. I don't understand how to – '

'I'll help you,' said Sally, glad of the opportunity to escape.

'I honestly feel those Eyeties should be shipped home,' Sheila was saying. 'They're just not responsible.'

'Who is?' replied Lucy.

'Would you like a drink?' asked Sally when they arrived in the spacious hallway of Conifers.

'I'd rather have some tea,' said Lucy. 'While you brew up I'll ring May.' She spoke lightly, as if nothing had happened, as if Solange had not fallen to her death, as if Tim had not been winched from the well, as if Peter had not fired his revolver into his mouth, as if she had never seen the photographs. Lucy felt anaesthetized, unable to believe what was happening, and as she dialled she had the strangest feeling that she would soon be back in the pavilion with the sandwich spread.

'May Latimer.'

'It's Lucy.'

'Yes?'

'I'm afraid there's been a – an accident.' Then she corrected herself. 'No, not an accident. I didn't mean that. I was wrong. Peter's shot himself. Up on the Clump. I'm so sorry. I – I just can't take it in.'

'Dear God. Not him!' Then May began to speak calmly, almost menacingly, as if she had to sort out a dispute between the children at school. 'There's a lot we can't take in, Lucy. I gather we've been summoned by your Frenchman. It's terrible for you and Sally and I'm sorry it worked out this way. I could never have believed that in a few days all our lives would be ruined like this. All we've strived for – just thrown away because of a lack of control.' May ended up by sounding artificial.

'Control?' Lucy was appalled. 'Is that how we should all be? Automatons?'

Sensing that she was in danger of losing an argument, May's tone became even more schoolmistressy, ruling out any further discussion. 'There's no point in continuing this conversation. I'm afraid there is a lot more to be explained, to take responsibility for. Martin and I will be at Gables at seven.'

'We're meeting at Conifers now. Sally – '

'I quite understand,' said May. 'Now I need some time to myself.' She hung up.

'I don't feel as if I'm in shock,' said Sally as she put the kettle on. 'In fact I feel nothing at all.'

'That's how I felt about Tim. That's the way I am now. I just don't believe any of it happened. They'll all come walking down the road soon. Late home from the pub for a warmed-up supper. The men. But I know the pain will break through. It's just a matter of time.'

'I expect that will happen to me,' said Sally. 'And then people will be telling me to take it one day at a time. Not make quick decisions. That kind of rubbish.' She paused and then said, 'Peter wouldn't have been able to take all the repercussions. It was best this way.'

'Can *you*?'

'Yes, I can take them. But I've got to get away from here.' Her voice rose again and she gripped the top of a chair until her knuckles were white. Lucy put her arms round her. 'I want it to hurt,' Sally said. 'Then I'll know it's real. Do you remember that day when the shed was set ablaze? You were staring at it, wondering what to do and then I ran over. I knew then.'

'It seems like years ago – not days.'

Sally went over to the stove and made a pot of strong tea. 'What's he like – your French detective?' she asked as they carried the tray into the lounge.

'He's been helpful and supportive *without* protecting me. It's because of Metand that I've been able to cope. Just. But now I want to concentrate on you.'

. 'Don't worry about me,' said Sally almost carelessly. 'I've been coping for a long time now. I'm not likely to stop.' She paused. 'It's all been a farce, hasn't it?'

'What has?' asked Lucy.

'The cricket club,' Sally replied, rather absurdly, but Lucy knew exactly what she meant.

Lucy remained in the chintzy lounge with its cricketing photographs while Sally took a shower. The room was large, with floral sofas and chairs, French windows opening on to a lawn that stretched down to the tennis court.

Photographs of Martin and Peter and Tim, as well as the rest of the village cricket team, dominated a grand piano, and on the lilac papered walls were a few framed prints, largely Impressionists; an ormolu clock ticked away the long minutes on the polished walnut sideboard.

'Do you want a shower?' asked Sally as she came back into the room.

Lucy shook her head.

'Will Metand stay at your place tonight like he did last time?'

'Just for tonight. We keep shuttling between France and England, and when I'm in one country I want to be in the other. I longed to be back here after Tim was found.' She knew they were talking brightly, as if they were watching the cricket, but it wasn't possible to accept the enormity of it all.

'And now?'

'I don't know. Have you got that drink?'

'We'd better be careful.'

'I only need one,' said Lucy.

As Sally went to the sideboard Alice came running into the room with Nancy Dexter. 'Did you find Mr Davis?' she asked.

Alice hugged her mother's legs. 'I want my daddy,' she said. 'Where's my daddy? Where is he?'

'He's gone for a walk,' Sally said absently, and Lucy tried to flash a warning glance at Nancy which didn't connect.

203

'Will Daddy be long?' demanded Alice.

'Nancy – will you take Alice upstairs.' Lucy tried to intervene gently. 'Mrs Davis has got some friends coming in for drinks.'

'Yes.' Sally kissed her daughter. 'What a nuisance. Never mind. I'll come and read you a story when they've gone.'

Mollified, Alice allowed Nancy to take her away.

Sally poured out two large Scotches and sat down on the sofa. Then she began to cry.

Lucy held her and thought of how they had all been only a few days ago. The Esher wives. Sally, the brittle tennis player, cocktail queen of Shrub Lane, inveterate avoider of the cricket pavilion sandwich-making, escaping into codeine sleep and unnamed illnesses. May, full of thumping good common sense, knowing her place, doing her job. And, of course, herself, who had grown so restless with her shadow Tim she had forced him into a journey and an opportunity which led to the bottom of a well. Two widows now in each other's arms. It was as if the war had never finished with their men.

Gently, Lucy released Sally.

'It's worse for you. You really loved Tim.'

'You loved Peter. Once.'

'When I began to understand about Baverstock I knew he was a hollow man. I'd always known he never cared for me.'

'When we got to France – just for a few hours – I saw fragments of the old Tim. Then he went away.'

'If he'd succeeded – if he hadn't been murdered – he'd have come back as the old Tim. I know it.' Sally sounded convinced.

'Perhaps. But I sent him to his death,' Lucy said woodenly.

'What would have happened if you hadn't?' She was unusually perceptive. 'He'd have worn away into nothing. You should see Tim as a hero. Take pride in him. He was protecting Peter and Martin. He just went back to war again, on their behalf.'

'The only thing is, I'm not sure if he died at the hands of the enemy.'

'Not *the* enemy,' said Sally sadly. 'I think you'll find it was *an* enemy.' They were silent for a while until she said, 'Peter was always the same. Jovial. Punctilious. Attentive.'

'I wish you could have told me,' said Lucy.

204

'So do I.'

The ormolu clock ticked on, relentlessly extending each second.

'It's all so incongruous,' said Sally. 'These prisons they were in. They had no self-expression.'

'Except their cricket,' Lucy reminded her.

'Think of the commuting. Those men travelling together, playing cards, making up a game. Except one of them won't. He won't be there ever again.' Sally paused. 'But of course the train gang will talk about him. It'll make them uneasy but they'll talk in hushed voices for weeks. They'll all be amazed, although secretly some of them might share the same feelings.'

'Can you imagine them admitting such a thing on the 7.43?'

'No,' said Sally. 'They could never admit anything. Even to themselves.'

The front door bell rang.

Martin was wearing an open-necked shirt, flannels and brogues. He looked extraordinarily young and totally devastated. May seemed dowdy beside him in her matronly Terylene two-piece, and her usual social smile was a travesty. Metand was with them, looking grey with fatigue, and Lucy felt a sense of incredulity that any of this should be happening.

'We met on your garden path, Mrs Davis. Inspector Frasier is dealing with – the details.'

'Can I get you drinks?' asked Sally.

May kissed her perfunctorily on the cheek and said, 'I think we should sit down and – and get on with it, don't you? I – I'm so terribly sorry about what's occurred. There aren't any more words to use – ' She broke off. Lucy realized that May, too, shared her protective disbelief.

'It's been waiting to happen, hasn't it?' said Sally. 'I could have spoken to Peter a long time ago and tried to reach him. I knew, you see. I really knew. The only intervention was Lucy's.'

'Yes,' said May venomously. 'And just see what she started.'

Lucy began to shake and Sally put her arm around her waist. The inability to accept the situation was over and the reality was raw and painful. 'Shut up,' she said. 'Just shut up. She *had* to do it. Had to stop this thing festering.'

205

'Better to fester,' May said viciously, 'than to explode all over us.'

Lucy thought of Peter's brains all over his face. Good old May, she thought savagely. As apt and to the point as ever.

They sat down again. May and Martin in opposite chairs, Sally and Lucy on the sofa while Metand leant against the table.

'We have four people dead,' he began. 'Graham Baverstock. Solange Eclave. Timothy Groves. Peter Davis.'

'Are you expecting any more?' demanded Sally. She finished her Scotch and walked defiantly over to the sideboard to pour herself another. May frowned and cleared her throat.

A long silence followed during which Lucy glanced at a photograph of the cricket team and then at another of Peter in his whites, smoking a cigarette and looking nonchalant.

Then Martin spoke quietly. 'Are you going to cross-examine me again, monsieur?'

'If I have to. But I was hoping you might save me that task.' Metand looked around him but his eyes didn't dwell on any particular face. 'After what has happened, I regret that I asked Mr Davis to think over his denial. It was an error of judgement. I should have tried to clear the matter up in the pavilion. Then perhaps – '

'No,' said Sally. 'Peter would not have been able to face exposure. If he was still here now, I'm sure he would have found a way of going to the Clump later.'

'He might well have been under arrest.'

'Then he would have dealt with the problem.' Sally sounded convinced.

We didn't know our husbands, thought Lucy. But how little we know each other, away from the roles we've adopted. Sally had become a realist. And May? She was about to be destroyed.

Martin stood up. There was a little pulse beating in his temple, but he didn't say anything for a long time. Then he burst into speech, staring straight ahead of him, his hands clenched, fingers locked together as if he was having to force out the words. 'I think I can save everyone a good deal of time. The discovery of the photographs was enough to wreck my future, so I might as well go the whole hog.' He glanced down at May who sat looking down at her lap, her face expressionless. 'I'm sorry.'

'It doesn't matter. Not now. I just want it to be over.' May's voice was a monotone, but the tears were pouring down her cheeks.

'You played a game with Lucy, didn't you, Mr Latimer?' said Metand. 'You were not on a business trip to Birmingham at all. When you phoned her in France you were close to Navise.'

Martin still gazed ahead, avoiding eye contact. 'I killed Graham Baverstock. Peter had made a mistake and begun a relationship with him. I'd warned him so many times since we got back. This was his first error of judgement. When Baverstock came to garden for Peter it was like Hersham had spewed out some kind of hell fire demon.' Martin paused, shuddering, as if he wasn't going to be able to continue. He coughed, cleared his throat and tried to start again but the words seemed blocked, as if he had a throat constriction. Then he forced them out once more, the sweat pouring down his face. 'He should have got rid of him directly he clapped eyes on the man. But the temptation proved too great. Peter risked everything he'd built up. With the law as it stands, Baverstock could have milked Peter for the rest of his life.' Martin paused for breath and then gave a sob, but there were no tears in his eyes. 'I had to do it. After all, I'd been trained in the army. It really wasn't difficult. Peter lured him up to the Clump and I was waiting there. Lucy and Sally were right about the burning shed. Peter set fire to it because Baverstock's attempts at blackmail were rather immature. That was the height of it – the shed. Peter had been holding out. Or trying to.'

The ensuing silence was a physical force.

Metand turned to Martin Latimer. 'Are *you* a homosexual?'

'I've always had – certain feelings.' His voice was so low that Lucy could hardly hear. 'I'm very ashamed of them.'

May's face was still expressionless.

'And what about Tim?' asked Lucy suddenly, desperately needing a reassurance that she couldn't give herself.

'No. He wasn't. But what he saw and what he eventually did broke him.' Martin seemed stronger now, as if by reassuring her he had recovered a tiny margin of self-respect. 'If it's any help to any of you, I loathe myself. I always have done.'

You put up a pretty good front, thought Lucy. So good that it was impenetrable.

'Was Solange blackmailing you as well?'

'She wasn't blackmailing anyone. It was only when Tim arrived in France that things ran out of control, as Peter and I always feared they would. It had always rankled with Solange that he was able to resist her advances, but the fact that she lost money as well rankled even more. I think there was an element of revenge on Solange's part over all this. Three young men had turned her down flat.' Martin turned to Lucy. 'At least you can remember Tim was never unfaithful to you.'

'Can you tell me what happened that night?' asked Metand. 'And this time I would like the truth.'

Martin spoke mechanically now, almost as if he was describing someone else's actions. 'It was the third day of our concealment at Pavilly. There had been no visits from the Germans and we all – Peter, Tim and I – had a false sense of well-being. Solange had withdrawn and was no longer making advances to us, and that was another reason for celebration. Particularly in Tim's case. We were in the wine cellar of the château and helped ourselves. It was like the last day of term at a boarding school. We knew we had to move on next day and go back to facing the dangers of the roads that never ever seemed to lead anywhere. Then Claude turned up with his friends Robert and Philippe and asked if they could join the party. They'd brought some more bottles with them and we made them welcome. We didn't know anything about Claude, except that he was Solange's husband and she didn't like him coming up to the château. But we'd guessed she was afraid of him.'

'Where was she at this time?'

'She wasn't around. Anyway – things went from bad to worse as we all got roaring drunk.'

'But not incapable,' whispered Sally.

Martin avoided her gaze and then began to speak with much more deliberation. 'Philippe had brought a football. We started to play a drunken game but there was no space. Claude decided there would be more room in the chapel so we went there.'

'With angels dying on the ceiling?' asked Lucy.

'Yes – it was a desecration.' He looked now as if he was at his own court martial, speaking woodenly but the emotion only just kept at bay. Once again, Martin gave the appearance of a reasonable man trying to explain the unreasonable, as if he was determined to distance himself from the reality of it all – and, indeed, from his own feelings.

Beside him, May's tears had been brushed away and she stared blankly ahead. Sally, meanwhile, was watching Martin with such focused disgust that Lucy wondered if she was going to get up and attack him. But she didn't move, sitting so rigidly that her fury was all too obvious.

'And what happened then?' asked Metand.

'We had a half-time break and there was more drinking – and some horseplay that got out of control. Solange must have come in without us noticing.'

'What was her reaction?'

'She was angry. But she had already calculated what she would do.'

'She took photographs?'

'With a view to turning the prints over to the Germans. After all, this was a rather juicier form of propaganda than the norm. Solange must have calculated that directly she saw what was happening. She'd had plenty of practice as a main-chancer.' Martin's voice shook, and he gazed down at Sally's expensive carpet as if he was searching for a way out in its deep, deadening pile.

'And then?'

'Claude obviously didn't want those photographs to go to the Germans because he thought he might be accused of being queer himself.'

'What were Claude and Tim doing while – the horseplay was going on?'

'They had gone back to the cellars, looking for more wine. When they got back Solange had just finished using her camera.'

'But what about Philippe and Robert? Were they willing participants?' asked Metand. 'Surely it would be very difficult to force them?'

'They were too drunk to know what was going on,' said Martin. 'When they began to realize, it was too late. Anyway, Claude went for Solange and she switched off the chapel lights. But he got them on again and began to knock her about. We tried to intervene but were too drunk. It was only Tim who seemed to sober up quickly. He dragged Claude away from Solange but he couldn't hold him for long.'

'So what did he mean, "Don't make me do it"?' asked Lucy hesitantly.

Martin was controlled again, speaking in a monotone, relieved to be no longer describing the 'horseplay'. 'Claude broke away from Tim and went for Solange again, holding her up against the wall of the chapel. He began to bang her head against it. Tim tried to stop him, but Claude was stronger than any of us, drunk or not. Probably stronger because he *was* drunk. So Tim got his service revolver out and threatened him. He kept saying, 'Don't make me do it', but Claude didn't listen. He just went on banging Solange's head against the wall. Then Tim shot him. I think he was trying to shoot Claude in the leg, but he wasn't sober enough for accuracy. He got him in the stomach, but by this time Solange was unconscious.' Martin was barely audible now.

'And the film?' asked Metand.

'We couldn't find it however hard we looked. She must have hidden it somewhere in the chapel while the lights were out, in some place that only she knew about.'

'What did you do to Philippe and Robert?' asked Metand.

'Tim didn't kill them. I took his gun and did it myself.' This time Martin must have paused for almost a minute, clenching and unclenching his fists, while Lucy looked on in part fascination, part bewilderment. The last of the men was cracking. Their fortress was finally in ruins. Then Martin continued. 'We dragged them out and dumped all three bodies in a ditch. It took a bit of time and we were terrified a German patrol might turn up. But we got away with it.' The sweat was pouring down his forehead and he kept wiping it away impatiently.

'So how did the rumour begin about collaboration?'

'They were already known to be collaborators,' said Martin.

'But surely the local people would have realized the executions were carried out by someone other than themselves?'

'They must have claimed the killings as their own – it wasn't a close-knit community so each family probably reckoned another had done it – and there was always the Resistance – the Maquis – to blame if necessary.'

'Of course,' said Metand. 'I should have realized that.' He paused and then asked him, 'Were you frightened Solange would blackmail you?'

'Of course.'

'And you searched the chapel thoroughly?'

'We never found the damn film.'

'Why didn't you force her to give it up?'

'She was in a bad state. Still unconscious and her head was bleeding. We took another risk by phoning a neighbour, although that was difficult because of our lack of French. Nevertheless, we managed to communicate that she was badly hurt. We were gone by the time he came. But we assumed he'd got Solange to hospital where she presumably received treatment for head injuries.'

'I wonder if that would explain her behaviour?' said Metand. 'Perhaps she had some brain damage.'

'Perhaps.' Martin shrugged apathetically.

'So there was no German capture, no set-ups, no bribery, no organized escape. That was all made up.'

'It was a strategy that Peter and I concocted. A last manoeuvre. Then, when we came home, it was just a waiting game. I felt I had myself under control, but I knew Peter was vulnerable, that he might succumb. We took up a fortified position but we knew the enemy were waiting, slowly moving towards us from the border-lands.' Martin broke down. There were no tears but muffled, gasping sobs which made everyone in the room freeze.

May gazed up at him, her lips trembling, as if about to say something but failing to get the words out. Did she pity Martin, Lucy wondered. Or was she condemning her husband for breaking the law as well as a social taboo that was about to damn their future, to terminate whatever might happen beyond this room.

'The border-lands?' asked Metand gently. 'Do you mean Hersham?'

Martin shook his head and fought for control. 'I mean any-where.' He paused and then added, 'Baverstock came, didn't he?' He spoke in such a low voice that Lucy could only just hear him.

'Let's return to the events in France,' said Metand impatiently. 'Solange took the photographs because she saw a chance of making a considerable sum from the Germans – just as she had for setting up the French whores?'

Martin nodded.

'So how did you leave France?'

'In exactly the way we've already described.'

'So there were no lies?'

'No.'

'You must have been waiting for Solange to blackmail you all these years. I'm surprised she held off, particularly as Anna had cancer. You could have paid for her treatment in America.'

'Just after the war, Tim had talked several times of trying to get the film from Solange but we put pressure on to keep him from going back.' Martin spoke slowly, unwillingly, and Lucy knew they were heading for the final, painful details that she had to hear but didn't want to hear.

'Why?' asked Metand. 'Didn't he stand a chance of success?'

'No,' Martin replied. 'I'd taken a discreet trip to Navise in 1946.'

'I would have thought you would stand out,' observed Metand. 'A wandering Englishman.'

'I wasn't wandering. I took care to stay in Honfleur and then made an expedition to Pavilly. I found the château had been badly damaged, the chapel ruined. I watched Solange. I watched her go in and out of that lodge for the best part of a day. She was greatly changed and I couldn't bring myself to approach her. In the end I took the most appalling risk and went to the Hôtel des Arbres. Peter had already found out that the original owners had left and the new proprietor, a Monsieur Leger, was pleased to welcome me. He showed me the photograph with great pride and gave me a print to take home.'

And Tim put it behind his books, thought Lucy. Had it been a flimsy piece of evidence that Navise's memory of the three Englishmen was still untainted?

'Leger was only too happy to talk about Solange. He told me she was ill. Mentally ill. But local people had no sympathy because they suspected she had been a collaborator too although there was no proof. She lived alone at the lodge. I was greatly relieved, and almost managed to convince myself that we were safe, but when I returned home and told Tim and Peter the situation sounded just about as dangerous as it always had. From then on Tim seemed to get worse. He was deeply guilty about Claude, horrified by what had gone on, unable to come to terms with any of it. Then there was Baverstock. Then there was Lucy.'

'So you followed them to Navise?'

'I stayed in Honfleur. But I phoned to check they'd arrived. I knew where he'd go.'

'Did you and Peter speak to Tim before he left England?'

'We didn't get the chance. He evaded us. Lucy was always there.' He turned to her and she could see that if Martin had suffered already then he was about to undergo the ultimate pain. Lucy almost felt sorry for him. She certainly couldn't summon up the righteous anger, the rage that she had anticipated. She still didn't know what had happened and Lucy wasn't sure that she wanted to.

'Tell me about France then. What did you do?' asked Metand.

Martin paused and the silence in the room was threatening. Then he burst into flurried, halting speech. 'I hid myself outside the lodge again and reckoned I could be in for a long wait. Fortunately Tim turned up quite quickly. Solange opened the door and he went in. After about half an hour he came out, looking distraught. He was about to walk back to the hotel when I caught up with him. Naturally, he was alarmed to see me.' Martin got up and walked over to the window. He gazed out into the darkening garden as if to some extent making himself witness the terrible events again. Lucy watched him with a mounting curiosity. She felt completely detached. 'I'd kept our secret. I'd kept it too long. So protection was the most paramount thought in my mind. I knew then that I would do anything to keep my marriage, my home, my job – my life as I've lived it here since the war.'

The cricket club, Lucy added to the list. The bullying.

'What reason did you give Tim?'

'That I wanted to help.'

'What was his reaction?'

'He was horrified. I asked him what had happened between him and Solange and Tim told me that she had the film and was going to hand it over to a local newspaper. In other words, she was enjoying playing with him. She said she'd been waiting for us. For a long time.'

'So she *was* afraid,' said Metand.

'She was also taking pleasure in the hold she had over us. Immense pleasure.'

'And then?'

'I told Tim that we'd both go and get the film. And that if she didn't give it up, we'd kill her.'

'And he disagreed?'

'He said he'd try to reason with her again. But I knew it wouldn't work and so did he. Then we had a row and Tim said that if I tried to harm Solange he'd call the police and give me up. He was the old Tim. The honourable Tim.' Martin was still keeping his back to them, gazing out unseeingly.

Lucy felt the first stirring of pride and of involvement with Tim. The detachment had gone.

'But *why* kill her? After all, as you say, what happened was an abberation. It was wartime and you were abroad. Did you have so much to lose?'

Martin swung round, and for the first time seemed angry, as if he had a point of view that his audience had wilfully chosen to ignore. 'I had *everything* to lose. If the film was released, I'd be arrested. So would Peter. There would be a trial, newspaper headlines, imprisonment. Not only would we lose everything but so would Sally and May. You can see the headlines, can't you. *British officers in sex scandal.* Of course we would have been all right if it had been the right kind of sex. But this was the wrong kind, wasn't it? The forbidden kind.' Martin's voice rose but more in fury than hysteria. 'I can't *help* what I feel. Neither could Peter. We were *born* that way.'

'You could have tried,' said Sally.

You could have gone easy on Tim, thought Lucy. But even she realized what a threat he had posed to the other two men. If only she could hate them, but her pride in Tim's unexpected strength and courage surmounted all her other feelings. She glowed inside for the love of him.

'What happened with Tim?' she asked.

Martin met her eyes, sounding as if he was an army official bringing her the news of his death. And, of course, that was exactly what Martin *was* doing. 'I told Tim we needed to talk and took him off for a walk in the woods. I didn't have a strategy until then. But I suddenly realized I had to kill both of them. Solange would enjoy playing games. Tim would be bound to protect her. If I killed him, I might be able to create a number of options to keep the police guessing for a long time. Hopefully for ever. I would make it look as if Tim had killed Solange and during the struggle she ripped away a fragment of his shirt. That was the first option. The second might seem as if *she* killed Tim and then committed suicide, trying to implicate him.' Martin's eyes didn't leave Lucy's for a moment. 'Tim wanted to get back to you and was sure you'd already be terribly worried. I told Tim I wouldn't keep him long and I didn't.'

May began to cry again, the tears rolling down her plump cheeks.

'Afterwards I slept the night in the car and in the morning I went to Pavilly, but Solange was out. There was another woman in the summerhouse and I kept out of sight until she drove off in a car. Then I broke into the lodge and waited. When Solange got back I insisted she should give me the film, but she said it had been destroyed. I couldn't tell whether she was playing games or not. In desperation I managed to persuade her to walk up to Pavilly and show me the fire damage, and when we got outside the château Solange told me that she had never destroyed the film, that she had been waiting for a time when it would come in useful as a weapon against us. Now that time had come. Apparently her friend Anna had cancer and Solange wanted to pay for this new treatment in America.'

So she *did* have that in mind, thought Lucy. Somehow she was glad.

Martin's voice slowed and he spoke as if he was finally surprised by his own actions, that for a long time he had not been able to quite believe in them himself. 'I hit her in a way that, once again, I'd been trained to do in the army. I think I broke her neck. Then I dragged her up to the fourth floor of the undamaged wing. She was very heavy, the opposite of poor Tim.' He paused. Still Lucy couldn't find the anger. His description had almost been tender. 'I wrapped the torn piece of shirt around her fingers and then took a long time levering her out of the window. Eventually I managed. Then I made my own search for the film, but, of course, it was fruitless. Solange had already decided what to do.'

There was another long silence and Lucy realized that Metand wasn't going to prompt Martin, who reached for May's hand. For a moment Lucy thought she was going to push him away. But she simply kept staring ahead and he eventually gave up.

Martin continued, his words tumbling over each other, the little pulse in his temple beating more rapidly. 'I killed Baverstock and Tim and Solange. I did it purely to protect myself and Peter. I knew that I had to, that in their different ways they would all three undermine what had been built up since the war.

I didn't want to accept how I felt sexually. I wanted to be normal. I wanted to forget Pavilly. Then Peter weakened so I didn't have any choice. Tim's attempt to try and make good the past only made me realize how fragile my identity was. I couldn't lose it. I couldn't lose everything.' He tried to take May's hand again, but she was still gazing ahead. 'Can't you understand?' Martin spoke now as if only he and May were in the room and he was desperately trying to reach her. 'It's the 1950s for God's sake, but nothing's changed since bloody Oscar Wilde. Why not? Why can't we say the name?'

'I can say it.' May spoke savagely. 'Homosexual. Queer. They're *just* names. Why didn't you tell me how you felt? Why couldn't we have tackled it together? It was the secrecy.'

'What do you expect in Esher?'

'I don't expect *anything* in Esher or Hersham or anywhere else. You should have told *me*. You would have been safe. But I wasn't important, was I? It was the cricket team, the job, your social standing. That's what you were obsessed with. You didn't give a damn about me.'

'Cricket teams,' said Sally woodenly. 'Filthy sandwiches.'

Thanks, thought Lucy. You never had a hand in making them, did you?

'Now you're really run out.' Sally laughed raucously.

'All that status,' continued May. 'You killed for it, didn't you?'

Lucy supposed that was the case but she still couldn't loathe him. Martin was like a little boy caught with his trousers down. Having done things.

'Is there any more?' asked Metand.

Martin started to say something and then stopped.

'François.' Lucy used Metand's first name without thinking.

'Yes?'

'Could you take him away.'

'Of course.' Metand walked across to Martin Latimer and lightly touched his arm. 'You'll need to come to the police station with Inspector Frasier and me. We will need a statement.' He turned to May. 'Your husband will spend the night in custody and you'll need to call your solicitor.' Metand turned to Lucy. 'It's over. At last.'

'I quite understand.' May's shoulders sagged. For once she was unable to find any common sense or any sense of belonging to anyone.

Martin walked over to the door with Metand by his side. Then he turned back to Lucy. 'It was Tim who was everyone's hero,' he said.

Lucy would always be grateful to Martin for having said that.

'After I've got the statement I think I'll take the night ferry home.'

Lucy Groves and François Metand were standing in the drive of Conifers while a police car drove Martin away. The sky had cleared and the stars were hard and bright.

'You won't stay the night?'

He shook his head. 'I'll telephone when you are needed. Probably in a day or so.'

'I shall miss you.'

'I'm very sorry about what has happened. It's all a profound tragedy.'

'If I hadn't forced Tim to France they would all be alive.'

'You sent him back to war again, Lucy, but at least you gave your husband back his self-respect.'

'Do you really believe that?' she asked too eagerly.

'Yes, I do.' They shook hands and then Metand walked to his car. He didn't look back.

Epilogue

4 August

The three women sat at their usual table in Caves Café.

It was Sally who had suggested the visit, and in a confused moment of bravado Lucy and May had agreed to join her. They had gathered at May's house, determined that what the men had done would not drive the women apart. 'One last coffee and revolting cake. Then there will be policemen to see, arrangements to make. But after that I'm determined I'll sell the house and go. Where I don't know, but if we go to Caves we could all three make a pledge,' said Sally.

'What would that be?' May had asked. She seemed to have aged a good deal in a few hours, but it was obvious that even she didn't want to be left alone.

'That we'll stick together, help each other out.'

Martin had been remanded in police custody and the newspaper headlines had gone into frenzied action.

BRITISH EX-ARMY OFFICERS SLAIN
NORMANDY KILLINGS MATCH BRITISH SLAUGHTER
KILLER CONFESSES TO FRENCH MURDERS
BRITISH EX-ARMY OFFICER'S SUICIDE LINKED TO FRENCH KILLINGS
KILLER ARRESTED – CLOSE FRIEND COMMITS SUICIDE
THE TRAGEDY OF SHRUB LANE
THE SHRUB LANE KILLER
YOUNG GARDENER'S MURDER BEGINS SLAUGHTER

Only the *Telegraph* had been a little more restrained, with a headline which read NORMANDY KILLINGS LINK TO CLUMP MURDER AND SUICIDE.

Martin Arthur Latimer, 32, of 15 Shrub Lane, Esher, was arrested last night in connection with the murder of Graham Alan Baverstock, 17, of 28 Walton Road, Hersham, Surrey,

218

Timothy Edward Groves, 31, of 12 Shrub Lane, Esher, and Solange Estelle Eclave, caretaker of the Château Pavilly, Navise, in Normandy, France. In a separate incident, a close friend of the Latimers, Peter Grant Davis of Conifers, Shrub Lane, Esher, was found dead at a local beauty spot.

'I shall be visiting Martin when I'm allowed,' May had explained tersely, as if she wanted to set a final record straight. 'I'm surprised you can bear to be anywhere near me, Lucy.'

'What Martin did had nothing to do with you.'

'If he could have only turned to me, then I could have helped him. We could have got through together.'

'That's what I like to think about Tim. And the way Sally feels about Peter. But it could never be.'

'Why ever not?'

'They had to keep the status quo. It was in-built, despite the fact that it was also their undoing. We weren't seen as equals. We were seen as in need of care and protection.'

'We're no longer in need of care, nor protection,' Sally had pronounced. 'Directly it's all over, Alice and I are going to Florence for a couple of weeks.'

'What about Nancy?'

'I've given her notice. She wouldn't have wanted to stay anyway.'

Lucy knew that however crazy Sally's idea of paying a farewell visit to Caves Café had seemed, it was definitely the right thing to do. With one collective piece of courage, they had told the ladies of Esher that they were still bonded together.

They sat at their usual table and drank their coffee in the same way they had always done. Only May began to look doubtful.

'Will you be having cakes?' asked the waitress, gazing at them as if they were pariahs.

'We always have cakes,' said Sally truculently. 'Why should this morning be any different?'

'No reason. No reason at all.'

It was not only the eyes inside the café that feasted on the three women. With studied casualness, passersby flocked to the mock Tudor windows to regard 'the tragic trio' as the press had dubbed them.

At the table of the tragic trio, however, conversation was surprisingly positive.

'I just want to get out of Esher for good,' said Sally. 'I hate the place. It's like being in aspic. Like being a flower and pressed in a book.'

Disapprovingly, May put a finger to her lips, concerned that Sally was talking far too brazenly and that the chatter around them had fallen away. It's like reading *The News of the World* aloud, thought Lucy. Last night she had cried herself to sleep and this morning she had woken to more tears and the realization of an agony that wouldn't end.

Lucy turned to Sally. 'I'm going to the Hôtel des Arbres,' she said.

'Where it all happened?' gasped May disapprovingly.

'I can be closer to Tim there. That's where he died his hero's death. I can't hate Martin. I want to, but I can't.'

May looked away.

'Could I come to Normandy?' asked Sally eagerly.

'Of course.'

'Peter only took you to Portugal just after Christmas,' May said disapprovingly.

'Yes. But that was the old life, wasn't it? The new is here now. Waiting for us.'

'He only took his life the day before yesterday.'

'Why don't you shut up?' Again, Sally's voice was deliberately loud.

'Please,' said May. 'It was a mistake to come. We've got to go. I have to get back. I'll be wanted.'

'Only by the police,' giggled Sally.

She's high on her own adrenalin, Lucy told herself. She was sure she hadn't been drinking.

May struggled to rise to her feet, flushed with anger and embarrassment and despair, but she was wedged in behind the table. 'Please move.'

Sally affected not to be able to hear.

'Please move. I want to get out.'

Suddenly she acquiesced, apologizing while May shakily rose to her feet. Bullies in the playground, Lucy thought. Bullies in the gossip shop. Is that what Sally and I have become, stripped of the identities our men bestowed upon us? Children again?

Lucy paid the bill and left a deliberately small tip. As Sally opened the door, she said to the woman behind the cash desk, 'It's a lousy day outside, you know.'

'Is it, madam?' she replied frostily. 'I haven't had time to take a look.'

'We have a lot of time on our hands,' said Sally sweetly. 'We're housewives out on a spree.'

'Really, madam?'

'Lucy, May and me,' Sally sang the last line and Lucy exploded with indecent laughter. May pushed past them and made her way out into the sun-soaked street that smelt of melting tar and exhaust fumes.

'You embarrassed me,' she said, walking too fast down the Cut. 'You let me down in public.'

The spree was over. Sally was almost in tears and Lucy felt weighed down with her grief. Why had they behaved like that, she wondered. It was demeaning.

'It was just a reaction, that's all.'

'What a reaction!' snapped May. 'You both made a terrible scene.'

'I'm sorry.' Lucy tried to put an arm round her waist, but she pushed it firmly away.

'You're hysterical,' said May. '*I've* got to live here. Alone. For a long time.' She began to cry and Sally and Lucy were penitent, although they knew she would never forgive them.

'Are we going to sit alone in our houses?' asked Sally.

'Just for a while,' suggested Lucy. 'Come round and have a cup of tea later. I've decided to go to France early tomorrow.'

'Commuting again. You should get a season ticket on that ferry.'

May's pace increased still further and then she slipped, saving herself by going down on one knee. She whimpered and they rushed to help her. Again, she tried to push them away.

'We're nothing without them. We're nothing without our men.'

'Yes we are,' said Sally defensively, but she was crying too.

Tim and I were comrades in arms, thought Lucy with a burst of pride. Then a forgotten few lines of poetry came into her head.

The men have marched away,
With a rattle of the drum,
Tiddly-um-tum-tum.

That seemed to say it all. Now the women must run the show.